CZECHMATE

The Spy Who Played Jazz

BY
BILL MOODY

Down and Out Books, LLC
3959 Van Dyke Rd, Ste. 265
Lutz, FL 33558
www.DownAndOutBooks.com

Cover design by JT Lindroos
Cover photos by Photography King and Harry Pehkonen

ISBN: 1-937495-30-2
ISBN-13: 978-1-937495-30-5

"Love the truth. Let others
have their truth,
and the truth will prevail."

*—Jan Hus, Czechoslovak
Reformation Leader, 1498*

Author's Note

The principal characters in Czechmate—Gene Williams, Alan Curtis, Lena and Josef Blaha—are like many of the events, entirely the invention of the author. The invasion of Czechoslovakia by the Soviet Union, however, is historical fact.

On August 21-22, 1968, combined forces of the Soviet Union and its Warsaw Pact allies swept into Czechoslovakia and crushed one small experiment in social democracy.

In the days following the invasion, Alexander Dubcek, the architect of what historians now refer to as Prague Spring, was arrested along with his entire presidium and taken to Moscow. Eventually, he was returned to Prague and installed as part of the new, Moscow-oriented regime and served for several months in this capacity. Later, Dubcek was gradually eased out, served briefly as Czechoslovakia's ambassador to Turkey before he was summoned back to Prague and ousted from the Communist Party in 1970.

On his first visit abroad since that time, Dubcek then 66, received an honorary degree from the University of Bologna on the occasion of the school's 900th anniversary. Speaking out for the first time on the events that followed Prague Spring, the former Czechoslovak leader denounced the Soviet invasion that resulted in "incalculable moral losses and economic stagnation" for his homeland.

On January 21, 1969, five months following the invasion, Jan Palach, a Prague University student walked into Wenceslas Square, site of some of the most pitched battles during the invasion. Before a horrified crowd of onlookers, Palach drenched himself in gasoline and set himself on fire in a tragic act of protest.

Until November 1989, when the Berlin Wall came tumbling down, Dubcek was retired from a lowly job with the Forestry Service and lived quietly with his family in Bratislava. The events of the early 1990s in Czechoslovakia have seen many of the sweeping changes Dubcek once dared to make in Prague Spring of 1968 .

Alexander Dubcek died in 1995.

PRELUDE

East Germany—May 1968

Hidden in the shadows, near the edge of the clearing, Keppler glanced at the luminous dial of his watch and silently cursed all Czechs.

Where was the man? Fifteen minutes overdue and now, even the weather was conspiring against him. He gazed at the sky and watched helplessly as pale slivers of moonlight began to seep through the cloud cover. Another few minutes and the entire clearing would be bathed in a soft glow. An altogether perfect night for a stroll with Helga.

For a moment, Keppler allowed his thoughts to linger over the silken thighs and ample breasts of the young girl waiting for him at the inn. Helga had proven to be a welcome diversion on this operation. He regretted he would have to end it so soon.

He jerked his mind back to the present, once again frowning at his watch. There was nothing to do, but check the drop and call it a night. Perhaps the delivery had already been made. Keppler hoped so. His legs were cramping and even thoughts of Helga were not enough to ward off the chill night air.

He was nearly to his feet when a sound caused him to freeze. Voices and heavy boots tramping on the sodden ground. Silently, he dropped to his stomach and pressed his body into the wet grass as the voices drew nearer.

He had waited too long.

Straining his eyes, Keppler peered through the foliage. He could distinguish the shapes now. Two of them, heads crowned with peaked caps and rifles slung carelessly over their shoulders. Coming right toward him.

East German border guards.

There was no time to pull back farther into the woods. His dark clothing, the shadows and undergrowth would have to be enough. Tiny beads of perspiration broke out on his forehead as the guards approached. The blood pounded in his ears as he tried to quiet his breathing.

The guards passed agonizingly close. One grunted and kicked at the foliage. Keppler held his breath as a tiny leaf floated through the air and settled inches from his face.

He listened to the fading footsteps, the muffled voices and after what seemed an eternity, the guards disappeared from his line of sight. Their voices became fainter until finally, there were no sounds other than the trickle of a nearby stream, the light breeze rustling through the leaves.

Releasing his breath slowly, Keppler lay immobile for another two minutes, then cautiously sat up and massaged some feeling back into his legs. He crawled a few feet away to a tree, rose to a crouch and scanned the clearing.

Satisfied he was once again alone, he moved off to his right, away from the tree to the stream. Lining up a point with the tree at the bank, he paced off seven steps and kneeled over the water.

He rolled up one sleeve of his shirt and slipped his hand into the water, recoiling slightly at its iciness. Working fast now, he felt around the stream bed and removed the second stone from the bank. In the hollowed out opening, his fingers closed around a small cylinder. He glanced around quickly, then replaced the stone in its original position.

Wiping his hand on the heavy dark twill trousers, he shook off the excess water and put the cylinder in his shirt pocket and buttoned it securely. He stood up and retraced his steps back to the tree. After one final scan of the clearing, he turned and headed back into the woods in a low crouch. Once into the woods, he began to jog, then broke into a full run.

Keppler would never know the contents of the cylinder that had nearly cost him his life, nor did he care. That was for others to worry about. It was just one more film canister like all the others. His own mind, flooded with the rush of adrenaline and relief, focused now on a large brandy, a cigarette and the warmth of Helga's bed.

Keppler would probably not even have been surprised to learn that the cylinder in his pocket contained the plans for the Soviet invasion of Czechoslovakia.

Prague—July 1968

In the Old Town square, Josef Blaha, white-haired, slightly stooped, his face covered in weathered lines, paused to gaze at the enormous clock on top of the town hall. Dating back to the 15th Century, it displayed not only the time, but the paths of the sun and moon.

Blaha watched, fascinated as always, as the hour struck. Two narrow doors in the clock face opened for the procession of the Twelve Apostles, life-sized wooden figures preceded by a skeleton. Blaha checked his own watch and smiled as he compared it to the clock. It was old and much used, but like the clock, it kept good time.

He turned out of the square and strolled slowly, but with some purpose, shoulders bent slightly as if he carried a heavy burden. Twenty years ago, on this very spot, President Gottwald sounded the socialist commitment of Czechoslovakia. The memory was still vivid in Blaha's mind. He sighed and felt a twinge of longing for the ideals of his youth, but he realized sadly, they were gone now, impossible to retrieve.

He turned on Pariska Street, a wide boulevard known to all Prague as tourist street, renowned as it was for the abundance of travel agencies and airline offices. Continuing on, he headed for the Intercontinental Hotel, Prague's most luxurious. Even at this hour, the street was alive with couples arm in arm, bustling groups of noisy students and workers, tipsy with beer and now heading home to the gray blocks of apartments.

Blaha studied their faces as he passed them, noting the lively eyes, the smiles promising contentment and hope, the voices ringing with gaiety. But he was struck only with a profound sadness for all of them.

Soon. Soon it would all be over.

He quickened his step as he neared the hotel. Then almost as what would appear to anybody watching, nothing more than an afterthought, he stopped at a news vendor to buy a copy of *Rude Pravo* from the old shabbily dressed woman in the kiosk. Blaha nodded to her as he placed the coins in the tray, acknowledging that the paper came from behind the counter rather than the copies displayed in front of the kiosk. He folded the paper and continued up the wide thoroughfare to the taxi stand.

A battered gray Skoda stood at the curb. The driver was slouched behind the wheel, a cigarette dangling from his mouth, a black cap all but obscuring his eyes.

"It's a very warm evening," Josef Blaha said.

"Aren't they always in July?" The driver sat up and started the engine.

"Yes, that is so." Blaha opened the door and got in the back of the taxi, annoyed with having to perform these childish rituals, but they were necessary. He was comforted only by the knowledge that this would be the last time he would have to endure them.

The taxi pulled away and headed for Wenceslas Square then turned across the Vltava River that winds through the center of Prague. As they crossed the bridge, Blaha glanced at the thirty Baroque statues silhouetted on the nearby Charles Bridge.

He closed his eyes as the taxi continued its journey toward the outskirts of Prague. Neither Blaha nor the driver spoke during the twenty minutes it took to reach a small deserted building in an industrial complex, long abandoned. Both got out of the taxi and walked along a path behind the building. They spoke quietly, their voices muffled by the light breeze.

"Well, old man, what have you got for me?" the driver asked. He was American, but Blaha always marveled at his flawless command of Czech. His features, hard and sharply etched were briefly illuminated by the flame of his lighter as he lit a cigarette.

"Something important," Blaha began. He avoided the American's eyes.

They too were hard, like stones.

"I hope so. Washington is getting pretty jumpy."

"They should be."

"What do you mean?" The driver had been gazing around, but now his head snapped back to peer at Blaha.

"The plans are genuine," Blaha said.

"What? You said they were a plant. Our reports are—"

"I don't care about your reports. I was wrong. Things have changed again." Blaha faltered. For a moment, he was unable to go on. He felt the American's eyes boring into him.

"Changed? You mean the invasion is on?"

"It's almost certain."

"Jesus Christ!" The American flipped his cigarette angrily into the darkness. "Almost? When?"

Blaha noted the American could not keep the alarm out of his voice. It gave him renewed resolve to continue. "When I know more, but not now."

"Not now? Listen I—"

"No, you listen," Blaha said, choosing his words carefully. "I will not meet with you again." He registered the American's confusion. "You nor anybody else will get anything more from me until I have a totally safe contact."

The American shook his head. "Oh, c'mon. I don't know what you're trying to pull, but you can't—"

"I can and I will," Blaha said. "A safe contact. Tell Curtis a safe contact or there will be nothing."

Blaha wheeled suddenly and stalked back toward the taxi, leaving the American in stunned silence. But he recovered quickly, caught up with Blaha, grabbed his arm and spun him around. "Do you know what you're doing?"

"I know exactly what I'm doing. I'm finished. This is the last time for me."

He jerked free of the American's grip. "Tell Curtis that too, but get me a safe contact. And hurry. Do you understand? Hurry." He got back in the taxi and slammed the door.

On the ride back to Prague, Blaha was aware of the driver watching him in the rearview mirror. His head rested against the seat and his eyes remained closed until they reached the Metro station. He sat up then, blinked, leaned forward and pushed some notes into the driver's outstretched hand. He got out of the taxi and left without so much as a nod.

The American watched Blaha until he disappeared into the crowd rushing for the waiting trains. Angrily, he jammed the car in gear and pulled away from the curb, nearly colliding with another car as he raced away.

Had anyone been close enough, they would have heard mumbling curses about Prague drivers and crazy old men.

ONE

London—August 15, 1968

"A musician." Walter Mead nodded and glanced at Curtis, bemusement spreading over his face like an uncomfortable mask. He stopped walking and looked at Curtis. "Risky, but I like it. It's original."

"That's right, a drummer," Curtis said. He pulled open the heavy glass door of the Soho jazz club and followed Mead inside. It was hot and smoky and already crowded. There were a dozen or so people in line ahead of them. Past the line, Curtis could see people were three deep at a long bar along one wall. From somewhere around the corner they could hear the sounds of recorded jazz.

Curtis paid the cover charge for both of them and guided Mead toward the bar. Arty, poster-sized photos of jazz greats adorned the walls. Mead pointed at one. "Charlie Parker and Miles Davis," he said. Inside, the tables were tiered and arranged in a semicircle facing the stage. For some reason it reminded Curtis of pews in a church. This was where tourists and London's faithful came to worship at the altar of jazz. Ronnie Scott's. At least that's what Curtis had been told. Curtis had never been a jazz buff himself. Some Dixieland maybe, but this modern stuff was too far out for him.

He'd made a table reservation, but with Mead's plane being late and the traffic from Heathrow, they were told they'd have to wait for the second set. They wouldn't need that long. Curtis ordered two lagers in pint glasses. He and Mead managed to wedge themselves near the back of the bar against the wall and through a smoky haze, still had a good view of the bandstand.

Three musicians—bass, piano and a saxophonist—were warming up, adjusting instruments, joking, checking out the crowd. Only the drummer was missing. All the tables were full and out of habit, Curtis scanned faces, trying to determine which were tourists, which were locals.

A gray-haired man in a blazer and light slacks walked on stage, said something to the pianist and they both laughed. He took the microphone off its stand and turned toward the audience, one hand shading his eyes from the bright lights.

"Who's this?" Mead asked. Somehow he'd managed to get his pipe going with one hand.

"Ronnie Scott. Owns the club. A musician too. Saxophone, I think." Curtis scanned the area around the bandstand, found who he was looking for just to the side, near the opening to the backstage area. "That's him, talking to the piano player."

Mead nodded and pushed his glasses farther up the bridge of his nose. The man was very young, less than thirty, almost boyish looking. Dark curly hair, easy smile. "Jesus," Mead said. "Not a care in the world, eh? A god dammed jazz musician." He glanced again at Scott as he began to introduce the musicians.

"...and on bass we have John Harvey deputizing for our regular bassist who has taken suddenly drunk." Scott's corny, but totally deadpan delivery brought a few chuckles from the audience.

"Is he kidding?" Mead said. He continued to watch the pianist and their man talking.

Curtis shrugged. "Tradition. Ronnie Scott is famous for his corny jokes. They publish them in one of the trade magazines every year. Ronnie Scott's ten favorites."

They watched as Scott turned once again to the band, nodded and made a last announcement. "In addition to our current bill, we have negotiated for," he paused briefly, "Miles." He let the audience digest this and listen to the murmurs of anticipation before he went on. "That's Miles Schwartz, a very fine clarinetist from Liverpool." The laughs were there again along with some moans and obviously some of the people had heard this one before.

"And don't forget our waitresses," Scott said, as a petite blonde with a tray of drinks passed in front of him. "I asked one the other night if she liked Dickens. She said she didn't know as she'd never been to one." There were more groans and a mock frown from Scott as he tapped the microphone.

"Seriously, we do have a special treat for you, ladies and gentlemen. In a special guest appearance with our own Graham Lewis this evening, the very fine American drummer—-but we won't hold that against him—who is, I believe, on his way to Prague for the International Jazz Festival. Please welcome, Gene Williams."

Over the applause, Mead and Curtis watched as Williams stepped on the stage and took his place behind the drums. He raised one of the cymbals and scooted forward. The pianist snapped his fingers for the tempo and they took off in a fast version of an old Broadway show tune that Mead recognized immediately.

Curtis sipped his beer and watched Mead study Williams. He seemed almost as caught up in the music. "What do you think?"

It was actually Curtis who had proposed the plan, worked out the details, amassed enough information to make Langley listen and send Mead over to see for himself.

Mead put down his beer, shook his head at the questioning barman and relit his pipe. He watched Williams, head cocked to the side, an almost pained expression on his face as he slashed at the cymbals. "If it's handled right, if there's cooperation, the risk can be minimized," Mead said. "Anyway, we don't have much choice. We can't afford to lose Blaha as a source."

He turned back toward the stage again to watch Williams. The young drummer was deep in concentration, eyes half closed, but a slight smile on his lips now. "And you think this guy is the best choice?"

Curtis shrugged and nodded. "He's the only choice. Consider him a gift." Even with the obvious drawback— running an untrained amateur into a hot spot like Prague—Curtis could think of a host of others—Blaha's demand made it a special case. A safe contact, a total stranger to the intelligence community. Curtis knew that's what the old man wanted and he could think of no one more a stranger than a jazz musician. Or, he reminded himself, one with better cover.

"Don't forget," Curtis said. "Blaha is a music copyist, which adds to the case for using Williams. It shouldn't be too difficult to get them together without arousing any suspicion."

Curtis hesitated for a fraction of a second, a pause that was imperceptible to the ear, but registered in his consciousness. No, it was too early for that. For now, it was enough to sell Mead on using Williams.

"My guess is Blaha's on to something big for him to pull this. He's never been demanding in the past. It's out of character, but he's kept his word. No contact since the meet he had in July and well, we need a break on this."

Mead took one last look at Williams. The drummer was in full flight now, hands a blur around the drums, playing a solo that had the attention of the other musicians as well as the appreciative audience.

"Let's walk," he said to Curtis.

They pushed out through the crowd and stuffiness of the club. Outside, it had started to sprinkle. Mead looked up at the sky and turned up the collar of his raincoat. "Doesn't it ever do anything, but rain in this fucking town?"

Curtis smiled in spite of himself. He knew it wasn't the weather Mead was angry about, but rather that he was going to have to approve Curtis's proposal. There was no choice.

They walked to Shaftsbury Avenue, then turned toward Picadilly Circus and were soon caught up in the theater crowd spilling out and clogging the already busy sidewalks. Turning toward Mead's hotel down Regent street, Curtis caught a headline at a newsstand.

WARSAW PACT FORCES

MASS ON CZECH BORDERS

Most of the pubs were closing, but the hotel bar was still open. Curtis and Mead settled in a corner table with a double Scotch each and managed to wrangle a few small ice cubes from the bartender.

Mead leaned back, took a long pull of his drink and peered at Curtis. "You know what I keep thinking? Hungary, 1956 all over again only worse. We can't afford to get caught out of this, Alan. We're up to our neck in shit in Vietnam and LBJ is pissing and moaning about the lack of solid information coming out of Prague." He shook his head and smiled ironically. "Some genius at State has convinced him we'd have at least two weeks' notice on anything like this."

Curtis looked up from toying with his glass. The tiny ice cubes had already melted. "I've been out there two years now. The people have been lulled into a sense of security with all of Dubcek's reforms and little static from Moscow," he said. "I don't think so."

"Neither do I," Mead said. "Neither does anyone on the Eastern bloc desk, but all we can do is provide information. We can't act on it. We want to protect Dubcek, but he's playing very hard ball with Moscow and they don't like it one damn bit." Mead downed his drink and signaled the bartender for another.

Curtis had already accepted the assassination of Alexander Dubcek as another Soviet option. Was it because this seemed the year of assassination? Bobby Kennedy, Martin Luther King, Alexander Dubcek? Eliminating Czechoslovakia's new leader would effectively cripple the government and put an end to the liberal reforms now taking place in Prague. On the other hand, it would also create a new martyr for the Czechs, something the Kremlin didn't need.

Mead nodded at the bartender and took his drink. "I think we're looking at a full-scale, armed intervention. There's no doubt the plans West German intelligence intercepted were genuine. Everything was there—troop movements, supply projections, equipment, the whole lot. And they have these Warsaw Pact exercises as legitimate cover." Mead paused for a moment looking out the window. The rain had increased now. "But something happened to delay things, set the timetable back." He shook his head again and looked at Curtis. "Maybe Blaha has the answer, huh?"

If he does, Curtis thought, *we have to go after it on his terms. It all comes down to using Williams.* "So this is a go, I take it." It wasn't a question. Curtis knew Mead had already decided, perhaps back at the jazz club or maybe even before he left Washington. He just wanted a firsthand look at Gene Williams. Mead wouldn't be here otherwise. Curtis smiled. The spy who played jazz. No one at Langley could have devised a more perfect legitimate cover than Gene Williams would have, and since the CIA had no jazz musicians available, it could only be Williams.

"When does Williams leave for Prague?" Mead asked.

"Tomorrow night. I've had him under surveillance just in case."

"I thought you might," Mead said. "Well everybody at Ronnie Scott's knows. Just go very carefully on this and let's hope he cooperates. This could blow up in our faces if anything goes wrong."

Curtis didn't need reminding that the Redskin Program was not one of the Company's great success stories. While it was true that select businessmen and tourists were routinely approached and sometimes encouraged to report any interesting conversations or even turn over photographs they took while traveling in Soviet bloc countries, they were never used in any operational sense, except in extreme cases.

"How are you planning to handle Williams?"

"He did a short stint in Vietnam, no combat, but knows the ropes on security, so I thought the patriotic pitch would be best and the Redskin fund will add a little sweetener."

"What about getting him with Blaha in Prague?"

"Roberts says Williams is bringing in some new music for the jazz festival so we can doctor it somehow so Blaha knows Williams is his contact, then have Williams insist Blaha do the copying of the parts for the band."

"Roberts is the Cultural Attaché, right?"

"Yeah. The Jazz festival is one of his pet projects. He fancies himself as some sort of jazz promoter. He's pretty friendly with the leader, convinced him his band would be even better with an American drummer."

"Roberts hasn't tumbled to any of this has he?"

"No way," Curtis said. "Although he tries. I feed him something once in a while to make him feel like he's in the loop and keep him off my back." Curtis put down his glass. He was suddenly very tired.

"Okay, but no rough stuff with Williams. If he doesn't go for it, well, we'll worry about that when we come to it. I want Grant with you when you make the pitch to Williams. I've told him if there's anything that bothers him, I mean anything, we scrub the whole project and start from scratch. Understood?"

"Sure, no problem. I agree."

"I'll be back in Washington Friday. I'll see if I can turn up more on Williams. The file is pretty light." He paused, remembering something. "Oh, and one more thing."

Curtis looked up. "What's that?"

"For God's sake keep Williams in the dark as much as possible. We want whatever Blaha is running, but we don't want some Goddamn jazz musician skulking around Prague thinking he's James Bond."

Curtis smiled at Mead. He spread his hands. "Sure, you know me."

"Yeah," Mead said. "I know you."

"By the way. What are we calling this operation?" Curtis stood up and shrugged into his raincoat.

"Czechmate."

TWO

Gene Williams woke up in Prague—or was it London.

He suddenly couldn't remember. Both cities figured prominently in his future, but nothing surfaced except the dull ache at the base of his skull and a parched dryness in his mouth. He lay quietly for a moment, listening for sounds, slightly disoriented, puzzling over the refusal of his mind to perform such a simple task.

He sat up with a groan as the dull ache became a sharp pain, a throbbing that moved up around his temple. Licking his lips, he opened his eyes to focus on his surroundings, but that too failed to strike any familiar chords.

It was a hotel room like so many others he had occupied in scores of cities and typical of those itinerant musicians can afford when they're paying their own tab.

A pale, threadbare carpet ran across the room and disappeared under a huge monstrosity of a wardrobe that took up almost an entire wall. A small table and chair stood next to the bed and held last night's clothes, carelessly strewn over both. In the corner was a sink. Gene gazed at it longingly. There was thirst-quenching water and aspirins above, but it was a long way across the room and the throbbing in his head was becoming more intense.

He continued looking around the room. The bathroom was...right, down the hall. There's a clue. He thought he had it now, but just to make sure, he got out of bed and carefully walked over to the window and pulled back the flimsy curtains.

Blinking at the light pouring in, he gazed down at the heavy stream of traffic crawling by several floors below. As far as he was concerned, its slow steady movement was right down the wrong side of the street. For an American badly hung over and not at all sure about being in England, it was a reassuring sight. The big red double-decker bus just turning the corner dispelled all doubt and restored faith in his memory. London it was.

He turned away from the window and managed to make it to the sink only a couple of steps ahead of dizziness that nearly made him stagger to the floor. He turned on the tap and leaned over the sink. There was a loud gurgling noise followed by what appeared to be brown water. He let it run for a minute until it cleared enough to fill a glass and wash down four extra strength aspirins.

He splashed water on his face, then drying with a thin hand towel, glanced in the mirror over the sink. He'd often been told how boyish he looked, but not this morning. There were dark circles under his eyes and his face was pale and pasty. Only the shock of dark curly hair falling over his forehead retained anything like its normal appearance. Turning away, he wobbled back to the bed, sat down and waited for the aspirin to work and cursed his own stupidity.

Everyone likes to think his hangovers are unique, a personal agony only he can understand. Gene's was. And he had proof, real medical evidence to support his claim. Irregular chemical imbalance, the doctor had told him when he was discharged from the army. A notation had been made on his medical certificate, but Gene was relieved to have some official name to put to it, some explanation for the dizziness and occasional blackouts whenever he had anything more than a couple of drinks.

In practical terms, it meant alcohol, even in small doses, affected him dramatically and made the mornings after an indescribable hell, so he generally steered clear of anything more than the occasional beer. He'd tried marijuana, but that was worse. Two quick hits and he was away, sometimes out of control, a sensation he neither liked nor could afford in his work.

In clubs, he sipped wine or drank mineral water in rock glasses and let everyone think it was vodka. That was less embarrassing than trying to explain his intolerance for one of the occupational hazards of the music business. It made him something of an oddity among his peers. He'd known plenty of musicians who could drink or get high and still manage to sound good. Gene couldn't. The sticks became rubbery on the cymbals and up tempos became an uphill battle.

Except for an intense love of the music that brought him mind-blowing exhilaration every time he sat down to play, Gene Williams only claim to kinship with the public's image of a jazz drummer was Krupa's first name. But, Gene mused now, Gene Krupa was something of a non-drinker, he'd heard and his much publicized brush with drugs like most of the media's treatment of musicians was greatly exaggerated.

Gene accepted his condition and learned how to handle it, but sometimes, when the occasion warranted, he slipped, disregarded the consequences and plunged into a bottle of Scotch with almost reckless abandon. The dues were heavy and he paid dearly, like he was doing now. If the pounding in his head was any indication, last night must have been more of a headlong sprawl than a slip, good reason or not.

It suddenly got worse as he discovered the room had a telephone. The shrill insistent double ring shattered the quiet and sounded to Gene like a fire alarm. He found it under his shirt and managed to silence it by the third ring. He took another sip of water and croaked a hoarse hello.

"Mr. Williams? Eugene Williams?" The voice was a woman's, sharp, clear and very business-like.

"Yeah."

"This is the American Embassy calling, Mr. Williams," the woman announced. "We have a message for you here. Would it be convenient to pick it up this morning?"

"A message?" His mind still wasn't functioning properly. He fumbled for a cigarette and tried to get it going with one hand. "Can't you just read it to me?"

No she couldn't read it to him, no she couldn't tell him who it was from and yes, he would have to come to the embassy in person to get it. All he wanted to do was lie down again.

There was a brief pause that sounded like she had put her hand over the receiver. Then she said, "Can we expect you sometime this morning?"

Gene sighed into the phone and surrendered. "Yeah, okay. I'll be there in about an hour or so." That would give him time to get under a long hot shower or soak in a tub, depending on what was down the hall, get some coffee and feel human again. "Wait, where is the embassy?"

"I suggest you take a taxi," the woman said, almost as if she'd been waiting for the question. "The embassy is in Grosvenor Square."

"Right. Taxi, Grosvenor Square," he repeated before he realized the woman had already hung up. He looked at the phone for a moment and then put it down.

He sat for another minute, smoking, thinking, intrigued and began to wonder. Except for a few musicians and possibly his younger sister Kate, no one even knew he was in London, much less where he was staying. As far as he knew, Kate was winding up a college graduation jaunt around Europe with some friends. She and Gene had promised to get together if their paths crossed, but he hadn't known he'd be laying over in London till he'd checked in for his flight from New York.

He was expected in Prague—everything was cool with his visa—so it couldn't be that. What then? Some administrative mix-up? Fully awake now and grateful for the slight relief as the aspirins kicked in, he realized the call had shaken him. Unexpected calls like this were like telegrams in the middle of the night. They usually meant bad news and Gene didn't want any bad news. Not now with things rolling so well. He lay back on the bed and tried to come up with an answer.

The London stopover was a no-extra-charge bonus package thrown in by the airline. He'd almost declined, but in the end, he decided to take advantage of the two day break in London to look up an old friend, a fitting celebration of his good fortune at being in the right place at the right time. The cardinal rule of the free-lance musicians.

The travel arrangements were courtesy of Pragoconcert, his next employer and the booking agency for the Prague Jazz Festival. He was due to check in that evening for a five-day guest appearance with a band known only to him as the Prague Jazz Ensemble. But anxious as he was to get to Prague, the chance to see Graham Lewis again and play even one night at Ronnie Scott's had been too tempting.

He hadn't seen Graham for nearly three years. They had met in New York when Graham was attending master classes in the mornings and haunting jazz clubs at night with Gene. London was all right, he decided. Compared to the frenzy of New York, it felt relaxed and perfectly matched his mood. His reunion with Graham was all he'd imagined and Ronnie Scott's club was definitely cool. When he'd been invited to play, the evening was complete.

There was talk of meeting some girls, but that had never materialized and then it was all a haze of going back to Graham's place for what must have been a lot of drinking and celebrating. But now this damn phone call. Short of ignoring it altogether—he couldn't do that, it might be Kate—there was only one way to settle it. He gave up finally, still puzzled and resentful of the intrusion and went off to explore the bathroom—down the hall.

***

The shower had turned out to be a trickle of lukewarm water, but it revived him enough to get dressed and go looking for coffee. The hotel, he remembered now, was near Paddington Station. He found it easily enough and got coffee at one of the many snack bars with stand up tables. He sipped his coffee, smoked, still nagged by the call.

In the station, the newsstands displayed the various London papers with the headlines about troop movements on the Czech border, but so what. It had nothing to do with him and the jazz festival. He simply didn't connect the two. He finished his coffee and found a taxi in front of the station.

"Where to Guv?" the driver asked.

"Ah, Grosvenor Square, American Embassy."

"Right you are, Yank. The driver slapped down the meter lever and Gene got in the spacious black taxi, wondering how far Prague was from the Czech border. For someone headed for Prague in a few hours, his knowledge of the country was virtually nonexistent. Jazz and politics simply didn't mix.

He was worried only about what kind of band he'd be playing with, would they dig him and what the drums they'd promised to provide would be like. All he'd brought were his own cymbals.

He leaned back against the seat and took in the sights as the driver negotiated the heavy West End traffic. Turning off Oxford street, the taxi finally pulled to a halt in from of a gray, stone monolith that took up one side of the square. Gene got out, paid the driver and jogged up the steps. At the top, he turned and looked back. The center of the square was a park, with stone benches and asphalt paths crisscrossing to the other side. At one end stood a statue of Franklin D. Roosevelt.

At the entrance, a Marine guard checked his passport and directed him to an information desk inside of the lobby. A young girl checked his passport again, wrote out a floor and room number on a slip of paper and directed him to the elevators.

On the third floor, he got out and found the office, knocked lightly before entering. Inside, he saw a man seated at a table reading from a file folder. He looked up at Gene with clear eyes and a quick smile. "Mr. Williams. Come in, please." The man stood and extended his hand. "I'm Alan Curtis."

Curtis was dressed well, his hair was cut fairly short and he wore stylish glasses. He sat down and motioned Gene to sit opposite him. Gene noticed then, another man standing near the window, watching him. "This is my colleague, Donald Grant," Curtis said. Grant only nodded.

"Am I in the right place?" Gene asked. "I got a call that there was a message for me. Gene's eyes flicked back to Curtis, took in the smooth even features, the glasses glinting in the harsh strip lighting. For some reason, car salesman drifted into his mind. A guy who might draw up papers on Jaguars or Mercedes in L.A. or Newport Beach.

He also saw what he thought was his own photo in the file in front of Curtis. He felt the first twinge of alarm then. The whole thing smacked of a suspect being called in for questioning, a witness asked to make a statement. Gene suddenly wished he'd simply ignored the call.

Curtis smiled. "Well, Mr. Williams, may I call you Gene?"

"Sure, whatever," Gene said, a little nervous now, glancing again over at Grant. "What about this message?"

Curtis briefly glanced at Grant. "Well, we wanted to make sure you'd come in. We needed to see you. You see we have a little problem and you're in a position, or will be very soon, to help us out." Curtis spoke with just the right amount of friendliness and solemn gravity to get Gene's attention.

"Oh, sorry," Curtis said. He reached inside his coat pocket and took out a small leather case, opened it and pushed it across the table.

It was a photo I.D. with Central Intelligence Agency across the top.

Gene glanced at it, tensed, sat up straighter and looked at Curtis. "Hey, what's this all about?"

Curtis put the case back in his coat. "I'm sure after I've explained, you'll understand why we got you down here under, well, rather false pretenses." Curtis smiled again in a disarming way. Nothing to fear from me he seemed to convey. He closed the file folder, but not before Gene confirmed the photo was indeed of himself.

"Bear with me for a minute, okay," Curtis said. "This is just routine. You see we monitor all U.S. citizens traveling to Eastern Europe."

Gene felt himself relax a little. So it was his visa and not bad news from home or anything about Kate. But why the file, his photo? The whole setup was weird. Surely the CIA didn't personally interview everyone going to an Eastern bloc country. Or did they? Gene had never been to Europe, let alone a Communist country, so what did he know.

"Is there some problem with my visa because I was—"

"No, nothing like that," Curtis said quickly. "In fact, your visa is better than a regular tourist visa, at least as far as we're concerned. Can we get you some coffee?"

"No, I'm fine," Gene said. He spotted a large clean ashtray at the end of the table. "Okay if I smoke?"

"Sure," Curtis said, sliding the ashtray toward him.

Gene lit up and listened impassively as Curtis went on.

"Let's see, the purpose of your visit is to appear at the Prague Jazz Festival, right?"

Gene didn't answer. If they knew where he was staying in London, they certainly knew why he was going to Prague and probably a lot more was in that file in front of Curtis. This was all just dressing, but Gene couldn't imagine where it was going.

"Okay," Curtis said, "I'm going to level with you, Gene. We've got a little problem and you're in a position to help us out. I don't know how much you know about us, Gene, but the Company doesn't always get good press these days."

Gene shifted in his seat. In fact, he knew a great deal about the CIA. His short stint with U.S. Army Communications often overlapped with the Embassy Center, and given the numbers employed there, some contact with agency personnel was unavoidable. *Curtis knows all this*, Gene thought.

"Much of our work," Curtis continued, "is pretty routine, dull even. Occasionally though, we call on one of our citizens. Someone like yourself who, for perfectly legitimate reasons, happens to be traveling to a country we have an interest in." Curtis paused and smiled again. "Your appearance at the jazz festival, for example, is what we call perfect cover to help us out with our little problem."

Gene looked away and locked eyes with Grant still watching everything from the window. He dragged deeply on his cigarette. Panic raced inside him. How to handle this? Shock? Outrage that he was being approached? Polite refusal? More than anything, Gene wanted to make the Prague festival. A major international jazz festival. He had a number of impressive credits, but that was not one and he wanted it badly. One phone call, he realized, and his visa could be revoked. That was all it would take to put him on a plane back to New York, the dream shattered if that's how Curtis wanted to play it.

"No offense, Mr. Curtis, but I'm just a musician. I don't see how I—"

Curtis pounced quickly. "I assure you, it won't interfere with your appearance at the festival in any way. I know it must be important to you and of course, there would be some form of compensation for your trouble. As I said, it's a small problem, no more than an errand really, but it would help us, help your country, if that doesn't sound too corny."

Gene briefly closed his eyes then stubbed out his cigarette. "I don't think so," he said cautiously. "I did my service already."

Curtis opened the file again. "Yes, Gene we know. Your record is excellent. Spec Four, communications, even a top secret clearance, which makes you an even more desirable candidate."

A desirable candidate? Gene could only stare hypnotically at the file. Curtis made it sound like an accusation. He guessed his entire life was in that file, but he was just as certain that there was nothing there remotely useful if Curtis wanted to get nasty. *Damn! Why me*, he thought as despair crept into his mind.

But Curtis didn't give up. He asked Gene questions about what he knew of the political situation in Czechoslovakia, Alexander Dubcek, the troop movements, even hinting at the possibility of a Soviet invasion. Gene couldn't answer any of them. With characteristic single mindedness, he had completely separated the two, but, of course, they were intertwined.

"There's the real possibility there might not even be a jazz festival," Curtis said. "Did you know that?"

It had never occurred to Gene.

"I don't know how your are on history, but we don't want what happened in Hungary in 1956 to happen now in Czechoslovakia. I'm sure you don't either, and with your help, we might be able to do something about it."

"My help?" Gene couldn't stifle a laugh. It sounded so ludicrous. A jazz musician stopping the invasion of Czechoslovakia. "I don't even speak Czech," he said.

"Not a factor at all," Curtis said. "A simple pickup and delivery is all we're talking about." Curtis narrowed his eyes then, boring into Gene who realized that look was to crumble the last of his resistance.

Gene felt cornered. Despite his initial resolve, he felt himself wavering. He was not a trained agent and they certainly wouldn't entrust anything really important or dangerous to a total amateur would they? He was going to Prague, so why not. But no, he caught himself quickly. That was precisely what Curtis wanted him to think. He knew there was more, much more that Curtis wasn't' telling him. Probably more than he wanted to know.

He was going to Prague as an invited guest, a performing artist. The idea of sneaking around doing whatever it was Curtis wanted him to do, didn't appeal at all. He sighed. If it meant losing out then so be it. If that was the price he had to pay then he wasn't buying.

"I'm sorry," he said. "I just really don't want to get involved in this. I appreciate your problem, but I don't think I'm cut out for this kind of thing." He searched his mind for more reasons, but came up with nothing. He lit another cigarette and avoided Curtis' eyes.

Donald Grant joined them at the table then. "Mr. Williams, I understand your reluctance. I know it's kind of a shock to be asked, even temporarily, to help us out, but we're not asking you to be a spy. It's more of a courier job really." He and Curtis exchanged glances.

"Suppose I'm just not interested?"

"Then you simply refuse."

"Okay, I refuse."

"Just a minute," Curtis said. "Before you refuse, I just ask that you hear me out. If you still feel the same way, we'll thank you for listening and you can be on your way. Fair enough?"

Gene shrugged. What choice did he have. He didn't want to piss off the CIA. "Okay, I'll listen, but that's all."

Curtis nodded and smiled. He poured himself a glass of water from a carafe on the table and offered one to Gene.

"We have a friend, Gene, a Czech, who as it happens is not an agency employee per se, but he occasionally does some things for us. We'd like to contact him. Since you're going to Prague anyway, we're hoping you might help us out, save the taxpayers some money and do yourself a favor at the same time."

Gene noticed Curtis said regular people, not spy or operative. Who was he trying to bullshit with that line. Save the taxpayers money? Give me a break.

"What do you mean, do myself a favor?"

"Well, naturally there would be some compensation for your time and trouble. We're authorized to pay you two thousand dollars, deposited in the bank of your choice. Tax free I might add."

Gene sat for a moment, his mind swimming in confusion. He didn't like the sound of the whole deal and he knew there was more. There's always more.

"Look man," he said. "I understand where you're coming from, but I just..." He paused and looked away for a minute, suddenly remembering a story by Herman Melville he'd read in college. "I prefer not to," he said.

Curtis sat back, allowed himself a smile and studied Gene for a moment. "Bartleby," he said.

Gene nodded.

"Well," Curtis said. "I gave it my best shot, but I understand, Gene, I really do. I appreciate you taking the time to talk to us though. No hard feelings. We're disappointed of course, but thanks for coming in."

And just like that he was dismissed. Meeting over. He tried not to let the relief show on his face.

Curtis stood up and offered his hand again. Gene jumped to his feet and shook with Curtis. Grant gave him a polite nod, but didn't say anything.

"Just one thing," Curtis said. "I'm afraid I will have to insist you keep our little talk confidential."

"Sure, no problem," Gene said. He was reprieved. Relief flooded his mind, erasing all traces of the earlier pounding in his head.

"Fine," Curtis said. "I do need you to sign this for me then. He produced a printed document from his brief and slid it across the table. "Government paper work, you know how it is."

Gene glanced at the paper. It was a statement concerning the National Security Act, a security debriefing. He didn't read it carefully. He'd seen something similar when he was discharged. What the hell. Curtis had to cover his ass. He signed and dated it and gave it back to Curtis. He headed for the door.

"Oh, Gene," Curtis said.

Gene paused, his hand on the doorknob. "Yes?"

"Break a leg in Prague, eh? I'm sure you'll enjoy the festival. It's quite an event and Prague is a beautiful city."

"Thanks," Gene said. "Thanks a lot."

He went out and closed the door behind him. He practically ran for the elevators and stabbed at the down button. He kept glancing back at the office door, expecting Curtis to call him back any moment. When the doors opened, he pushed the lobby button and leaned against the back of the car. He closed his eyes and let out an enormous sigh.

On the way out, he smiled at the girl in the information booth, he smiled at the Marine guard and didn't even cringe when someone called, "Have a nice day."

He jogged down the front steps two at a time, crossed the street and paused in the square only long enough to give the statue of Franklin D. Roosevelt a mock salute before walking quickly toward Oxford Street. Glancing in shop windows, he decided the CIA wasn't so bad after all. They had a job to do and maybe it was necessary to use a private citizens once in a while. He clapped his hands together. But not me, baby.

Curtis had given him a lot to think about, however. He didn't know a damn thing about what was going on in Prague and maybe it was time he found out. At a newsstand near Marble Arch, a *Time* magazine with Dubcek on the cover caught his eye. He grabbed it and three newspapers. He still had a few hours before his plane and across the busy intersection, Hyde Park looked inviting. He could laze away the afternoon, grab something to eat and catch up on Prague politics.

He could hardly wait to get there.

* * *

"Melville?" Donald Grant said.

Curtis shook his head. "Hey, he's not dumb. I thought he'd buy it."

"So what now?" Grant said.

Curtis didn't answer right away. He got up and walked over to the window. He glanced down in the square and caught a glimpse of Gene Williams melting into the crowd. He looked at his watch. "We'll let him think about it for a while then hit him again. He turned back to Grant. "Did you get the backup stuff I asked for?"

"Yeah, it's all ready," Grant said. "Mead said no rough stuff though, remember?"

Curtis smiled. "Yeah I remember, but he won't know unless you tell him."

"That's true," Grant said. He was smiling too.

THREE

Prague—August 16, 1968

In the office of the Czechoslovak Communist Party Central Committee, Eva Simenova looked at the wall clock for the third time in fifteen minutes. Eva was young, pretty, and as always, annoyed at having to work on a Saturday. She'd worked for the Secretary for more than seven months now, and except for the occasional extra hours, she was content with her job and knew she was better off than many twenty year-old girls in Prague. Lately though, there seemed to be more to do than usual. Secretary Indra was keeping the staff busy at all hours. Eva felt especially proud that she had been singled out for praise and even given her own key to the office.

Normally, she didn't mind the extra work, but today was different. If they had to work much longer, she was going to be late for her meeting with Jarda. Just thinking about him made her eyes sparkle. Jarda was so handsome and Eva was sure he really liked her, maybe even enough to marry her.

She sighed wearily and resigned herself to at least another hour with files and letters, hoping Jarda would understand. She had even thought about asking Secretary Indra for permission to leave early just this once, but he'd been in his private office the entire morning. He seemed to spend more time than usual in there lately and everything seemed more secretive.

Besides, like many of the girls, Eva was frightened of the Secretary. She could never say exactly why, but there was something about him that gave her the chills when he looked at her, so she nearly jumped out of her skin when the door to his office flew open and he clapped his hands loudly.

"It's getting late, ladies and I've decided you all deserve an early day. So finish up what you're doing and let's all go home. Quickly now," he said and clapped his hands again rapidly.

Eva and the other girls needed no prodding. Squealing like school children let out of class early, they gathered up their things and scurried out of the building. Outside, the late afternoon sun was warm and beautiful. Eva's mind was already on how she and Jarda would spend the evening. A quiet romantic dinner she decided, then perhaps a stroll along the river.

From up the square, she could see the tram approaching. As she fumbled in her purse for change, she suddenly remembered she'd left her lipstick in her desk drawer—the expensive one Jarda had given her from the Tuzex store. She raced back up the stairs, opened the door and stopped suddenly.

Secretary Indra was hunched over the telex machine, obviously having just completed a transmission. He turned to her as she came in. "What are you doing here?" he shouted, his eyes blazing at Eva.

Eva froze. "I'm sorry...I forgot my—"

"I don't care what you forgot you stupid girl. Get out! At once!"

Struck with fear by the Secretary's outburst, Eva's eyes darted to the telex as an answering message began to spew out of the machine. The Secretary's eyes followed her gaze and the distraction was enough for Eva to grab her lipstick and flee the office. She raced back down the stairs just in time for the tram.

Out of breath, she dropped gratefully into a seat and puzzled over the Secretary's strange behavior. And all because of a telex message from Moscow? She knew about those. Everybody did.

It was her job, wasn't it?

***

In Hyde Park, Gene Williams bought a box lunch at a crowded snack bar and staked out a deck chair along the edge of the serpentine. The enormous park was crowded with office workers, shoppers with packages and carrier bags and the usual throng of tourists taking advantage of the bright sunshine that had just broken through.

Gene worked his way through the lunch, alternately reading and watching the ducks and swans splashing around in the water, clamoring for scraps of food, boldly stomping out of the pond, demanding attention with their insistent quacking. Gene gave the remains of his dry sandwich to one exceptionally loud chorus and settled down with a cigarette to continue his education on Prague politics.

He was drawn to several articles. There were a number of profiles on Alexander Dubcek, recounting his meteoric rise to power and his current position that at 46, made him the youngest Communist leader in the world. But even a quick scan confirmed Alan Curtis' assessment: Dubcek was in trouble with Moscow.

There was also a recap of the Hungarian uprising in 1956 that Curtis had alluded to. The parallels between that and what could happen in Czechoslovakia were obvious and well-drawn. Several columns were devoted to assessing, evaluating and predicting the Soviet's next move by informed Kremlin watchers. The general consensus was that Dubcek would eventually bend under the pressure and Moscow's hard line policy would be restored. Of the massing Warsaw Pact troops, most writers were of the opinion that it was all for show, a bluff designed to intimidate Dubcek. The exercises were an annual affair, they reasoned, and no one seemed unduly alarmed or thought that they signaled the probability of an invasion.

Gene put aside the articles, his head whirling with facts and opinions he could never hope to sort out. He felt better informed, but chose to believe those that took the bluff theory route. The jazz festival would take place as scheduled. He wondered if Curtis was being a bit dramatic.

"Gene? It is you, isn't it?"

Gene turned in his chair at the sound of the vaguely familiar voice and found a small, slim man peering down at him curiously. He wore a straw hat and clutched a large cigar in his hand.

It took Gene a minute to recall the name. He hadn't seen George Stevens in years. Mary must be nearby somewhere. They never went anywhere alone. Old family friends. George was an insurance broker, Gene remembered, and also very boring, but his residual good humor won out.

"Hello, George. How are you?" Gene pulled himself out of the deck chair.

George Stevens beamed and pumped his hand vigorously. "Hey, Honey, look here. It's Gene Williams." He waved to a slim woman coming down the path toward them in a stylish pants suit. Her hair was pulled back and a pair of oversized sunglasses perched on her head. Of the two, Mary was the easier to take, but Gene cringed at the prospect of spending his last couple of hours in London with either of them.

"Hello, Gene, good to see you," Mary said, smiling broadly and leaning close to kiss Gene on the cheek.

"Well, isn't it incredible," George said. "Small world I always say." He grinned at Gene and adjusted the camera slung over his shoulder. He wore a bright sports jacket, dark green slacks and white shoes. His loud voice was already drawing curious stares.

Gene sighed. "Yes, I guess it is. You two just sightseeing?"

George bobbed his head enthusiastically. "Got it all right here boy," he said patting his camera. "My God what a city this is, Gene. Mary and I have just been soaking up the culture, haven't we, Honey." He turned toward Mary for confirmation.

"Oh, George, Gene doesn't want to hear about boring old London when he's headed for mysterious Prague." She took in Gene's surprised look. "Your mother told us you were going to Prague before we left. It's a big jazz party isn't it?"

"Festival," Gene corrected her. "How are the folks?"

"Oh, they're fine. In fact they're meeting us at the airport when we go home."

"When is that?"

"Tomorrow," George said, glancing at his watch. "When do you leave, Gene?"

"Tonight."

"Have you seen your sister?" Mary asked. "Your mother said she was traveling around Europe as well."

"Yeah," George said. "We would have loved to show Kate around London."

Gene managed to suppress a smile. It had been a game when he and Kate were kids—avoiding the Stevens. "No, I haven't caught up with her yet. She's with some friends."

"Well, c'mon, George," Mary said. "We've got things to do. Nice to see you Gene. Any message for the folks."

"Tell them I'll try to get home after Prague."

"You go on, honey," George said. "I want to have a little man to man with Gene."

Mary shrugged and started up the path. George put his arm around Gene's shoulder and they began to walk slowly behind her. His voice took on a conspiratorial tone. "Now listen, Gene. You want to watch your step out there in Prague. You'll be right in the thick of the Commies."

Gene nodded. "Sure, George, but don't worry. I was invited, remember. And I'm only going out there to play music." Even as he said it, Gene felt another rush of relief. It had been so close. He wondered what George would say to hear about his near recruitment to the CIA.

"Yeah, I know," George said. "But you remember what I said, eh."

"Sure, George. Take care."

He watched for a minute as George caught up with Mary. She turned and gave a final wave before they both disappeared in the throng of people. Gene glanced at his watch. It was time for him get back to the hotel and pack. He turned across the park and thought about dinner in Prague.

* * *

They came twenty minutes after he returned to his room—Alan Curtis and Donald Grant, both looking less friendly now. Later, he would think they must have staked out the hotel or had him followed the minute he left the Embassy. He couldn't have been more surprised to see them when he answered the knock on the door.

"Hello, Gene," Curtis said, walking past him into the room. From Grant he got another bland stare, as he shut the door behind them.

Gene stood for a moment, unsure and feeling that alarm in his mind again. Curtis pulled out the chair from the table and sat on it backwards, leaning his arms over the back. "Sit down, Gene," he said, indicating the bed. "I'm afraid we have some bad news."

Gene's suitcase was open on the bed. On top were some music score sheets, an arrangement a friend in New York had given him on the chance it could be used at the festival. He moved his bag aside and sat down, looking at Curtis.

Ten more minutes and I would have been gone, he thought. *But no, they would have found me, had the plane delayed.* His reprieve had been short lived and now they were going to pull the plug.

"What do you mean bad news? Let me guess. My visa has been canceled, right?"

Curtis looked amused. "No, nothing like that. It's a personal matter. We thought we'd better come in person since you went to the trouble of coming over to the Embassy this morning."

"I didn't come because I wanted to. Remember? What personal matter?"

"Had any thoughts about changing your mind?"

Gene glanced over at Grant. *Here's my out. Just say yes, sure I'd be happy to become a temporary spy.* "No, none at all."

Curtis sighed and shook his head. "Well I'm sorry to hear that, Gene I really am. Aren't you sorry too, Donald?"

"It is very disappointing," Grant said.

"You see, Gene, with a little cooperation from you, we might be able to help you out with your problem."

"My problem." What was it going to be? An irregularity in his passport? An anonymous phone call from the Czechoslovak Embassy.

Well, Curtis could do whatever he wanted. Gene wasn't buying today. "Don't tell me. Let me guess. Owing to my membership in the Democratic Party, the Czechoslovak government has decided I shouldn't be allowed in the country."

"It's not funny, Gene." Something in Curtis's tone told Gene Curtis wasn't lying. He patted his coat pocket and produced a photo copy of what looked like a newspaper clipping. "We just got this, official confirmation from Madrid. This was in yesterday's paper."

Gene took the clipping. There was no way of telling what paper it had come from. He began to read and suddenly felt like he'd been kicked in the stomach.

> UPI, Madrid. Spanish police here today reported the arrest of Katherine Williams, 21, U.S. citizen from Vista, California. Williams is reportedly being held and charged with illegal possession of narcotics. No arraignment date has been scheduled, pending further investigation. The U.S. Embassy is making inquiries into the case.

Gene read it and read it again, not wanting to believe, but it was there, right in front of his eyes. He felt a wave of nausea sweep over him, his throat tighten. Little sister Kate, who never touched anything stronger than coffee, in a Spanish jail on drug charges? Kate was an athlete—swimming, surfing, tennis, you name it, Kate did it. But drugs? No way. This had to be a mistake.

He looked up at Curtis then, saw his expression, his face hard and set and knew it wasn't a mistake. Curtis knew it too. "This can't be right. I know my sister. This isn't her scene. She—"

"Maybe you don't know her as well as you think." Curtis said.

It was seeing the now half smile on Curtis' face. "Fuck you, Curtis!" He sprang off the bed, but Grant was behind him pinning his arms. He struggled for a few moments, consumed in impotent fury, then slumped back.

"Okay, let him go," Curtis said. Gene jerked free of Grant and glared at Curtis. The clipping had dropped to the floor in the scuffle. Curtis picked it up. "Sorry," Curtis said. "I didn't mean it the way it sounded, but we see it all the time." He got up and paced around the room. "Tourists, college students going abroad for the first time, even businessmen occasionally. They think their American passport makes them immune from the laws of other countries. Granted, this is not much, but sometimes foreign authorities like to make an example. Your sister was just unfortunate to be caught."

"No way," Gene said. He could only think of Kate, alone, frightened, lost in a Spanish jail.

"The point is," Curtis continued, "maybe we can do something about this. Speed things up, a quick trial if she's charged, light sentence, maybe even outright release."

Now he was getting it. The friendly patriotic pitch hadn't worked so they'd let him stew for a couple of hours before they brought out the big guns. The formalities were over. This was the real game, only it wasn't a game and Gene didn't know there were no rules. "You did this," he said to Curtis, a strange feeling of unreality seeping through him.

Curtis sighed and glanced at Grant. "No, Gene, I'm sorry you think that, but one thing we do not do is plant drugs on unsuspecting tourists. We had absolutely nothing to do with your sister's arrest."

"We just want to help if we can," Grant added.

"Oh, fuck you, too. What is this good cop, bad cop? We all know you set this up." But Gene knew that instant he was going to do whatever necessary to get Kate free and back home safely.

"I think you're being a bit dramatic, Gene," Curtis said.

"Am I? And you guys are just loyal, dedicated civil servants, right? You wear American flags in your lapels, go to church on Sundays and eat apple pie." He stood up then. "Why didn't you just frame me?"

"Because your medical records state you have an intolerance for alcohol and drugs." Curtis' voice was matter of fact now. "It just wouldn't wash."

Gene sat down again and bowed his head. "What do you want me to do?" he heard himself say.

"Fine," Curtis said. "I knew we'd come to an understanding." He seemed almost cheerful. "Naturally, the first thing we do is see about getting your sister released. We have, shall we say, certain influence in these matters."

"I bet you do. Just make it go away."

Curtis seemed not to hear. "Don't forget the compensation I mentioned this morning. I think you'll find it quite generous, given the little we're asking you to do, plus aiding your sister."

"You can use the money for her," Gene said. "Bail, bribes, whatever it takes. Just get her out." He glared at Curtis, hating him and all he stood for "Let's just get on with it."

Curtis seemed not to notice or care. He quickly took on a business-like tone. "Okay, here's the rundown. It's very simple really. About two months ago, West German Intelligence came up with this." He took a small object out of his pocket. "Know what this is?" It was a small metal container with a screw top used for 35 mm film.

Gene shrugged. "Film, I guess."

"Microfilm to be exact." He returned it to his pocket. "On it were detailed plans for the Soviet invasion of Czechoslovakia. Everything but when. That's what we don't know. More recently one of our sources in Prague came into some new information that we think just might give us the missing factor in this equation, or, and this is what we're really hoping, that the whole operation has been scrubbed. I don't think I have to tell you how much we'd like that to be true."

Gene lit a cigarette and listened. Overwhelmed that he was being drawn into a world he had no knowledge of, no conception. Agents, microfilm, invasion. Curtis' words frightened him.

"There's just one problem, Gene," Curtis continued. "Our source in Prague refuses to pass on this information through normal channels. He wants a totally safe contact, someone without any intelligence connections." He pulled his chair close and pointed at Gene. "Someone just like you, Gene."

"But why?"

Curtis looked away. "Frankly, we're not entirely sure. He may be overreacting to the show on the borders, think he's under suspicion, it's hard to say. But he's adamant about a safe contact and this is where you come in. No one suspects you of being anything, but what you are—a musician. Perfect cover. Our source is happy, we get the information and you've done your country a service."

"How does he know I'm his...contact?" It was strange even to say the word.

Curtis smiled and seemed pleased with himself. "That's the beauty of the whole thing. He tapped the music sheets on top of Gene's suitcase. "Music." He smiled again as if he'd just explained the meaning of life. Gene stared back at him blankly.

"Our source, his real job is music copyist. That's his cover, although he was doing it long before he came to work for us. Good reputation, does fine work so I'm told, often for the Prague Symphony." Curtis picked up the pale green music sheets, covered in penciled notes. "This is for the festival, right?"

Gene shrugged. "It could be, but the music may already be set. A new arrangement would have to be rehearsed. I can't just go in and demand—"

"You'll have to," Curtis said, looking at the score. "How does this work?"

"This is the conductor's score. It's sent to a copyist who uses it to make individual parts for each instrument in the band. During a rehearsal or performance, the leader can refer to the score, follow along, see what each instrument is playing."

"Okay, after the parts are copied, the score is returned with the parts?"

"Yes, in case the arranger wants to make changes later."

Curtis sat down again looking at the score. "All we want is to let our source know it's you he's to contact. Is it possible to change something in the score, do something to the music that only a music copyist would pick up on as unusual, so he'd know it's our signal? It would have to be subtle. Something out of the ordinary, but at the same time, not be noticed by a layman even if he were looking right at it. See what I mean?" Curtis looked at Gene expectantly.

Gene stared at the score, thinking, an idea forming in his mind. If this source was as professional as Curtis claimed, any minor mistake would be routinely picked up and corrected. Arrangers were not known for neatness and good copyists corrected errors in notes, key signatures or sharp and flat signs. But there was a way, he realized. Something that would leap off the page like a red flag.

"We could change one of the clef signs."

"I don't follow you," Curtis said.

"Look," Gene said, pointing to the score as Grant came over to look as well. "At the beginning of each line there's a clef sign for every instrument. These first five are for the saxophones so they have a treble clef sign." He pointed to the S-like symbol. "See, the sign is the same for the trumpets. Now the trombones are bass clef instruments, different." Again Gene pointed to the symbol that looked like a capital letter C written backwards with a dot in the middle.

Curtis looked up from the score as if waiting for the punch line of a joke. "So, what are you suggesting?"

"Here, in the rhythm section parts. The piano is treble clef, but bass and drums are bass clef. If that sign is wrong or deliberately changed, a copyist would, I think, pick it up immediately. One thing arrangers do not do is confuse clef signs. If we put a treble clef on the drum part and with the music coming from me, he should know it's some kind of signal."

Curtis looked at Grant and smiled. "That's it then. You've got it." He looked in the desk drawer and found a pencil and handed it to Gene. He and Grant both watched as Gene erased the bass clef sign on the drum part and wrote in a treble clef symbol.

But even as he replaced the original symbol, Gene wondered about the seemingly unnecessary precautions. He realized there was a lot Curtis wasn't telling him. He folded the music and put it in his suitcase.

"Now, the important thing is for you to get this music to our source as soon as possible after you get to Prague. His name is Josef Blaha. If anyone questions you about it, you can just say, oh I don't know, you heard about him through friends in New York. You'll have to think of something. I'll leave that to you. After that, he'll probably contact you quite openly. After all, it wouldn't be unusual for him to confer with you about the music."

Resigned, Gene nodded. Curtis seemed to have thought of everything. But he could only think how complicated Prague was going to be now. Making excuses, lying, secret meetings and still try to give a good performance with the band.

"The car is here," Grant said, looking out the window.

Gene looked at his watch. It was getting close to plane time, but Curtis had obviously thought of that too.

"We have a car to take you to Heathrow and don't worry about the room. We'll take care of it."

"What a guy," Gene said.

"Hey, c'mon, Gene. I can't tell you how valuable this is to us. And one other thing. Leave your sister to us. Don't even contact your family yet. It might, well, hamper our efforts. But don't worry. We'll get right on it." He handed Gene a business card. "If absolutely necessary, you can contact me at this number in Prague."

Gene took the card and absently put it in his shirt pocket. Curtis and Grant headed for the door. "Hurry it up, okay. We'll be outside."

Gene nodded and finished gathering up his things.

"Oh, one more thing, Gene. Don't worry, this will all be over before you know it."

* * *

"Well what do you think?" Curtis asked Grant as they left the hotel. A dark green Rover was idling at the curb. Curtis held up five fingers for the driver.

Grant shrugged, his eyes roving about the street. "It should work. That bit with the music beats anything we could have come up with, but Williams? I don't know. He's a wild card. You might have some trouble there."

"Yeah, I know," Curtis agreed, "but he can be handled."

"I hope you're right," Grant said. "Well, it's your show from here. I'm just glad I'll be back in Washington when he finds out that story about his sister is a plant. What's he going to do then?"

"By that time, it won't matter. We'll have what we want and the money should soften the blow. He'll understand."

"You think so?" Grant looked skeptical.

"You just tell Mead we're a go. I'll get word to Arnett in Prague." He laughed. "I just remembered something. Arnett hates jazz. He's going to love tailing Williams. Can you picture that?"

Grant smiled. "Not unless that band knows some Johnny Cash tunes."

FOUR

"What is the purpose of your visit to Prague, please?"

"I play jazz, man," Gene Williams said. He took off his sunglasses, trying to hide the anxiety churning inside him. Just be cool, don't overdo it. No one knows, but still, we don't know who's watching. Keep smiling, be casual.

The passport control officer frowned at Gene's photo, then back at him. He looked a moment longer, then stamped it, handed it back and motioned him along to customs. Gene let out an audible sigh of relief and hoisted his suitcase and cymbal bag on the counter where several customs officers were opening and checking arriving passengers.

He lit a cigarette and surveyed the crowded terminal. He was in Prague. Well almost. His eyes were everywhere at once, taking in the passengers arriving on various flights, listening to the mix of languages. He saw no familiar faces, nothing to worry about. Yet.

He watched as the customs officer went through his bag, scarcely touching the music sheets on top. He unzipped the cymbal bag and took out one of the cymbals, a 20-inch K Zildjian, as Gene looked on protectively. The customs officer looked up at Gene and smiled. "Boom, boom, yes?"

"Yeah," Gene said. "Boom, boom."

What did baffle the officer was the round rubber pad glued to a piece of plywood. He looked at Gene again for an explanation.

"Practice pad," Gene said. He took it with him everywhere, along with an old pair of chipped sticks. The pad was just right for hotel rooms, to think, to relax. Better than worry beads.

"I rather think you'll have to give him a demonstration."

Gene turned toward the voice. A tall slim man in a rumpled brown suit was smiling at him.

"Gene Williams isn't it? I thought I saw you on the plane. You were at Ronnie Scott's the other night. Bloody good too. I'm Philip Hastings." He held out his hand to Gene. "Don't look so worried," Hastings said. "You're one of the reasons I'm in Prague"

"What? I—"

"It wasn't by accident. I go to Ronnie's all the time. I'm an absolute jazz nut you see, so when my paper's music critic took ill, I was elected to be his replacement. I'm afraid my first assignment is to interview you."

"Your paper?" Hastings' burst of information was too much for Gene.

"Sorry, I forgot. You're American. Well, I don't mean that either." Shaking his head in embarrassment, Hastings took a newspaper out of his satchel. "Here," he said, thrusting it at Gene. It was folded to a profile on Alexander Dubcek. The photo and byline was Philip Hastings.

Gene felt himself instantly relax as they shook hands. He turned back to the customs officer, who was by then peeling the rubber back from the wood on the practice pad.

"Whoa," Gene said. He took the pad and set it on the counter. There were several curious stares from onlookers who'd stopped to see what all the commotion was about. Gene took a pair of sticks out of his cymbal bag.

"What would you like to hear, man?" Gene winked at Hastings. "How about some Charlie Parker?" Gene tapped out a quick march cadence, twirled the sticks like a gun fighter and offered them butt end first to the customs officer. He was grinning now, nodding his head in understanding. He quickly closed Gene's suitcase, marked it with a piece of chalk and put the pad and sticks back in the cymbal bag.

Gene Williams was in Prague. Perfect cover.

He stood a few feet away, waiting for Hastings then they made their way to the arrivals hall. "I rather think you're expected," Hastings said, pointing to a man holding up a cardboard sign with Gene's name on it.

They walked over to the man. "That's me," Gene said, pointing to the sign.

He was suddenly struck by the notion that probably no spy had ever made a more obvious arrival. Grudgingly, he began to see the logic and cleverness of Alan Curtis's plan.

"Where's Jan Pavel?" Gene asked, hoping he was pronouncing the band leader's name correctly.

"Pavel no come," the man said, exposing a mouthful of gold teeth. "Pavel say, you come with me." He was already reaching for Gene's cymbal bag.

"You going into town?" Gene asked Hastings. "Save your cab fare." It would be a simple matter to determine if Hastings was who he said he was, a genuine jazz fan, a reporter, or another of Curtis's recruits, primed with a crash course in jazz to keep an eye on Gene. He wasn't sure which would be worse, but he wanted to find out.

Being trapped with a pseudo jazz fan is every musician's nightmare. They usually toss off a couple of familiar names—Duke Ellington, Miles Davis, Dave Brubeck—but eventually reveal themselves when they announce their favorite trumpet player is Herb Alpert.

"Well, thank you very much. That's very kind," Hastings said, accepting Gene's offer. "It'll save me tracking your down later, since I've been assigned to you." Hastings took in Gene's surprised look. "Don't' look so worried. For the interview I mean. My paper wants to know how an American drummer gets invited to Prague to play with a Czech band."

Minutes later, rolling down the Lenin Highway toward Prague, Gene learned that Hastings was indeed his paper's political correspondent and a very knowledgeable jazz fan. "When my colleague took ill, I was assigned to cover the jazz festival and you seem to be the story." Hastings took out a pen and pad from his bag and began to take notes as Gene filled him in.

During the early summer, Gene found himself in a trio backing an unremarkable singer with a very remarkable bassist named Tomas Kodes. Gene and Kodes had hit it off immediately and soon became friends. "Tomas was on leave from Jan Pavel's band, working on a scholarship. Pavel, he said, wanted to have a guest American drummer and it was my gig if I wanted. Just being at the right place at the right time," Gene said. He wondered now how true that was. Did his recruitment go back as far as Tomas? Was he part of the plan?

Hastings had a pipe going by this time and the sweet aroma filled the taxi. Hastings nodded, made some more notes on Gene's background, his credits and his future aspirations. "So this is your first time at a major jazz festival, eh?"

"Yes," Gene said. He looked away then, out the window as the car sped into Prague. He decided to take advantage of Hastings' expertise and turned the tables on the Englishman. "Tell me about Alexander Dubcek."

"An extraordinary man, Dubcek. He's made great strides for the country and the people worship him. Still, he's making a lot of people nervous. Some say he's moved too quickly to suit Moscow and I'm afraid they might be right. But, that remains to be seen. He still might pull it off."

"Pull what off?" Gene asked, realizing just how politically naive he was.

"His liberalization program—abolishing censorship, easing travel restrictions—socialism with a human face he calls it. I have to applaud all that, but it hasn't gone down very well with the Kremlin. Dubcek's walking a tightrope. One slip, one step too far, well, Hungary was not so long ago that people don't remember."

Gene listened carefully, trying to digest Hastings' mini course in Czechoslovak politics and the tenure of Dubcek's career in office. "You think there's really a chance of an invasion?"

"Those troops on the border, you mean?" Hastings shook his head. "Rubbish. Sheer bluff. The Warsaw Pact exercises take place every year and someone would certainly know if an invasion was in the cards. You can't keep that kind of thing secret, can you? Especially not in Prague. The city is swarming with spies from every country, more than you and I could imagine. Even yours, if you don't mind me saying so."

"Oh, yeah," Gene said. "Well, I'm just here to play music."

He wondered what Hastings would say if he told him he was sitting next to one of those spies and someone did know about a potential invasion. Despite what Alan Curtis had told him in London, Gene drew some comfort from Hastings' inside opinions and analysis. But he wondered again why this man called Josef Blaha was refusing to pass along information through normal channels. Recruiting an amateur, was, it seemed to Gene, risky for Curtis and desperate for Blaha to ask for one. Something was very wrong, something that frightened Josef Blaha very badly.

They neared Prague as dusk settled over the city. Lights aglow, the air was warm and muggy and the city's spires were silhouetted in the light sky. Gene found it hard to believe he was here for any other reason than to enjoy the city and play music. But, of course, he was and everything about Prague reminded him how much he didn't know, how much he'd have to be on guard. That was perhaps something Hastings could help him with.

As the car bounced over some tram tracks, Hastings gave the driver directions to his hotel. "You speak Czech?" Gene was surprised at the quick exchange between Hastings and the driver.

Hastings shrugged. "Enough to get around. Leave a message at the hotel," he said as the car ground to a halt. "It's the Alcron. Let me know if there's anything I can help you with. I know Prague quite well."

Gene hesitated a moment then said, "Well, there is one thing. Is there some way you could check on a story in another paper, in another country?"

"Where?"

"Spain."

Hastings considered. If he found Gene's question strange, he didn't show it. "I don't' see why not. Something specific?

"I'll let you know," Gene said. "Try to make one of the rehearsals. I'm sure Jan Pavel might have something for you on me being here."

"Good idea." Hastings waved and shut the door.

Ten minutes later, the driver deposited Gene at the Zlata Husa Hotel. The Golden Goose, the desk clerk told him. It had a certain old world elegance, but neglect was the word that struck Gene as he stood in the ornate lobby. He surrendered his passport, a formality the clerk assured him and followed an aging bellhop in a military style uniform to his room.

Once inside, Gene smiled at the spacious room that faced Wenceslas Square. For once he was on somebody else's tab and it was a generous one. He explored the room, unpacked and decided to venture down to the hotel's dining room. There he learned his first Czech word: *Pivo*, beer and managed to make his dinner choice through a series of hand gestures and valiant efforts at English by the waiter. He smoked a couple of cigarettes over strong coffee then decided on a walk around the square.

The wide street was crowded with couples, students, clusters of men engaged in animated conversations, huddled around stalls selling hot sausages and pickled cucumbers. Trams clanged up and down the cobblestone boulevard to the far end of the square where a statue—St. Wenceslas astride a horse—looked out over all.

Continuing toward the statue, Gene took in the colored neon signs on the restaurants and kavarnas, the faces of people who appeared to have a real zest for life. They certainly didn't look like a nation under the shadow of invasion by a foreign power.

He stopped suddenly in front of a travel agency as a poster in the window caught his eye. PRAHA—1968. It was for the jazz festival and among the list of names he found Jan Pavel's displayed prominently. Just below was his own.

He stared at it for a moment, feeling the rush, as if he had reached some great plateau. Hundreds of hours of study and practice, countless gigs for next-to- nothing pay or recognition, one nighters in band buses, and now finally, he had arrived. The culmination of all his goals in music was right there on that orange and black poster.

He smiled at his reflection in the window. But the brief rush of elation was quickly dampened by the face reflected behind him. Standing just a few feet away was a stocky man with close cropped hair. He appeared to be studying the tram schedule, but Gene was sure he'd seen the man in the hotel restaurant and near the clock tower just a few minutes ago.

Was he getting paranoid? Letting his imagination get away from him? He continued his stroll, stopping every now and then to look at something in a window and every time the man was nearby.

Welcome to Prague. Okay, Gene thought. Curtis' watchdog? It made sense. Czech? Russian? That was more than enough speculation to send him back to the hotel. He took out the practice pad and went through a ritual of exercises as he stared out the window at the lights of Wenceslas Square.

Later, he drifted off to sleep, thinking of the first rehearsal and wondering about his sister Kate, somewhere in a jail in Spain.

***

In his office at the American Embassy, Alan Curtis pushed aside a stack of file folders and glanced at the wall clock facing him. The position of its hands, told him two things: the reception for the trade delegation was only an hour away if everything had gone as planned, Josef Blaha would have the music Williams had brought for the festival.

Curtis loosened his tie and opened the last of the files stacked on his desk. It was routine, but he wanted everything cleared. The next few days would be busy ones. His assistant had already gone over the material, but Alan Curtis' reputation for thoroughness never faltered. It was a creed that had served him well and one he had followed since his college days.

Scanning the open file before him, Curtis frowned and squinted at the typewritten sheets. Noting the high points, the salient details reminded him of the words of Langley instructor. "Intelligence work is sometimes no more than examining a weather report, checking a position on a map, or simply reading a local newspaper," he'd said. "Anything that might increase the likelihood of making the right decision at the right time."

Curtis wrote it down and committed those words to memory. He stopped for a minute letting his mind fall back to the circumstances that brought him to where he now sat. He lit a cigarette and hoped his most recent decision would be added to the list of those he'd been making for twelve years. Thirteen if he counted the year he'd accepted the CIA's offer of a career in intelligence.

Korea, university, graduating at the top of his class guaranteed Alan Curtis the pick of job recruiters that swarmed the campus. But as far as he was concerned, the offers guaranteed only average salaries and uninteresting corporate jobs.

Curtis had cultivated a political science professor he rightly suspected of being on the Company payroll. Displaying just the right mix of earnestness and dedication, he garnered an interview with an impeccably dressed man toting a pigskin attaché case. His suspicions about the professor were confirmed when the interview took place in his office. Curtis congratulated himself on his first important judgment of character.

The pigskin case talked; Curtis listened. "A young man with your capabilities could have a very rewarding career with us," he'd said. The Company was never mentioned once. That was understood. Curtis cut several days classes to complete the voluminous application forms and the day after graduation, security clearances behind him, Curtis headed for Langley to begin indoctrination courses at the sprawling CIA complex.

Curtis was a quick study and soon endorsed the criteria by which to judge what is and what is not permissible in dealing with friends and enemies of the United States. His own embellishment to the course was a rather personalized form of pragmatism. After a second phase of training, he was assigned to the Iran desk as communications officer, servicing requests from the field, waiting for his own first outside assignment. He bided his time, learned from the old hands and in the process, received excellent ratings.

Vienna was the next stop as assistant case officer. He debriefed defectors, received kudos for two minor successes and learned from one blown operation. Other assignments followed, broken by a year's study of Slavic languages back in Washington. By then, his superiors had duly noted the ease and elegance of manner with which he conducted himself at social gatherings. Curtis was quietly installed on the Prague Embassy staff, where suspicions went around that he was "one of those," even though he was listed as a Foreign Service Reserve Office in the State Department's *Biographic Register.*

Problems, solutions, decisions—they were all second nature to Alan Curtis. He rarely questioned his own judgment, at least not until now. On this one, he felt himself wavering and he didn't like the feeling of limbo, drifting, second guessing himself, but always coming back to the same place.

Was using Gene Williams the right decision?

When Arnett had reported Josef Blaha's demand, Curtis had been incredulous. The old man was bluffing, had to be. But deep down, he knew Blaha was serious. Curtis had waited, but when Arnett had checked the usual drop sites, there was nothing. No signal for a meeting, no answers to Curtis' requests. Blaha had simply shut down, gone underground.

Of course he could be found, threatened—perhaps using his granddaughter as leverage—but Curtis knew in the end, it wouldn't work. Blaha might roll over, but he would simply go through the motions and there would be nothing of value coming out of such tactics and precious time would be wasted. No, he realized he would have to at least attempt to satisfy the old man's demands.

Curtis had requested copies of visa applications for the next thirty days and sifted through the assembled dossiers of journalists, businessmen, émigrés with Czech surnames visiting relative, tourists, businessmen headed for the Brno Trade Fair and even a prominent movie actor. He had been left with only one name: a jazz musician. None had Gene Williams' perfect cover and access. How more a stranger to the intelligence community could a jazz musician be? Simple, straight forward, an invited guest to the Prague Jazz Festival.

Curtis had feigned slight interest to Warner Roberts, the Cultural Attaché. "Oh yeah," Roberts had said, taking full credit. "It's a big thing. American drummer with an all Czech band. Hasn't been done before."

Neither had a musician been used as a spy either. A random name off the CIA's zombie list of potential Redskin candidates, routinely compiled, but seldom utilized and with good reason. Curtis didn't need reminding of the times the Company had been burned.

An elderly missional couple headed for West Africa was so horrified at being approached by the CIA, they had complained to their congressman and later to a crusading columnist bent on making a name for himself by blasting government agencies.

Another traveler, an opportunistic young man on a tour of the Soviet Union, agreed enthusiastically to report anything and everything he encountered on his stay in Moscow. But when he returned, instead of presenting himself for the debriefing, he organized his own lecture tour: How I Spied for Uncle Sam. It played in a number of cities and the agency was not amused. It took a flurry of diplomatic cables and denials to discredit the young man and restore Soviet-U.S. relations.

In addition, even willing recruits—which Gene Williams was not—were generally not advised that by simply being briefed by an intelligence agency prior to their arrival in a foreign country constituted espionage and made them liable for charges by that country. This was common knowledge in intelligence circles and often capitalized upon by the KGB.

Despite all these negatives—Curtis could think of many more—the situation in Prague called for extreme measures and if ever there was a special case, this was it. Curtis sighed and closed the last of the files. He leaned back in his chair and let his eyes roam over the office, taking in the functional furniture, the inevitable telex machine and finally, the obligatory portrait of Lyndon Baines Johnson.

"And you think you've got problems," he said aloud to the painting.

It was all there, neatly documented and cataloged, all the signs for an impending disaster. Months of research, logging information, following up on tips, overheard conversations, all pieced together to form the fabric of Prague. But the hole in this fabric remained. It was a situation that required unorthodox measures, gut level instincts. *Yes*, Curtis thought, *even something as crazy and dangerous as using a jazz musician to gather intelligence.*

There was no question in Curtis' mind that Josef Blaha had discovered something so vital and so frightening that he simply no longer trusted his usual contacts. There could be no other explanation for the old man's requests. No, check that, demands. He wasn't giving it up until they were met. It had to be a definite date, a confirmation, some new piece of information that couldn't have been anticipated, something perhaps no one had even imagined. Curtis could feel it.

Were the Soviets coming or not? And if they were, when? Tomorrow? Next week? Curtis signed again and lit another cigarette, blowing a cloud of smoke toward Johnson's portrait. His thoughts went round and round, but always came back to the same fact: he was dependent on Gene Williams to fill in the blanks. A musician whose cooperation and control was based only on his belief that his sister had been arrested and was now being held in a jail in Spain.

Curtis had hoped the arrival of the orange diplomatic pouch would reveal something more about the young musician, some practical leverage that he could apply, but evidently, Walter Mead had found nothing of further use. The pouch contained only routine papers and triggered the memory of a story Curtis had once been told about an ingenious CIA officer and his KGB counterpart.

They had convinced each other that life would be much more simple if they exchanged diplomatic bags, photocopied their contents and then concoct a story to explain their great stroke of luck in securing information. Unfortunately for both, their superiors saw through the flimsy plan and acted accordingly. The Company man was allowed to resign; the KGB operative was never heard from again.

Curtis shook his head. *They must have been crazy*, he thought, *and dammit, so am I.* But, he reasoned, Mead could have stopped him cold, scrubbed the entire operation. He didn't. Reluctant or not, he had approved Williams and now they were committed. And if Curtis needed one, there was another reason for rationalizing the idea of using Williams.

Keppler, the German agent who had intercepted the invasion plans was dead, murdered and found near the Czech border. The connection between Keppler's death and Blaha's demands was too much to be a coincidence. Curtis never believed in coincidence.

But an amateur? A musician? Someone had once told Curtis the only difference between an amateur and a professional was dedication. It wasn't ability that mattered, just dedication. For the moment anyway, Curtis could be sure of that much from Gene Williams. But what if Williams somehow managed to discover that the story about his sister was just that, a story? Well, Curtis would deal with that and Williams when this was all over.

Curtis cleared and locked his desk. But before he turned out the light and left his office, he gave Johnson's portrait once last look.

"Lyndon, you old bastard, let's hope I'm right."

***

Josef Blaha was exhausted. His eyes burned and his back ached from the many hours he'd sat hunched over the large work table he used when he worked at home in his small flat in Old Town.

He ran his long slim fingers through his white hair, took off the wire-framed spectacles and rubbed his eyes, trying to massage some life into them, feeling every one of his sixty-eight years.

The table was littered with the tools of his craft. On one corner was a neatly stacked ream of music paper, heavy enough to withstand a thousand foldings, repacking and still retain the necessary stiffness when laid out on music stands. Next to the paper were two bottles of black ink, a tray with several osmoid-tipped pens and an X-Acto knife for errors. This was the one item rarely used. Josef Blaha did not often commit errors.

As a copyist, his reputation in the music circles of Prague was beyond reproach. Josef Blaha was as much an artist as the musicians who played from his meticulously copied parts or the composers who casually dropped off their scores for the Blaha magic. For many years, Blaha was the choice of the Prague Symphony. It was left to him to translate the scrawled pencil sketches into beautifully copied individual parts, sometimes numbering over a hundred. It was painstaking, tedious work, turning a blank sheet of music paper into a work of art. But in recent years, Blaha had scaled down his schedule and workload. He was simply tired.

Still, he did the occasional favor for a favorite conductor or composer, and of late, there were small accounts with radio stations, chamber groups, even dance bands. It was work he considered child's play even if the pay was good. And now, more and more, pop music, imported from the west and even more inane. A musician himself, Blaha could sympathize with the plight of trained musicians forced to play elementary arrangements for mediocre singers. It was an insult to the artistry of these musicians, but like musicians everywhere, what choice did they have? Work was work.

This morning Blaha was annoyed at having to work so early. He'd been up half the night, but there was a special reason and this was perhaps the most important job of his career. It was now nearly noon, but he would be finished soon and Jan Pavel would have his music for the afternoon rehearsal.

The thought of his old friend Jan Pavel brought a smile to his lips. They had studied together at the conservatory. The factory incident had cut short Pavel's promising career; not enough talent his own. But both men had continued to pursue music in their own way. Jan the rogue, Blaha called him now, intoxicated by the taste of American jazz and he had done well. He was glad for his old friend. No, he didn't mind doing a favor for Jan Pavel, even though he was puzzled by the request.

He had accepted this job for another reason that had nothing to do with friendship. Or did it? No, he was sure Pavel had not followed the same path. Jan had been a resistance fighter during the war, but music, not the cause, had been Jan's passion.

Blaha leaned back in his chair, stretched his arms overhead and returned the spectacles to his weathered face. He examined the score before him once again. He was nearly finished. The saxophone, trumpet and trombone parts were already complete. Only the rhythm sections parts remained uncopied.

Grudgingly, he had to admit the harmonic structure of the composition was brilliant and displayed an inventiveness, almost daring in the chord progression. He did not entirely understand modern jazz, but he knew this arranger had more than a cursory knowledge of Ravel and Bartok.

But in this score, he was looking for something other than musical excellence. Somewhere in this score, buried among the maze of notes, rests and other musical notations was a signal. A signal that would measure the first step in releasing him from the dreaded secret that plagued his every waking hour. A secret he desperately wanted to be rid of once and for all. Somewhere in this score was his freedom, he was sure of it.

He'd had more than enough lurking around the back streets of Prague, leaving bits of information in out of the way places, making hurried, innocent appearing meetings on park benches and always, always, looking over his shoulder. He did not regret his decision to become involved, but now there had been enough. He owed that much to his granddaughter Lena and his beloved wife Hanna. How long had it been now?

It was she who had triggered his desire for reprisal. They had killed her as surely as if they had gunned her down in the street. The Communist takeover of Czechoslovakia in 1948 had been too much for Hanna. Barely recovered from the ravages of war, they had stamped out her last remaining will to live. It had happened to so many of their friends and now it was happening again.

Lena had already endured enough hardship having lost both her parents in an automobile crash, but now, at 24, she had blossomed into a beautiful, bright young woman with her whole life ahead of her. They had found each other and together, he and Lena, had coped. But what did the future hold for Lena?

Perhaps she could get away, go to America, have a new life. They owed him that much. But he would do no more. He could no longer jeopardize Lena and they were getting too close. For himself, he no longer cared. But for Lena, he must stop. Enough damage had already been done. Discovery of his involvement with American intelligence would spell disaster for both of them.

This would be his final act.

He knew as soon as Jan Pavel told him the arrangement was for the young American, they had met his demands. This was at last, the contact he'd been waiting for—someone totally safe. He could afford no more meetings as he had chanced in the past. They were too dangerous despite the precautions and he was sure on one occasion, he had been followed. Perhaps he was already under suspicion, so he had demanded and Curtis had complied.

He had to admire the cleverness. A musician. Where had they found him? It was perfect. He wondered if the young American—what had Pavel called him? Williams?—was being used in some way, unaware of the risks involved? Probably not. They would tell him only what was absolutely necessary. And if anything went wrong? Well, he was not an operative so they could deny any knowledge of his activities. Enough speculation he thought, bringing his mind back to the task at hand.

He had checked and double-checked the parts already copied. There was nothing unusual in any of them. Hastily sketched perhaps, but correct nonetheless. Scanning the piano part again he found the same was true there as it was for the bass. There were only chord progressions written above the staff and diagonal slash marks in each measure to indicate the bassist was to play a walking, four beats to the bar bass line.

He'd scarcely looked at the drum part. It was even sketchier and from a copyist's point of view, the easiest to do. Again the diagonal lines, which to the drummer meant he was only to keep time. There were the occasional rhythmic figures, accents that mirrored the brass section and an occasional spot with the word "fill" penciled in above the staff, the odd one word idiom of jazz that meant the drummer was to play some improvised solo at that point.

He frowned at the score. Had he been wrong? There seemed nothing out of the ordinary, nothing that could be construed as a signal. But there had to be. Anyone in Pavel's band could have copied this score, yet Pavel had said the American had asked for him by name. However respected his work was in Prague, Josef Blaha didn't flatter himself by assuming Williams had heard of him in New York.

No, someone had instructed William to ask for him by name. Who? Pavel? He hadn't seen or heard from Pavel in years and he was certain his friend was not involved. But where then was the signal? He must be sure. He scanned the drum part again, still finding nothing until—wait. Something caught his eye. There, in the beginning. His finger traced down the page then back to the top.

And there it was, so obvious now that he saw it. Hidden in plain sight. The American was a drummer. Why hadn't he seen it before?

The clef sign at the beginning of the part was wrong. Any fool knows drum music is written in bass clef and yet, there it was, clearly penciled in: the S-like treble clef sign. And something else. He reached for the heavy magnifying glass and saw tell-tale signs of erasures.

Hurriedly now, he once again checked the other parts. All the clef signs were correct. Only the drum part was wrong. This was the work of a skilled arranger, one who would not make such a careless error. It had to have been deliberately changed by Williams himself, under orders from Curtis.

Blaha let out a relieved sigh. Satisfied now, he took a blank sheet of music paper, his hand gliding across the page skillfully, effortlessly. The page came to life with the swift sure strokes of the pen. Completing the part, he returned his attention to the top of the page. The space for the clef sign was still blank. With a quick flourish, he added the treble clef sign, not correcting the error on the score.

It was now left only to impart his own message

Josef Blaha knew exactly how he would do that.

FIVE

Lunch was in a noisy basement tavern off Wenceslas Square called The Tiger. Several tables were pushed together to accommodate the band and various assistants. Plates of steaming pork and dumplings were quickly brought from the kitchen. The inevitable chilled mugs of Pilsner beer stood by every plate and most of the musicians gulped them down like water. It took some explaining and interpreting for Gene to convince the band he couldn't drink more than one.

"But *pivo* is good, yes?" Bartek, one of the saxophonists, wanted to know.

Gene grinned and held his glass up in a mock toast. "All right!" the band shouted and pounded on the table. He was already one of them and he'd only met them for the first time earlier that morning.

When Gene had arrived with Jan Pavel for the ten o'clock rehearsal, most of the musicians were already engaged in the familiar rituals. But now there was an air of seriousness, Gene thought, as he watched trumpeters oil valves and wipe down their horns with soft cloths. The saxophonists paced around, their cheeks puffed out, blowing scales and adjusting reeds. One of the trombonists, the bell of his horn pointed toward the floor, worked the slide up and down like a pump. Crouched over the keyboard of a nine foot grand piano, the tuner repeatedly struck a note, tightened the hammer-like tool on a string,and listened like a doctor taking a patient's heartbeat. Nearby in the harsh glare of the stage lights, the pianist stood by impatiently, hovering like an anxious relative.

As introductions were made, Gene shook hands with everyone and began to match the unpronounceable names with faces and instruments. He saw behind the shy smiles a unanimous expression of expectancy. We've been waiting for you, their eyes said questioningly. The American drummer, come perhaps to change the band's sound?

The drums were already there as promised, a Czech brand, Amati. Shiny jet black and seemingly fine. "The drums are for you," Jan Pavel had said. "Later, the director would like to meet you."

"Sure," Gene said. "This is really cool. Thank you." He sat down at the drums, took his own cymbals out of the bag and secured them to the stands. He felt the weight of a dozen curious stares as he took out sticks, adjusted the height and angle of the snare drum, the height and tilt of the cymbals. The next few minutes, he knew would set the tone for his entire stay.

The newspaper clipping Alan Curtis had given him was still in his pocket, wrinkled from folding, refolding, numerous readings that he still found hard to believe. Drug charges. His Sister. It just wasn't possible. He suddenly wished now he'd given it to Philip Hastings.

Somewhere in Prague, perhaps at this very moment, Josef Blaha was pouring over that music score he hoped he'd been clever enough to fix, to let the old man know he, Gene Williams, was his safe contact.

And now, he must—he had already by insisting Blaha copy the music—deceive Jan Pavel as well. He knew he'd been less than convincing. Pavel had instantly known something was wrong. He knew Blaha, they were friends, but he also knew Gene couldn't have known this. Was Pavel part of this too?

He tapped on the cymbals and felt the sneaked glances from the band. One particularly intense gaze came from the heavily bearded bassist. A huge barrel chested man. Imre, Jan had told Gene, came from a family of gypsy musicians. It would have been a disgrace if Imre had not chosen and pursued a career in music. As it was, he was something of a black sheep for choosing jazz over the family's traditional gypsy folk music.

He studied Gene and cradled his bass in one arm and nodded appreciatively as Gene warmed up on the drum set. The Lucerna Hall was flooded with light and a number of technicians scurried about, running cables, checking spot lights and microphones. The enormous seating area remained in darkness. Stretched across the hall's ceiling was a huge banner that read: PRAHA 1968.

Gene had a fleeting thought for the man who had been following him the night before. Was he sitting out there somewhere in the shadows? *Concentrate*, he reminded himself. *This isn't some club gig. This is genuine, a major league, prestigious, international jazz festival.* He took a deep breath. *One thing at a time. New band, new music and everyone wants something from you.*

"Okay," Gene said, looking up, catching all the band watching him and smiling. Jan Pavel's Prague Jazz Ensemble was almost a big band. Five saxophones, three trumpets, trombones and rhythm section of piano, bass and drums made it the size of Maynard Ferguson's Birdland Dream Band.

They'd settled down for the morning rehearsal, going through five arrangements, each more difficult than the other, after that first get acquainted blues chart with the Count Basie like flavor. Despite the obvious acceptance and enthusiasm of the band, Gene was constantly on alert, dealing with the first sight reading he'd done in a long time. Two of the charts, reminiscent of Dave Brubeck, featured complex time signatures and tempo changes, but somehow, Gene managed to make it all swing. Finally, Pavel called a break for lunch.

"Yeah, Gene, we kick ass, yes?" Bartek the baritone saxophonist grinned and clapped Gene on the shoulder. Gene agreed. If this was any indication, they'd blow the house down. In the walk over to the Tiger restaurant, every member of the band hand said something or smiled to let him know, make him feel at home. Gene was elated to be part of such a unit, however short his stay might be.

Dessert at the Tiger came with laughter and camaraderie. Gene's initial impression of the band was soundly confirmed. There seemed to be no stars, no personality conflicts, no ego problems and Jan Pavel seemed to be liked and respected by all. That was not always the case with big band leaders, but Pavel presided over everything like it was his family.

The meal was punctuated with road stories, back slapping and leering, flirty, suggestive, but harmless bantering with the waitresses. Gene watched and tried to answer the questions he was bombarded with about the American jazz scene. He took in the nodding comprehension and sometimes awe on their faces as Bartek translated his answers. The universal language cliché about music ran through his mind and almost erased the secret role he was playing. Almost, but not quite.

It constantly pulled him back, like somebody tapping him on the shoulder, reminding him that now, the band represented his cover, the real reason he was here, as Curtis had put it. In addition to being a musician, he was also an actor. Well prepared, but playing a role that was a deception to everyone he came into contact with. For his sister Kate, he must be convincing.

After lunch, they straggled back to the Lucerna Hall in twos and threes, heavy with food and beer, spurred on by the anticipation of new music. News of the arrangement Gene had brought had spread through the band. Direct from New York and the band was clearly excited at the prospect.

When Gene arrived, he found Jan Pavel talking with a young girl standing by the piano. The spotlight blinked on and off as the technicians continued the lighting checks. He saw her first in darkness, then bathed in light, then dark again. A flash of buttery yellow hair, smooth skin and nearly as tall as he was.

"Ah, Gene," Pavel called to him. "Please, this is Lena Blaha, Josef's granddaughter."

Gene hopped up on the stage. Closer now with the house lights back on full, he took in the greenish eyes, dancing with curiosity, the slight tilt of her head and the long tanned legs beneath the short cotton skirt.

She smiled and offered her hand. Her voice was soft, lightly accented, but the English was precise. He searched his mind for something clever to say, but all that came out was, "Hi. Gene Williams."

"Hello, Gene Williams. Jan has been telling me about you and how much you are helping his band." Her expression seemed to say, *Why does an American come to Czechoslovakia?*

"Well, I don't think this band needs any help," Gene said. "Are you a jazz fan?"

"Yes, but my grandfather doesn't quite approve I'm afraid. He thinks I should only listen to classical music."

Gene smiled. "Well, you can tell him jazz is America's classical music. We even have royalty—Count Basie, Duke Ellington." Gene winked at Pavel, but the leader seemed confused by the exchange. Gene and Lena both laughed.

"I'll have to remind him of that," she said. "But my grandfather is very set in his ways."

"So I've heard," Gene blurted out without thinking and regretted it immediately.

"What?" Lena's eyes clouded over and she became solemn.

"Nothing," Gene said, trying to be casual again. "Is this the new music?" He pointed to a stack of parts on the piano. He felt interest in her gaze or was it challenge. How much did she know? he wondered.

"Yes," she said, recovering quickly. "He was going to bring it himself, but he had...he had some other things to do."

Gene glanced at the music. Yes, he thought, like avoid being seen with me. Special delivery. Of course Blaha would not come, not yet. Too obvious. Was Lena sent here to check him out? Was she supposed to signal him in some way?

Gene opened one of the copied parts and glanced over it. "Your grandfather does beautiful work."

Lena held his gaze. "Yes, for Jan, for you, he did a special job."

"I understand," Gene said. "Please tell him I appreciate it very much. I would like to thank him in person." He paused, sensing what he hoped was understanding in her eyes. "Can you stay around? Maybe after the rehearsal you could show me around Prague or I could meet you later and—"

"I'm afraid not," Lena said quickly. "Anyway, you are busy." She looked at Pavel for confirmation.

"Yes," Pavel said. He turned away to assemble the band.

"Goodbye, Jan." She said something else in rapid Czech and Pavel nodded. "Nice to meet you, Gene Williams." Then she walked off stage.

Gene watched her go. She had the easy fluid movement of a dancer. She turned to look back at him once before disappearing through a side exit and caught him still looking at her. He waved briefly and all he could think about was how he wanted to see her again.

The new arrangement was quickly passed around and Gene went back to the drums. His eyes immediately went to the clef sign on his part.

Unchanged. Message received. Josef Blaha understood he was to be his contact.

Now, somewhere in the music there should be a signal for Gene. A time, a place. He skimmed over the part, but saw nothing out of the ordinary. Like a hundred other drum parts, it was a sketchy skeleton for the drummer to improvise on, fill in gaps in the arrangement.

Jan counted them in now, a medium up tempo. Accents on the eighth measure, then again at measure thirty. Gene glanced over at the trumpets. They were muted here, not accented. Gene got a questioning look from Pavel. They continued to play Saxes getting more confident, mastering the fingering.

Okay, unnecessary accents at measure eight and thirty 8:30? But where? A hotel, a park? Curtis said it could be anywhere. Pavel stopped the band to rehearse the trumpets alone, to get them through a phrasing problem.

Clever or obvious? So obvious no one would notice. There, in the coda section. Four big chords, the lead notes beautifully penned in the spaces of the staff with the fermata, the hold sign over each note. Like an upside down U with a dot in the middle. The notes were C A F E. Cafe. But which one. There must be hundreds in Prague. Then suddenly he knew. At lunch somebody had mentioned a jam session that night at a local club.

"Hey, Bartek," Gene called. "What was the name of that jazz club we're going to tonight?" Trying to keep it casual, just a matter in interest.

"Reduta," Bartek said. "We go, yes? Nice girls and..." His voice trailed off, muffled by the sound of the trumpets.

Josef Blaha is a professional, Curtis had told Gene. He'll know what to do.

Cafe Reduta, eight thirty tonight.

Then it's over.

***

In the rear of the Lucerna Hall, beyond the view of anyone on stage, Karel Arnett sat in one of the hundreds of empty seats, smoking, squinting at the stage, bored out of his mind. Jesus, how many times are they going to play that one number? Nothing but a bunch of fucking noise anyway. He ground out his cigarette and leaned on the chair in front of him.

He glanced around the deserted hall. He had a cover story if necessary, but no one had questioned his presence and he made sure Williams didn't see him. He knew he'd been made the other night. He'd have to be more careful. Curtis was worried about it, but he knew what he was doing. He lit another cigarette and thought about the evening ahead, keeping tabs on the young drummer.

Well, at least the music was back from Blaha. That part had gone okay and should make Curtis happy. He remembered Lena Blaha coming in with the music. The old man had been holding out on him. He had no idea Josef Blaha had a granddaughter that looked like her. *No wonder he keeps her under wraps. Great ass, long legs. Jesus.*

Arnett peered at the stage again. He could just make out Williams' features. *Cocky bastard. Jesus, a fucking musician. We need a pro on this, not some fucking jazz musician. Curtis must be losing it. Williams could screw it all up and then we'd all be in the shit, especially Curtis.*

If Williams falls, I'll be there to catch him, Arnett thought.

***

A short walk through the cobblestone streets of Old Town brought Gene Williams and the saxophonist Bartek to the Cafe Reduta. The music filtered up from inside and bounced off the walls of the narrow slit of an alley in such a way that nearing the club, Gene thought he'd walked right into a speaker.

They walked down the curved staircase into the basement club, past a long bar that ran the length of one entire wall. The club was much larger that he imagined and crowded with wooden tables, crammed together in clusters forming a maze of aisles for the young student waitresses to negotiate with trays filled with mugs of the inevitable amber beer. There were candles on the tables and lantern lights spaced along the walls at uneven intervals. Through a haze of smoke, a feeble spotlight cast a dim glow on the bandstand that left several tables in darkness.

"Bulgarian," Bartek said, nodding toward the band. A quartet struggled with a Thelonious Monk tune. "Hovno," Bartek said, dismissing the saxophonist. "Shit. C'mon, Gene. We drink some beer then we play."

Bartek shouldered his way through the three-deep crowd, clamoring for mugs of beer and plates of thick sausages. Besides himself and Bartek, Gene spotted several other members of the band. Except for concerts, the Reduta was the only place for live jazz in Prague and the only place where guest musicians were welcome to sit in, Gene had been told.

The Bulgarian group finished to light applause, scraping of chairs and clinking of empty glasses, but it was obvious the crowd had come to hear something more. With Jan Pavel's musicians in the house, word had filtered around the visiting American drummer would be joining in.

Gene took a beer from Bartek and looked around the club. The poor lighting and smokey haze would have made it difficult to spot Josef Blaha—if he was there. *He'll find you.* Gene could still hear Curtis' voice in his head, as if he was still in London. Was that only two days ago? Why hadn't Curtis contacted him? What was happening with Kate? Who was he to contact if something went wrong? The questions swirled about in his mind, but were overshadowed by the biggest question of all: what if Blaha didn't show?

"Gene, you drink one more *pivo*, yes? Then we play. A piece of pie." Bartek already had his case open and was assembling the cumbersome baritone saxophone.

Gene laughed. Except for Jan Pavel, Bartek was the only band member who really spoke English. He claimed to have learned from American soldiers when he was a young boy, but murdered the pronunciation and always got the familiar slang phrases just a little bit off. "Piece of cake," Gene corrected him.

He watch Bartek speak to a young blond-haired man. A polish pianist, Gene was told. Another friend of Bartek's, a bassist was already on the band stand tuning up to the piano. There was a buzz in the club as Gene and Bartek took the stand. Gene sat down at the drums and the group was filled out by a chubby trumpeter, blowing silently, fingering the valves of his horn. Bartek tried a couple of preliminary phrases to test his reed. Satisfied, he turned to Gene. "We play some blues, okay?"

Gene glanced at the bassist, who was studying him from the corner, one arm around his bass. The pianist glared at the keyboard as if it were some puzzle he had to solve. The audience suddenly quieted as Bartek snapped his fingers for the tempo. Slightly up, but not too fast for a groove.

The rhythm section opened for two choruses. Getting used to each other, looking for the groove, settling down, feeling each other out. They were joined by the two horns and the simple line was stated. It already felt good to Gene. The bassist boomed out a solid walking line. Head down, eyes closed, the pianist fed chords to the horns like a salesman distributing sample brochures. Here's one you might like. No? Try this then.

Feeling the pulse, bearing down on the ride cymbal, Gene reined everybody in as Bartek leaned into his horn and took the first solo. Chest heaving, rocking on his heels, Bartek let loose with a half dozen blistering choruses. The trumpeter, head tilted to one side, listened to what Bartek had to say, pondered, allowed himself a smile or two and nervously toyed with his horn, wondering perhaps how he could top Bartek, decided he could not and smiled his appreciation instead.

The intensity built steadily as Gene pushed, prodded Bartek with accents and beat out a tattoo on the ride cymbal. Bartek responded, then finally backed away slowly with a slight bow to the applause and shouts of approval as he surrendered to the trumpeter.

Smiling and nodding, Bartek turned toward Gene and grabbed a mug of beer someone had brought to the stage for him as the trumpet player began his exploration. Unhurried, making his debt to Miles clear, he rode the crest of the rhythm section as the intensity built again. Waves of chords flowed from the piano and were underlined by the bass lines, rock steady, glued to Gene's beat. Together they laid down a carpet of sound for the trumpet to walk on.

Gene could feel trickles of sweat over his eyes as he squinted at the trumpet player stepping away from the microphone, his journey ended for the moment. Gene brought the volume down to a whisper as the pianist began to unravel the keyboard in his own way. Gene and the bassist came together as one in the final chorus, playing riffs and figures as if they'd worked together for months.

Trading sticks for wire brushes, Gene laid down a fluffy beat for the bass player's story as he struggled with wood and strings and calloused fingers. The horns reappeared for twelve bar exchanges with Gene. Bartek, mocking, challenging; Gene answering, twisting Bartek's phrases until they were his own, then Bartek's once again.

The theme was stated for review, then they were out. With the final chord and cymbal roll still ringing, they all knew whatever they played the rest of the evening, they were bound together by this first journey. The audience shouted their approval. A tray of beer appeared on the stage. Cigarettes were lit, fingers massaged, mouth pieces adjusted and they decided on the next tune. A haunting ballad by Bartek, some old standards, more blues and a muted Miles-like rendition of a Broadway show tune earned the trumpeter respect from all. After a little more than an hour, they were intimates, joined by a common bond that would be recognized and shared again whenever they met.

Gene followed Bartek off the stage and maneuvered between the tables. His shirt was soaked. Nodding quietly, he acknowledged the smiles, the slaps on the back, the glasses raised in toasts. He was drained, but elated, buoyed by the electricity in the room and the part he had played in its creation. Then it all ended too quickly.

"I congratulate you, Mr. Williams. You play very well." Gene felt a tug on his arm. He turned and saw a slightly stooped old man with nearly white hair peering at him with blinking eyes. "I wonder if I could speak to you about the music I copied?"

"Mr. Blaha?"

Blaha nodded and looked around nervously. He was carrying some sheet music. "Come, let us sit over here." He indicated a table in one corner of the club. On the bandstand, a trio had taken over, the pianist valiantly trying to emulate Bill Evans.

Gene followed Blaha to the table. They sat down and the old man again looked around as if he were expecting someone. He held the music in his hand, suddenly looking as if he had only discovered the flimsy pages and wondered how they got there.

"I took the liberty of copying some of the pages for myself," he said. "It's an interesting composition." He spoke louder than necessary until the trio was rolling into their second tune. Then his voice dropped to a whisper "Curtis has sent you, yes?" His questioning eyes behind the small glasses were full of desperation and glinted in the candlelight.

"Look, Mr. Blaha," Gene began. "None of this is my idea. I want you to understand that. I'm just a musician, nothing more, but I had no choice. My sister is in trouble, still is for all I know. Curtis agreed to help her if I—"

"Yes, of course, that is how they work," said Blaha. "How much did he tell you?"

"Curtis? Nothing. Just that you're to give me something and I'm to pass it along to him."

"Yes, Curtis, but you must be..." Blaha paused and looked at Gene. "Not here though. Can you come tonight? Later?"

"Sure," Gene said, "the sooner the better as far as I'm concerned. I just want out of this. Where?"

"Yes," Blaha said. "It will be over soon." He shook his head and nodded at the stage. The pianist was nodding to the drummer to pick up the beat. "In one hour at the Charles River Bridge. Do you know it? The one with the statues."

"I'll find it."

"Good, but you must come alone."

"Sure, okay. Whatever you say." Now that the moment was here, Gene didn't know what to feel. His eyes remained on Blaha. Whatever the old man had discovered, it was frightening him to death.

"Well young man, it's been interesting talking to you." He had raised his voice again. "Perhaps as my granddaughter says, I should listen to more jazz." He got up from the table, then stopped, turned back and whispered to Gene.

"Be careful of your own."

Gene wasn't sure he'd heard right, but it was too late. Blaha was gone. He could see him weaving his way through the tables toward the exit. He'd even left the music on the table.

Be careful of your own? What was that supposed to mean?

***

Williams was gone. Karel Arnett scanned the club frantically, but there was no mistake. Jesus Christ. Two minutes to take a piss and the sonofabitch takes off.

Arnett sprinted up the stairs two at a time and out the door. He looked both ways up and down the alleyway. Call Curtis? No, not yet. Not if he could catch up with Williams before the meet with Blaha. That had to be what they were talking about in the club. He stood for a moment, running a hand through his hair, trying to decide what to do next. Goddamn fucking unpredictable jazz musicians.

Where? Blaha's place? No, they'd never go there. He had to find Williams before the meeting unless—wait a minute. Williams had to return to the hotel sometime. He could just stake it out, pick him up there. Yeah, Curtis wouldn't have to know anything. He smiled and lit a cigarette and jogged back down the stairs.

"Hey, Milos," he said to the barman. "You like jazz?"

"No." He gave Arnett a stony stare and rang up his bill. "Classical, you know Bach, Beethoven."

Arnett nodded his head and smiled. "That's what I thought. Good man, Milos. See you."

Outside, Arnett stood for a moment, looking up and down the alleyway then started walking back to Wenceslas Square and Williams' hotel. Yeah, maybe Williams was back already. He liked that scenario.

He began to whistle the Johnny Cash tune, "I Walk The Line."

SIX

The Charles River Bridge links Old Town with Mala Strana and is normally busy with pedestrian traffic—tourists, hand-holding couples, artists with sketch pads, families and black market money changers—all fascinated by the gallery of thirty statues of saints that line the parapets on the bridge.

But after midnight, Gene Williams stood alone and the gallery in stone, blackened with age and weather, seemed to lend only a ghostly presence. Gene gazed into the black water of the Vltava River lapping gently against the bridge. Thirty minutes and still no sign of Blaha. He turned away from the river. Above him was Prague Castle and the three soaring spires of St. Vitus Cathedral.

He paced and nervously tapped the rolled up pages of music Blaha had left on the table at the Reduta against his leg. Where was he? Maybe he wasn't coming. Maybe he changed his mind. He unfurled the music pages, suddenly wondering why Blaha had made extra copies of the score. Cover, of course. The old man had to have a good excuse to come to the club and what better one than to discuss the music. He rolled it up again and peered over the railing of the bridge, seized by impotent rage and frustration.

He glanced at his watch again. There was nothing to do, but go back to the hotel. It wasn't his fault Blaha didn't show up. How long was this nightmare going to drag on? He wanted to talk to Curtis, see what was happening with Kate, find Blaha, get it all over and done with so he could go back to just being a musician. Reluctantly, he began to walk back across the bridge toward his hotel. If only he knew where Blaha lived he could try...wait a minute. The music.

He unrolled the sheets again and flicked his cigarette lighter. They do it in New York. Why not Prague? He found what he was looking for near the bottom of a page. All copyists use them, a stamp with their name and address—and Josef Blaha was no exception. J. Blaha Kotlarska 32. There was also a telephone number. He tore off the corner with the address, folded up the other sheets and put them in his pocket.

He started walking again, this time faster, instinctively knowing what he was about to do was wrong, but unable to resist the impulse.

He had to get this over with once and for all. If it meant him going to Blaha, so be it. At least it was worth a try.

Across the bridge, he headed for the lights of Wenceslas Square and found a taxi easily enough. He showed the driver the address and was surprised when they turned around back toward Old Town. The taxi dropped him at the end of a narrow street and the driver pointed to a drab apartment building near the corner. Gene held out money to the driver and let him take the fare on the meter. He waited until the taxi pulled away, then went inside the apartment building.

One dim bulb illuminated the entrance. Glancing around to make sure he was alone, he used his lighter again to make out the names on the mailboxes. Blaha was on the second floor. He mounted the darkened stairs and found number four on the left side of the landing.

He stood for a moment listening at the door, listening to the voice in his head that said this was crazy. There was no sound from inside. All he could hear was the sound of his own breathing. He knocked lightly on the door, then pulled his hand away, surprised that even that light pressure was enough to open the door, apparently already ajar. He opened it farther and peered into the apartment. He looked around the hallway. No sound from any of the other flats. Everybody was asleep. *Like I would be if I had any sense*, he thought.

"Mr. Blaha?" he called softly. Nothing. Something was very wrong. Every instinct told him to back out, shut the door and forget the whole thing, but the compulsion persisted.

Inside, he closed the door quietly behind him and let his eyes adjust to the darkness. There was a small couch just in front of him by the window, a table and chairs. To his left was the kitchen. The rest of the room was in shadows, but then something caught his eye. A sliver of light from another room. He called again, but still no answer. He thought of all kinds of explanations. Blaha had come back, decided to do some work, left the door open by mistake, fell asleep. He debated again whether to investigate further, but the light drew him like a moth. He called once again before he pushed open the door. And then he found Josef Blaha.

He saw the music scattered on the floor first, as if it had been swept off the large table then tipped over on its side. A bottle of ink was overturned and had spilled onto some pages of music. To the right was another smaller table, also overturned. The source of light was the small desk lamp that lay on its side on the floor facing toward the door.

He could feel his heart starting to pound as he looked around some more. The whole room was in chaos. He backed up and felt something hit against his back. He turned to look, then reeled backward as if he'd been pushed.

Josef Blaha's body turned slightly on the rope around his neck, blood trickling from the back of his head. His face was contorted, bloated grotesquely. Gene kept backing up and tripping over the desk chair, falling back, his eyes still on Blaha.

Fighting panic, he got to his feet, the bile rising up in his throat. He ran blindly out of the room, one hand over his mouth and found the kitchen, bent over the sink, retching uncontrollably. He felt beads of sweat on his forehead, yet his body was chilled. He found a glass on a shelf over the sink, turned on the tap and rinsed his mouth out, breathing hard, blood pounding in his ears. He leaned on the sink for a couple of minutes, then walked back in the room, though every instinct made him want to rush out, sprint down the stairs and get as far away as fast as he could.

Don't touch anything. Don't touch anything. But he already had. He went back to the sink, ran the water till it was clear, then used a dish towel to wipe the tap clean. Holding the glass he'd used, he rinsed it and turned it upside down on the counter.

It was several minutes before he could walk steadily. Several minutes that his mind raced in panic, confusion and fear. He suppressed the almost overwhelming urge to bolt down the stairs into the night. He forced himself back in that room he would never forget. He avoided looking at Blaha again. God, he'd been talking to him just an hour ago.

He made a quick search of the room, but had no idea what he was looking for or how he would recognize it if he did. Somebody else had been looking for something too, but they obviously hadn't found it. Found what? What was Blaha to have given him? He would never know now. There was nothing here, but a collection of music supplies and Josef Blaha's dead body.

What should he do? Report it to the police? No, there was too much to explain. He was a foreigner in a strange country, a Communist country. Josef Blaha was a spy and this was—murder. No, just get out of here.

He went back to the front door and looked out in the hallway. Still nobody, no sounds. He used his shirt tail to wipe the doorknob and closed the door gently behind him and crept down the stairs to the front entrance. He checked the street, but saw no one. He began to walk away from the building, then broke into a jog. At the corner, he turned and began to run.

***

It was all starting to go wrong.

Alan Curtis sat in the windowless code room of the U.S. Embassy, smoking idly, listening to the monotonous hum of the teleprinter squatting against the wall. He tried to visualize Walter Mead's reaction to his most recent request.

It was now thirty minutes since his last transmission to Langley, relating the news of Josef Blaha's death and the possible discovery of the murder—and that's what is was, murder—by Gene Williams. Curtis had been careful to emphasize the word possible in his message to Mead. Blaha had been hanged, but shot in the back of the head by a small caliber gun beforehand.

Josef Blaha had gotten too close and Walter Mead had been right, Curtis reflected. Running an amateur was risky, unpredictable. The ploy with the music had gone exactly as planned, the Reduta, a logical place for the initial contact with Williams, and even if Arnett had lost him, he'd been on the scene. Everything had been covered. Or so they thought.

They hadn't figured on Blaha setting up a second meet at another location. They hadn't figured on Arnett losing Williams and they hadn't figured on Williams going off on his own to Blaha's apartment. That was the only explanation. Blaha would never have told Williams to come to his apartment and obviously no fall back instructions had been given.

And now, their best source was gone. No information had been passed and they didn't know any more than before Williams was brought in. It was all falling apart unless they could salvage something out of all this and still make use of Williams. If Langley bought it, well, he would know soon.

As if to answer his thoughts, the teleprinter rumbled to life and brought Curtis to his feet as the keys beat out the coded message. He stood over the machine and watched it unfurl a foot of yellow paper and inscribe a two line string of numbered code groups. The clattering ceased almost as quickly as it had begun, then returned to the earlier low hum.

Tearing the sheet from the printer, Curtis went back to the desk and quickly deciphered the cable.

```
CONTINUE AS PLANNED CZECHMATE PROJECT
```

VIA ALTERNATE SOURCES. FULL BACKUP.

MEAD

Curtis returned the code book to the safe near the desk and shredded the cable as he considered its contents. He sat down and lit another cigarette and put his feet up on the desk.

They were still alive. Now there was a way. Williams and the girl. Blaha's granddaughter Lena.

Whatever Josef Blaha had uncovered was lost forever, taken with him to his grave. But his murder made his importance all the more clear. Whoever had searched that apartment hadn't found anything, nothing had been passed on to Williams—Arnett was sure of that much—so that left only the girl. With Williams help, she would find it or at least point them in the right direction.

Not a bad assignment, Curtis thought, remembering Arnett's description of Lena Blaha. Strange, in all the time he'd worked Blaha, he'd never seen his granddaughter.

He sighed and stubbed out his cigarette. All he had to do now was keep Williams in line.

* * *

At the Soviet Embassy, Colonel Dimitri Polokov, KGB, Chief Military Attaché, added the final items to the daily briefing memo that would be delivered to the Director of the STB, the Czech Secret Police.

—Security leak eliminated.

—Investigate possible connection U.S. citizen, Eugene Williams.

—Initiate surveillance and search of Williams' hotel room.

—Continue surveillance of Lena Blaha.

Polokov frowned as he reviewed the memo for several minutes until he was at last satisfied. Impatiently, he initialed it and returned it to a locked drawer in his desk and left the office.

There was something else, he thought, as he hurried down the steps to the waiting staff car. *What was it? Yes, of course.* It suddenly came to him as he passed one of the secretaries, a pretty young thing who flashed him a warm smile.

I must remember to write my daughter.

***

It was like quicksand, Gene Williams decided, pulling him down deeper with every step. A simple errand, Curtis had said. Just pick up something from one of theirs and pass it on. He'd made it sound so simple. Now it was a nightmare. Murder. In his wildest speculations about what would happen in Prague, murder—discovering a murder—had never entered his mind.

Now, as morning light moved over Prague, Gene was discovering fear. He'd slept badly, waking up several times, seeing Josef Blaha's body in his mind, swinging from the rope, his unseeing eyes. He squinted his eyes hard shut, willing the vision to go away.

He took the practice pad and a pair of sticks out and sat on the edge of the bed, the pad on a chair facing him. While he gazed out the tall windows facing Wenceslas Square, he went through his daily warm-up routine. Single stroke rolls, beginning slowly, gradually increasing the speed until the sticks were a blur, never bouncing more than a couple of inches off the rubber pad, holding it at that speed then slowing until his wrists turned up one slow stroke at a time.

He watched Prague come to life for another day. The trams and buses crowded with people moved up and down the wide boulevard, collecting and depositing passengers in the dazzling sunshine that promised another hot, muggy day. Continuing to play on the pad, his eyes burned and his throat was raw from too many cigarettes. When he stopped for a minute and massaged his wrists, he glanced at his watch. Nearly eight o'clock. The hotel was waking up too. The sounds of doors opening and closing, snatches of muted conversation, guests making their way down to breakfast and a day of what? Sightseeing? Business? What was his day going to bring?

He felt a strange sense of isolation, aloneness in this foreign city. As far as he knew, nobody had seen him enter or leave Blaha's apartment, but could he really be sure? Anyone at the Reduta could have been assigned to watch him. Certainly Curtis' man had been there. And anyone, especially if they were asked by the police might remember seeing him talking to Blaha or leaving the club. Anyway he looked at it, he could be seen as a prime suspect in the murder investigation of a spy working for American intelligence.

For the hundredth time, he cursed himself for the impatience, the impulsiveness of last night. When Blaha hadn't shown, he should have simply gone back to the hotel. How different things would have been. But no, he had to strike out on his own and now he was in a worse position than ever.

He was in Prague for the CIA and the full impact of that had only struck him as he'd stared at Josef Blaha. He was their courier, their contact, whatever they called it, and now the man he was to have met was dead. Murdered.

What was Blaha to have given him? Papers? Film? Names? What could be so important, so vital that it had cost Blaha his life?

He stopped the sticks on the pad and lit a cigarette. He felt a new surge of panic and fear surge through him. What if whoever killed Blaha knew or even suspected he was Blaha's contact? If they hadn't found whatever they were looking for, they might assume Blaha had passed it on to him.

He went to his bag and searched for the card Curtis had given him in London. Could he just call Curtis, simply walk in the embassy and ask to see the CIA man? Why hadn't Curtis contacted him, especially in light of what had happened to Blaha? Surely Curtis knew about it now. Gene had to talk to somebody.

He thought of the reporter, Philip Hastings, but no, there would be too much to explain. Hastings would want the whole story and Gene wasn't ready for that. Wait. Jan had told him about a reception tonight at the embassy. Curtis had to be there for that. Yes, that would be the logical way.

He walked over to the sink and splashed cold water on his face and looked in the mirror. Just get through the day. Stay cool, keep a low profile. Do nothing to draw attention. Just see what happens. Rehearsal this afternoon, reception tonight.

He dressed hurriedly, wanting to get out of the room. There was nothing there, but bad dreams and panicky thoughts. He went down to the restaurant and found Jan Pavel already there, pouring over the morning paper. Jan saw him and waved.

"Ah, Gene, you are up early, yes?" He motioned for Gene to join him. "The Reduta was good?"

"Yeah, lot of fun," Gene said, sitting down.

A busboy hurried over with a carafe of water and was quickly joined by a waiter in a black suit and bow tie.

"You will eat something?" Pavel asked.

"No, just coffee for now, thanks."

Pavel studied him with troubled eyes. "Something is wrong?" he asked.

"Huh? Oh no, just tired I guess. I didn't sleep very well. Probably just excited about the festival."

"Ah yes," Pavel said. "The festival is very important for my boys." He reached across the table and touched Gene's arm. "And for you too, eh?"

"How do you mean?" Gene asked, surprised by the question.

Pavel smiled and shrugged. "There will be reporters, critics, you can, how do you say it? Make name for yourself." Pavel's eyes twinkled. "In Europe, with my band. Perhaps you will stay even longer, eh?"

"Longer?"

Pavel's expression grew serious. "Gene, you are very good for my band and we are all very happy to have you here. I know the boys would like to have you stay." He waved his hand toward the window. Outside, the sidewalk was already jammed with people, some hurrying purposefully, some dawdling before shop windows. "Prague is not New York, but the life is not so bad here and the music, that is the important thing, eh?"

"One thing kind of bothers me, Jan?"

"Tell me and I will fix it," Pavel said quickly, then smiled. "Ah, I know, the politics." He leaned across the table and spoke quietly. "The Communists, yes? But that is changing too, Gene. Dubcek, he is—"

Gene smiled. "No, I didn't mean that. Your regular drummer. I mean what happens with him if I stay?"

Pavel looked relieved. "Oh, not to worry. He is on vacation with his family, full money and even a bonus. Even if you stay longer, when he comes back, he will play percussion—vibraphone, tympani—whatever is necessary for the radio work."

Gene nodded. It had been something that had been bothering him. The politics? Well, he had a whole different slant on that now. But how could he tell Pavel he wanted out of Prague as quickly as possible. In just a few short days, his whole life had changed, but Jan Pavel had nothing to do with that and he owed the bandleader his best effort.

"I don't know yet, Jan. I'll just have to see how it turns out," he said, managing a weak smile. He busied himself spooning sugar in his coffee.

"Good," Jan said. "Oh, I forget. These are for you." Pavel dug in his briefcase and brought out two envelopes. "This is the official invitation to the artists' reception tonight." It was large and heavy and embossed with the seal of the United States.

Gene barely glanced at it. He stared instead at the other envelope. Flimsy paper, yellow with a cellophane window and came from the telegraph office. Pragoconcert was handwritten across the front. Word of Kate?

Before Gene could open either, the waiter came to the table and spoke to Jan. "Excuse me, Gene, I have one phone call." Pavel got up and headed for the hotel lobby.

Gene turned over the envelope in his hands wanting to rip it open, but not with Pavel still around. He glanced up as Pavel came back, looking ashen.

"Gene, is terrible." He sat down obviously shaken.

"What is it?"

Pavel looked up. "Josef Blaha, my friend. He is dead. That was his granddaughter, Lena. So terrible, the police, he..." Pavel's voice trailed off and he got to his feet, gathered up his briefcase and papers. He put some money on the table. "I must go. I have many things to make this morning and now this. Rehearsal at four o'clock, Gene. Ahoy." And he was gone.

Gene sat very still for a moment. So there it was. He tried to imagine what Lena was feeling. He opened the telegram, shaking his head disbelievingly. He felt the same shock as when he'd read the newspaper clipping in London. His hands were shaking as he looked up.

The restaurant was nearly full now. People drinking coffee, eating breakfast, talking happily. It was a perfectly normal world, or so it seemed. But it was not normal at all.

He felt the sudden urge to laugh as his hand closed over the telegram, crushing it into a ball. Relief and then anger swept through him on one rushing wave. He dropped the balled up telegram on the table, pushed back his chair and bolted from the dining room, crashing into a waiter as he hurried out. The waiter dropped a tray and dishes and cups flew everywhere.

In the hotel lobby, he stopped for a moment, strangely disoriented, only vaguely aware of the desk clerk's curious stare. Had he spoken to him? Gene looked at him, then started for the door when the clerk called him back. He was holding the phone in his hand. "Mr. Williams."

"What?" He turned on the clerk almost accusingly.

"A call for you," the clerk said, pointing to a bank of telephones along the wall. "Number three."

Gene stared blankly for a moment, then spun towards the phone and snatched up the receiver. Curtis. Exactly who he wanted to talk to. "This is Gene Williams."

"Hradcany Castle. Twelve o'clock." The voice was muffled, difficult to understand.

"What? Who is this? Hello. Hello?" The line was dead. He stared at the phone for a moment before hanging up. He glanced at his watch, then at the desk clerk who was still watching, eyeing him curiously.

***

In the restaurant, they were still cleaning up the mess. One of the waiters was angrily overseeing two busboys as they swept up broken cups and plates and they were just as angrily denying they had not been at fault.

Karel Arnett got up, walked past the table Gene and Pavel had occupied and scooped up the balled telegram as he went by. His orders were clear, but he wanted to see what had set Williams off. He had a hunch this might be more important.

Arnett stopped in the lobby and on a shelf under the telephones, smoothed out the crumpled telegram and read it quickly, a smile spreading over his face. Shaking his head and sighing, he dropped a coin into the phone and dialed Alan Curtis at the embassy.

"Curtis, it's Arnett."

"What's up?"

"The whole game. We got a problem. Your drummer boy just got a telegram—from his sister."

"Oh Christ, that's all we need."

"Want me to read it to you?"

"No, bring it over."

"Right, I'm on the way." Arnett hung up the phone and walked out of the hotel. He could always pick up Williams at the rehearsal.

Sticks, Arnett thought. *Curtis will love that.*

SEVEN

The tour was standard fare sightseeing: a quick look around Prague by bus. Through Old Town, across the Vltava River to Mala Strana, Wallenstein Palace, and finally, the Heights and The Royal Castle Gardens of Hradcany.

Gene slumped in a rear seat of the tour bus, ignoring the multilingual commentary by the smartly uniformed young girl. His mind was on only one thing—a showdown with Alan Curtis.

He'd boarded the bus after confirming with the hotel that its route would take him to the castle grounds. Mingling with tourists, he decided, was the safest bet and the least conspicuous means for the meeting with his anonymous caller, although there was no doubt in Gene's mind, the caller was Alan Curtis. There was no one he wanted to see more. Curtis could play his spy games, but now he was going to pay.

He'd wandered around aimlessly for a couple of hours after the call, turning things over in his mind, trying to clarify his position, which had once again changed abruptly with Kate's telegram.

Kate was safe and always had been. He should have kept the telegram, thrown it in Curtis' face

Hi, Sticks, the message read. *Sorry I missed you in London. Good luck at the festival. Love, Kate.*

He smiled, thinking of the nickname Kate had tagged him with when he first took up drums and the endless arguments they'd had over it. He'd always hated it, but Kate had refused to give it up, even after he began playing professionally.

It was all so clear now. The newspaper story Curtis had shown him in London, the whole story about Kate's arrest was total fabrication, a carefully orchestrated scenario and he'd fallen for it. The cold war was a good name for it, he decided. The CIA could probably rig anything. Why hadn't he seen through it? The blind amateur neatly and thoroughly manipulated by professionals.

He'd been duped, but now that Kate was safe, that was all that mattered. And with Josef Blaha dead, he was in the clear with Curtis, of no further use to the CIA. Yes, he'd been at the murder scene, but no one knew that, maybe not even Curtis, and now, he had a score to settle.

Gene was an amateur, but a very angry one now as the coach climbed the serpentine hill toward the castle.

"...the symbol of Prague and all Bohemia," the guide intoned. She sat facing the passengers, a microphone in her hand, watching everybody craning their necks to see out the window.

The city stretched below, magnificently beautiful in the dazzling sunlight, deserving of the name the city of a hundred spires. The bus labored up the incline and finally pulled to a halt near the Strahov Monastery.

"The monastery was founded in the twelfth century," the guide continued. "It is now the home of National Literature." She stood up. "Now if you'll follow me please." She stepped off the bus and stood waiting as the passengers got off.

Gene waited, lagging behind the crowd as they left the bus. He found it easy to lose himself as the guide assembled everyone for the tour. They were mostly well-dressed Germans and French, weighted down with shoulder bags, cameras and guide books.

Gene drifted out of the courtyard among the cluster of buildings in the gardens surrounding the Monastery. The tour group caught up with him once near Wenceslas Chapel, but he trailed off again and took a seat on a stone bench and lit a cigarette.

The call had been brief, only a time and place, so he guessed he had only to make himself visible. He glanced at his watch, letting his eyes roam over the passing faces, hoping to spot Curtis first. The sun was hot. Even with sunglasses, he could feel its glare and the heat bearing down on his shoulders.

Then, a familiar face emerged out of the throng of tourists, coming toward him now in long strides. He stood up and stared.

"Hello, Gene," Lena Blaha said.

***

"There's a slight problem," the Czech said. He had a broad face, wide-set dark eyes that rarely blinked. He was dressed in a well-cut dark suit.

The American was instantly defensive, wary. His face knitted into a frown, weighing, calculating. "A problem? Now look, I've done all I can—everything you wanted."

The Czech didn't look at him. He brushed an imaginary speck of lint off his cuff. "That is not the problem. We are satisfied with your progress. No, it's something else. This musician of yours, Williams."

"What about him?"

"Exactly. He was seen with Blaha, at the nightclub."

The American shrugged. "So? What about it? Probably talking about the music he did for the band. Williams brought a new arrangement for the festival. Blaha did the copying. Pavel told me himself he is, was, a friend of Pavel's. Nothing unusual about it."

"I'm afraid I don't share your confidence," the Czech said, his voice taking on an edge now. He wasn't used to being disputed, certainly not by the American. "Williams was also seen at Blaha's flat."

"Before?" The American shifted forward on his chair.

"No, after." The Czech paused and looked at the American, watching him digest the information. "Perhaps, as you say, it is nothing. But we think it prudent to investigate further." The Czech stared at the American unblinkingly. "You will find out what you can." He was pleased to note the American realized it was an order, not a suggestion.

The American sighed and looked away. "Yeah, sure, I see what you mean. It's probably nothing though."

"Let us all hope so," the Czech said. "The time is drawing near."

* * *

It was cooler on the Heights, above the Castle. Below, the river, a gleaming molten ribbon, knifed through Prague. The air over the city shimmered in a haze of heat and the trams far below, shuttling along the embankment, looked like toys.

Lena leading, they walked up the steep path from the castle to a spot among the trees the tourists had yet to discover. She had not spoken, having greeted Gene's astonished look with only a nod, indicating they should walk. He had simply followed, still too stunned to speak himself.

Lena moved with fluid grace. Her pleated skirt swirled around her long legs. She wore open-toed sandals, a white, loose fitting blouse that further accented her complexion. *She wasn't just pretty*, Gene thought. *She was beautiful.* But even in the bright sun, her face was pale and drawn. Her eyes were red and had lost their sparkle.

As if by mutual agreement, they stopped. Gene sat down and leaned against a tree. Lena settled herself on the grass next to him.

"Thank you for coming," she said.

"It was you who called?"

She nodded. "I'm sorry to disappoint you. You were expecting someone else weren't you."

"I was expecting..." He faltered, confused by her calm manner. If she knew about her grandfather, and of course she must, she was a very cool one.

"Yes, Curtis perhaps? Alan Curtis?" She turned toward him and eyed him coldly now, then looked away quickly. "Forgive me. That wasn't fair. Of course you were expecting Curtis."

Gene remained silent, preferring to let her speak. It was all happening too fast.

"Curtis is not coming. He doesn't even know we're meeting."

"Okay, what's going on here, Lena? Are you telling me you work for Curtis too?"

"And you don't?" Her eyes flickered with anger for a moment, then she turned away. "Yes, but not like you think. I helped my grandfather." Mentioning him made her tremble, but she fought it, tried to maintain control. "Last night he was killed, murdered, but of course you know about that already." Her voice was flat, almost a monotone as if she were simply reciting facts.

"Lena, I—"

"No, let me finish. It's all right. I want to tell you." But it wasn't all right. The words choked out of her. Her eyes brimmed with tears and then she fell against him. A shudder went through her body as she collapsed.

Instinctively, Gene folded her in his arms until she exhausted herself. Finally, the trembling ended, the tension drained away and she sat up and rubbed her eyes. Sniffing and wiping away the tears, her breathing returned to normal.

"I'm sorry," she said. "I thought I'd already finished with that."

"No, it's all right, Lena. It's all right."

"I knew he was going to meet you last night. I was afraid. I..."

"You knew?"

"Not at first, but when Jan Pavel called and my grandfather insisted I deliver the music personally, I knew it must be you he'd been waiting for. He was very worried and upset lately. More so than usual."

Gene sighed, watching Lena compose herself. He lit a cigarette. "There's no reason for you to believe this, but until a few days ago, I had nothing to do with Alan Curtis, the CIA, none of it. I was tricked into the whole thing by Curtis."

"Tricked? How?" There was again, the disbelief in her voice.

He told her everything. How he'd been approached in London, been convinced his sister was in danger and finally about the telegram. "Until then I was just a musician, coming to Prague for the festival." He sighed and took a deep drag on his cigarette. "I don't know how any of this works. Last night I discover a murder, this morning I find out my sister was never in any trouble and here I am, sitting on top of Prague with a girl I thought I might be taking to dinner." He turned and looked at her. "And now, you tell me you're in deeper than I am."

Lena looked away, out over the city, suddenly lost in memory. "Some time ago, I discovered that my grandfather was working for the Americans. He'd already been through so much, I think it was his way of getting back, doing something." She shrugged, threw her hands up. "People do things for all kinds of reasons."

Gene watched her, sensing her need to vent. He sat quietly and listened.

"He would be gone from home at odd times and then come back acting strangely distant. I thought he was in some kind of trouble, but he wouldn't talk about it, so one afternoon, I followed him. It was very difficult, almost as if he knew I was there. It was only later that I realized it was not me he was trying to elude. He took taxis, got on and off trams, went in and out of department stores and always left by a different way than he'd entered. Somehow, I managed to keep up.

"Finally, he bought a newspaper and went to a small park and just sat down on a bench. I didn't know what to think. He was there for almost an hour and yet, never looked at the paper once. He just sat there, waiting.

"I felt awful spying on him like that. I kept moving, afraid someone would notice me, then I laid down on the grass and pretended to nap. Finally, another man appeared. He had a newspaper too and sat down next to my grandfather. They didn't speak, but they did switch papers. A few minutes later, the other man left and soon after that, so did my grandfather. I stayed there for a while, trying to figure it out, then I went home."

Gene pictured it all in his mind, like a scene from a movie. He looked around, but they were still alone.

"I couldn't stand it any longer," Lena continued. "When I told him what I'd seen and asked him about it, he got very angry, but eventually, he told me everything and admitted he had been working for your government. I pleaded with him to let me help, but he got even more angry and said it didn't matter anyway. 'Forget what you saw, Lena. It's nearly over.'"

She stood up and walked a few paces away then turned back to Gene. "I didn't know what he meant. I still don't. But now, there's something I must do."

Gene saw the anger and hurt in her eyes. "My grandfather was murdered, Gene, for whatever it was he was doing, whatever he found out. I'm sure of it. I want to know why. What was it that was so important that he had to be killed? Why was he not protected? Please understand me. It's not revenge, it's just, I have to make some sense out of all this. It's the only way I know."

Gene didn't trust himself to look at her. "Why are you telling me all this?"

She took a deep breath. "I want you to help me. With my grandfather gone, there's no one else."

Gene looked in her eyes then, but couldn't hold her gaze. He looked away, fumbled for another cigarette, his mind racing. "I think you're making a mistake, Lena. I'm very sorry about your grandfather and I wish we'd met under different circumstances. But me help you? I'm in enough trouble myself. Besides, I wouldn't know where to begin."

"I would," she said. Her face was set in determination, her eyes challenging.

"How?"

"My grandfather was meant to give you something. Names, information, it could have been anything. He was waiting for you, but I'm sure there's a record of it somewhere. There were places he left and picked up things, around the city. Dead letter drops he called them and I know of two such places."

"Have you looked?" Gene asked, half not wanting to know.

"Not yet."

Gene nodded, thinking. "If you know about them, then somebody else might too. It's too soon."

"Yes," Lena said. "I thought of that."

"There was one thing he said to me, at the Reduta. I didn't understand."

"What? What did he say." Lena turned toward him, excited.

"'Be careful of your own.' He started to leave then turned back to say that."

Lena studied him. "Is that all?"

"Yes."

Lena sat down on the grass next to him. "If he was being watched, chances are I am too," she said. "But you, if I showed you where the drop points are, you could—"

"No, Lena, I can't. I think it would be a mistake. I know it's hard, but let it go, forget it."

"Please," she said quickly. "It's all right. I understand. It was unfair of me even to ask you." She managed a feeble smile, but he saw the disappointment in her eyes. "It was very kind of you to listen. I thank you for that." She stood up and brushed off her skirt.

Gene stood up too. He was so drawn to her, but it was already clear he'd dropped several notches in her eyes. "I wish I could help, Lena, I really do."

Her shoulders slumped and she stared at the ground. "What will you do now?"

She made a faint show of confidence. "I'm not sure, but please don't worry. I'll be fine. I have relatives in Plzen. They are coming to help with the...the arrangements. I don't want to stay here now."

"Sure, I understand. Look, maybe we can...is there something I can do?" But she had already asked and he had refused.

"No," she said quickly. "I must go. Perhaps I will come to the festival. I would like to hear you play one time." She smiled again and he felt he was drowning, feeling a premonition that if he didn't do something, say something, he'd never see her again.

"Goodbye, Gene." She turned and began to walk back down the path toward the castle.

Goodbye, Lena, he whispered quietly. He stood for a moment watching her go, feeling awkward, helpless, and suddenly filled with self-loathing. He'd tried to turn down the CIA and lost. And now he'd rejected a naked plea from a beautiful girl and had been let off easily.

If he didn't give the performance of his life at the festival, Prague would be a total waste. But there was still Curtis and the score to settle with him. His anger returned briefly and gave him some comfort.

***

Colonel Alexis Savin poured himself another tumbler of vodka and stretched back on the hard bunk in his temporary quarters near the Czechoslovak border. He was tired although there had been no physical activity since the Warsaw Pact exercises had begun to wind down. No, it was mental tiredness, the pressure of keeping his men finely tuned, ready for action he knew many of them anticipated.

Out the window in the fading light, he could see the T-54 tanks silhouetted in the dusk, poised in readiness. Huge iron monsters that somehow seemed like part of the landscape. Behind the tanks, trucks and armored vehicles, the men under his command were bivouacked and also waiting. Impatient, irritated, many of them only young boys, waiting for something—what, they themselves didn't know—to release their growing frustration. Poised like parachutists, jump lines hooked up, the door open, only to be told, not yet. Wait.

Why shouldn't they be on edge? Savin thought. They had been on these damn maneuvers since May. They had done their job, flexing their muscles for the benefit of the western world and their eastern brothers just across the frontier.

But, it hadn't worked. The people of Czechoslovakia were not cowering in fear and Alexander Dubcek was defying the Kremlin, so the orders to pull out were countermanded even before they could break camp. But still, they were held in check and the men were bored, homesick, spent and cruelly deprived of a return home and a well-deserved leave.

Savin turned from the window as there was knock on the door. "Come in," he barked. A tall, blonde haired young officer stood at attention in a sharply creased uniform.

"Excuse the intrusion, Sir," Lieutenant Kiryanov said. "I have a request to make."

Savin eyed the young officer. Bright, educated, ruthless, ambitious, the Soviet soldier of the future. Ready to slaughter some workers for the cause are you Lieutenant? That's your future only you don't know it yet. That's what all your training will go for. Mowing down helpless Czechs.

"Yes, what is it?" Savin sat down on the bunk, not at all embarrassed that he was dressed in only fatigue pants and undershirt.

"Well, sir," Kiryanov began cautiously. "It's the men. There were two more fights this evening, in the mess."

Savin looked at Kiryanov. He knew the Lieutenant was wary, seeing his unshaven face his careless dress, the glass of vodka in his hand.

"Sir, you know their condition. In my opinion, I think they need a break. We've been here so long, a little diversion would perhaps be in order."

"In your opinion?" Savin swung off the bunk, vodka splashing out of his glass as he confronted the young officer. "You dare to question the decisions of command?" Savin agreed with him completely, but he couldn't resist the opportunity to put the young officer in his place.

"Of course not, Sir. The decisions of command are always correct and to be obeyed without question," Kiryanov replied quickly with mechanical precision. He had reflexively assumed the position of attention again.

"That's better, Lieutenant. What is it then?" The fool was so easily intimidated. Savin sat down on the bunk again.

"To town, Sir. I thought perhaps some of the men could go into town this evening." He watched Savin's half reclining body on the bunk, the half empty glass on his chest, the vodka bottle on the floor.

Savin waved his hand. "Yes, to town. Let the men go into town. Let them get drunk if they can find something decent to drink. Let them find some women. Let them eat. Let them go." Savin stopped suddenly, aware of his rambling. "Report to me in the morning, Lieutenant. Dismissed."

"Yes, Sir. Thank you, Sir." Kiranyovov's salute went unseen, unacknowledged. Savin was hardly aware that he was gone.

Obeyed without question. The decisions of command are always correct. The lieutenant's words echoed in his mind and jabbed at his conscience like probing needles. Were they right? If they were, why didn't they do something instead of sitting out here in the countryside waiting, always waiting.

Those fools in the Kremlin, this time they'd bring the world down on all our heads. Hadn't they learned from Hungary. Didn't they know the world would clamor for their downfall if their insane plan was put into action? Of course they did. There was no other explanation for the delay.

Savin could hardly believe it when he'd first heard of the decision. An invasion. For what? To stem a counter revolution was the official line when really, it was only a country trying to live their own brand of Communism. What was wrong with that? Did they think the Czechs would welcome them. Fools, all of them. The Czechs were tough. They would try everything short of military resistance. Even Dubcek knew that would be futile.

No, they wouldn't resist militarily, but there would be bloodshed nonetheless. The students, workers, the old people who had seen it all before, felt the Nazi boot, in the end, they would all be crushed, just like Hungary twelve years earlier.

Savin had seen it then. He'd been there too, but not as a colonel. It had shaken him, confronting those hate filled eyes in Budapest. *Why are you here?* the eyes asked. We are your comrades. Oh yes, Comrades. As long as you do exactly as Moscow tells you.

The plans had been in readiness for months now, but still, the order had not come down and the strain was beginning to tell, on the commanders as well as the troops. They were all wound so tightly, something had to give soon.

Savin drained the remainder of his vodka and lay back on the bunk. He was not fooled by the meetings in Bratislava and Cierna. The rumors had filtered down despite what was said officially.

Dubcek must go. The movement must be put down at all costs.

Well, my learned Kremlin brothers, it's going to cost you dearly. And I, Colonel Alexis Savin, remain at your disposal for better or worse.

He reached for the bottle on the floor and held it up. A toast—to Alexander Dubcek. He put the bottle to his lips, but it was empty. Angrily, he hurled it across the room, sent it crashing into the wall where it shattered.

Sleep was the only escape and it came quickly.

***

For perhaps the tenth time, Alan Curtis stared at the crumpled telegram from Kate Williams. Even flattened and smoothed out on his desk it retained scores of creases. Something else they hadn't figured on. It was going more wrong all the time.

Conscious of Arnett's almost smirking expression opposite him, Curtis looked up. "Don't look so pleased," he said. A one in a thousand chance. How could they have predicted this?

Arnett spread his hands defensively. "Okay, I admit it. I'm not sorry the little drummer boy is out of it." He looked at Curtis for a long moment. "He is out isn't he?"

"Not necessarily," Curtis said.

"C'mon, you can't be serious. This blows your control. Getting his sister out of trouble was the only thing keeping him in line. Williams wouldn't piss on you if you were on fire now."

Curtis leaned back in his chair and looked at Arnett. "Didn't you tell me you were sure Williams was at Blaha's apartment, that he'd discovered the body? Oh, and that was after you lost him at the jazz club."

Arnett flushed. "Couldn't have been anything else. He was white as sheet when he came back. He looked sick, like—"

"Somebody who's just seen a dead body."

"Yeah, but so what? I don't follow you."

"Don't you think the Czech Police would like to have a few words with Williams if they knew he'd been at the murder scene. And don't you think the STB would find it informative to learn Williams was a stringer for us?" Curtis' voice was cold and hard.

"Jesus, you'd really do it, wouldn't you. You want him that badly?"

"You better believe it. We still don't know what Blaha was running and Williams still has an in where we don't."

"You mean the girl? Blaha's granddaughter?"

He had to follow it to the end or at least until it was too late and then it wouldn't matter. But there was another reason he had to keep Williams on track, a reason he couldn't tell Arnett or Walter Mead, or anyone. Not yet.

"Exactly. She had to know something about her grandfather's work, but she'd hardly cooperate with us now. Williams might turn her though."

Arnett shook his head. "You want me on tonight?"

"No, I'll see Williams at the embassy reception. I think he'll be kind of anxious to talk to me, don't you?"

"I think he'd like to have your balls."

EIGHT

Gene woke up groggy, as if he hadn't slept at all. He was almost late for the afternoon rehearsal. By now the music was familiar, the band getting it under their fingers, making it come together. But Gene knew he wasn't on top of it, wasn't focused. Jan Pavel gave him several questioning glances when he missed a figure here, a break there. His lackluster performance affected the band too. He was the drummer. Gene should be inspiring the band, kicking them along, providing the punch, but his heart wasn't in it. He was dragging them down, making everybody sound tired. Finally, in frustration, Jan Pavel threw up his hands, called a halt, made a short speech and sent everybody off.

"What did he say?" Gene asked Bartek as everybody was packing up their instruments.

"Pavel say go think about the festival, remember why we're here."

Gene nodded and suddenly lashed out at a cymbal and slammed his sticks down.

"You okay, Gene?" Bartek asked. He walked over and picked up the sticks and handed them to Gene. "You need these," he said.

Bartek and a young trombonist talked Gene into dinner at the hotel. Despite himself, he was amused by Bartek's tales of life on the road in Czechoslovakia. Gene tried to join in, realizing Bartek's translations were for his benefit, but his mind was elsewhere. He couldn't get Lena Blaha's hurt pleading eyes out of his mind.

He picked absently at his food and finally begged off with a headache and went up to his room, leaving Bartek to puzzle over his behavior. He stripped off his clothes and filled the huge tub with water as hot as he could stand it. He eased himself into the steaming water, leaned his head back against the edge of the tub and put a hot cloth over his face. He closed his eyes, letting the warmth steal through his body.

What would happen to Lena now? She'd mentioned relatives somewhere. Would she leave Prague? It took no effort to bring her image to his mind. He hardly knew her, but the attraction had been immediate, drawing him to her in a way he hadn't yet figured out. Even in grief for her grandfather, she was beautiful. Dangerous thought, he mused, remembering her lithe body and dancing eyes. Getting involved with Lena would mean more complications, more entanglements and he was leaving soon anyway wasn't he? He wanted out as soon as possible. He would simply have to forget Lena.

There had been only one serious relationship in his life thus far and she'd married Gene's best friend. Well, he could hardly blame her. Life with a lawyer was a much more secure proposition than with someone on the road, in the jazz life that did little to strengthen relationships. The rest had been short term affairs, one night stands, taken up when they were offered, no strings attached. A cocktail waitress in Detroit, an airline stewardess in San Francisco. He could barely remember the names or faces now. Drummer freaks, jazz buffs who hung around, the last ones to leave while he packed up his drums. The road was littered with casualties and sex was the main objective.

Music had been the driving force in his life for so long, Gene couldn't remember thinking or feeling otherwise. It left little time for anything else, so he'd resigned himself to being a loner, at least until he met someone who understood that.

Was someone like Lena that person? He laughed, dipped the wash cloth in the warm water and wrung it out over his face. Who was he kidding? The last thing she needed was a drummer on the way out of town. He berated himself again for turning her down, but what else could he have done? He probably wouldn't see her again. He could have said yes, but then where would it go?

When the water cooled, he roused himself from the tub, dried off with a large towel and began to shave. It had all happened so fast and so unexpectedly. One minute he was an invited guest to a jazz festival; the next, there was Curtis, Kate, Blaha's murder, Lena—all crashing down on him in the space of a couple of days.

He stopped shaving for a moment, his face half covered with lather and stared at his reflection in the mirror. What would tonight bring? One thing was sure: he would have a showdown with Alan Curtis. Maybe he could get Curtis to help Lena. They owed her that much for her grandfather's service.

He was still plagued with thoughts about the murder. Suppose he had been seen? If any connection could be made between him and the crime scene, he could be in real trouble. He visualized a headline: AMERICAN MUSICIAN HELD IN PRAGUE SPY MURDER.

He finished shaving and went to dress for the reception, pulling out his one and only suit from the wardrobe. It was slightly wrinkled, but it would have to do, embassy reception or not. He dropped it on the bed and then stopped suddenly. He spun around and opened the wardrobe again, staring inside. The light jacket was still there, two shirts, but...somehow different. Weren't they on the other side before? Yes, that was it. Was it his imagination or had they been moved?

He felt his heart began to pound faster and he checked the things he'd dropped on the bed, the night stand, his open suitcase. Everything was just as he'd left them—almost. Some things had been touched, moved, looked at perhaps, but whoever had done it, had been too careful in replacing things in their original position. He sat down on the bed, unable to accept it for a moment, but there was no doubt.

Sometime, very recently, his room had been searched.

When? This afternoon while he was with Lena? He tried to brush the thought away, but she was, after all, the granddaughter of a spy. During the rehearsal, knowing he would be out for at least a couple of hours? While he was in the bath? He hadn't heard anything, but he'd been half asleep, lost in thought. Yes, somebody could have come in while he was soaking in the warm water.

He sat wrapped in the towel, smoking, going over in his mind more possibilities. Curtis or one of his baby sitters? No, not Curtis himself. He'd send someone. Check out Williams' room. Maybe he did get something from Blaha. He put out the cigarette. *Fuck this. Goodbye, Prague.*

He dressed quickly in the suit, hastily knotted his tie, suddenly eager to get out of the room. Get to the embassy early, catch Curtis before the party was in full swing. *The sooner the better*, he thought as he took the elevator down to the lobby.

He walked outside and stood for a minute in front of the hotel, aware of a strange new feeling, his senses more alert. Taking the coach tour to meet Lena had been instinctive. Who else besides Curtis' watchdog was tracking his moves? He scanned the faces of people hurrying past the hotel. Was it his imagination or did they suddenly seem hostile now, suspicious, threatening? He took a couple of deep breaths. *Okay man, let's not freak out. Settle down.*

Several people did glance at him curiously, there was no mistake about that. The suit. Of course, that explained it. It was not expensive, but it was well cut, fit him perfectly. Its purchase represented an impulsive act of extravagance nearly a year ago, he remembered now. He didn't care much about clothes as long as they were comfortable, but every man should have one good suit. Kate had insisted. Even if her brother was a shaggy haired jazz musician. She had helped him pick it out. Yes, that's what the curious glances were about. It wasn't the kind of suit that could be bought in Prague where, as far as Gene could tell nothing, but drab gray was sold.

He tried out a smile. Settle down. Nobody knows anything. But his room had been searched. He wasn't imagining that. Or was he? Maybe the maid just moved things, rearranged. He debated for a moment whether to go back inside and check, but what could they tell him?

He checked his watch. The band bus had probably already gone. He started to look for a taxi then suddenly decided to take a tram instead. The desk clerk was helpful, even wrote down the name of the stop to show the driver, and told him the exact fare he would need and produced a pocketful of coins.

Across the square, he joined an anxious crowd of commuters and somehow felt more secure in the company of strangers. No one took any notice as he boarded the tram. It was crowded with tired shoppers and workers, carrying stringed carrier bags or large loaves of bread loosely wrapped in paper for the evening meal. Gene made his way to the rear doors and stood gripping the hand rail, studying the faces of the passengers.

What was it like living in a country like this day after day? Most of the people wore blank expressions, unseeing eyes that stared straight ahead, but then so did everybody on the Seventh Avenue Subway in New York City. Looking around, Gene saw most were dressed in drab suits, work clothes, cheap cotton dresses. What fueled their lives? What made these old women cackle with laughter? Were the blank looks masking the despair felt under a Communist regime? Who knew? Certainly not Gene Williams.

The lights came on as dusk settled and the old tram rattled along the cobblestone street. *Four stops*, the desk clerk said. Klarov Street. He got off and crossed through the heavy traffic as night time Prague came to life. He found the large building without too much trouble and stopped for a moment, taking in the sign in bold lettering: **United States of America**. *Step in here and you're the same as on American soil*, Gene thought. But as he walked into the courtyard and up the steps, he remembered the last words he'd heard from Josef Blaha.

Be careful of your own.

An officious looking Czech with a name tag glanced at his invitation and checked his name off a list. He directed Gene up a long staircase to the great hall. He could already hear the hum of conversation and music coming from inside. Vintage Duke Ellington. *Very appropriate*, he thought as "Take the A Train" echoed about the room. He went inside and discovered the party was well underway.

The hall was long; a high ceiling that could easily accommodate a hundred or so people. Along one length of the room were glass French doors that opened out onto the inner courtyard and spaced at intervals of ten feet or so. From the ceiling, hung large crystal chandeliers. In one corner was a grand piano, probably used for private recitals and tonight perhaps an impromptu jam session. At the opposite end of the room was a large buffet and next to it, a makeshift bar manned by a platoon of white-jacketed waiters dispensing large mugs of foamy beer and an assortment of wine and liquor courtesy of the embassy commissary.

Gene made his way through the crowd, scanning faces, looking for Alan Curtis. He spotted several band members and Jan Pavel in one corner deep in conversation with a man in formal dress, smoking a large cigar. Bartek waved and pointed. He and the young trombonist had already cornered three young girls at the bar. There were musicians and officials and snatches of conversations in several languages taking part in the festival plus the usual bevy of guests, friends and hangers on who had wrangled an invitation. Gene passed the formally attired embassy staff and judging from their numbers, everybody must be present. Everybody but Alan Curtis.

"Gene." He turned at the familiar voice and saw Philip Hastings pushing through the crowd, hair askew and carrying two mugs of beer. "I saw you come in," he said, reaching Gene. "Here, take one of these." He held out one of the frosty mugs to Gene.

"How's it going, Philip?" It was getting warmer by the minute. He took a long pull of the beer.

"Not too bad." Hastings downed half of his and smiled. "Ah, that's the ticket. He held up the mug, looking at the golden amber liquid. "This is the only Embassy bash I've been to where beer is the featured drink, but in Prague, what else?"

Gene nodded. "Sorry I haven't called you, but, you know, rehearsals and all."

"I can imagine. I'd hoped to get by, but I'm afraid my coverage of the festival is going to be rather limited." Hastings smile suddenly vanished.

"How's that?" Gene tried to concentrate, but his eyes roamed around the room. *Where the hell was Curtis?*

Hastings dropped his voice slightly. "I'm afraid things are heating up around here and my paper's ordered me to stay on top of new developments. I don't want to alarm you, but there are serious rumors floating about that the Soviets are coming in."

Gene stopped, the glass halfway to his lips. "Are you sure?"

"No, of course I'm not bloody well sure. Nobody is. But I've got several sources I'm trying to track down to confirm things."

Across the room Jan Pavel caught Gene's eye and motioned him over. "Look, Philip, can we get together, tomorrow maybe? At your hotel?"

"Don't see why not. I'll be out most of the morning, but I'll be back by lunch time." Hastings studied Gene closely. "Is something wrong? Is it about that newspaper article you wanted me to track down? I just—"

"Oh no," Gene said quickly. He'd almost forgotten he'd asked Hastings to check on it for him. "Don't worry about that. Listen, I see somebody I have to talk to. I'll catch up with you later, Philip." He moved off toward Jan, leaving Hastings puzzled in the center of the room.

Gene fought his way to the bar. Duke Ellington had surrendered to Count Basie and the music was much louder now, blasting in the background as he reached Jan and the man he'd noticed earlier.

"Come, Gene," Jan said. "This is Mr. Roberts, the Cultural Attaché. He is very anxious to meet you. He is a big fan of our band." Pavel beamed at both of them.

"Well, well, Gene Williams. I've been hearing some great things about you, boy," Roberts boomed. "Just call me Warner." He held a drink in one hand and a large cigar in the other. He stuck the cigar in his mouth and held out a beefy hand to Gene.

Roberts was not tall, but he had broad shoulders. His tuxedo jacket fit tightly around his thickening waist and was flecked with cigar ash. His face was flushed and his eyes dark and rheumy, but alert. Gene guessed he'd had several drinks already.

"Okay, Warner," Gene said shaking hands. Roberts brought to mind a small time politician at the opening of a shopping mall. "I guess I have to thank you for being here."

Roberts grinned. "Well, I won't pretend I didn't have a hand in it." *He had a slight southern or Texas accent*, Gene thought. "Had to help out ole Jan here." He slapped Pavel on the back. "He's been telling me great things about you. Yes, sir, great things."

Gene didn't know why, but he disliked Roberts immediately.

"I hope Jan isn't working you too hard," Roberts went on. "Prague is quite a city." He leaned in closer to Gene and half whispered. "How 'bout these Czech girls, eh? Ever seen so many blondes with big tits?" Roberts punched Gene on the arm and threw his head back in a hearty laugh.

Gene glanced at Pavel, hoping he hadn't heard Roberts. "Well, I've been pretty busy," Gene said. "Have I met the embassy staff or are you it?"

Roberts gave him a quizzical appraising look, puffed on his cigar before he answered. "Well, there's Ambassador Beam, of course." He pointed to a tall figure in the center of the room talking with several people. "Hell, all these people in monkey suits are embassy staff. And...hey, there's another one. You really should meet him." He leaned closer to Gene again. "Just between you and me, this one is our cloak and dagger guy, if you get my drift." He winked at Gene. "Hey, Alan," Roberts shouted over the music.

Alan Curtis turned and headed toward them, his eyes fastened on Gene.

"Alan, say hello to Gene Williams. He's the hot drummer I told you about, playing with Pavel's band at the festival. Best advice I ever gave you, right Jan?" He slapped Pavel on the back again, almost spilling his drink. Jan managed a smile, but looked uncomfortable.

"I think Jan can get along just fine without me," Gene said. "He has one hell of a band."

Pavel smiled his thanks while Gene and Curtis went through the charade of pretending to meet for the first time.

"Alan here is our mystery man, Gene," Roberts said. "Right, Alan." Roberts winked, but got only an icy stare from Curtis that sent him off to find another drink. He left, tugging Pavel along with him. "Be right back," he called.

Gene faced Curtis. "I want to talk to you right now."

Curtis looked around quickly. "I'm sure you do." The taped music had stopped now, but someone had begun to play the piano and people were beginning to move in that direction. "Not here though," Curtis said. "C'mon, we'll go outside." He took Gene by the arm and they skirted the people beginning to crowd around the piano.

They went through the French doors, down a marble staircase and along the ambassador's formal gardens toward the orangery. The sounds of the party filtered down through the windows.

"Okay," Curtis began, turning to face Gene. "I know you've got a beef, so let's get that over with and—"

"Fuck you, Curtis."

"Now hold on."

"No, you hold on." The pent up raged spilled out of Gene in waves. "I'm sure you know I got a telegram today from my sister. Remember her? How are the negotiations going with the Spanish police? Oh that's right, you didn't need to bother with that, did you because she's not in Spain at all? She's back in California, which is where I'm going to be very shortly. So you and the CIA can go fuck yourselves." He spat out the words, but Curtis showed almost no reaction.

Shaking, Gene dug in his pocket for a cigarette and lit it. "What kind of people are you anyway? Is this how it works? Blackmail anybody who doesn't go along with your little plans?" He watched Curtis, head down pacing around, listening in silence. It angered Gene even more. He grabbed Curtis by the arm and spun him around.

Curtis shook him off and glared. "Are you through?"

"You're damn right I'm through. As soon as the festival is over, I'm out of here."

"Now you listen, Williams. We're not talking about some band you're quitting. There's a couple of things I'm going to lay out for you." His eyes fastened on Gene. "You've had your say, now I'm going to have mine."

"What's the point," Gene said, dropping his voice. "Blaha is dead. I'm no use to you now."

Curtis ignored him. "First, the telegram. Yes I know about it. We couldn't risk you refusing. That was the reason for the cover story about your sister. That's how important it was and still is. Am I getting through to you? Do you really think we'd go to all that trouble if it wasn't?"

"Cover story? Is that all you can say? Man, that poor old guy is dead. Doesn't that mean anything? You guys are unbelievable."

Curtis sighed as if he were explaining things to a child. "That poor old guy as you call him was a pro. Blaha knew the score, the risks." Curtis paused. "We're sorry about it too, but we cut our losses and go on. That's how the game is played." His voice, his gaze was steady, unapologetic.

"Well, it's not a game to me and I'm taking myself out. We are done." He started to walk away, but Curtis grabbed him and pulled him back.

"You're done when I say you're done," Curtis said. "If you have any ideas about taking off, keep this in mind. Under International Law, anyone briefed by an intelligence agency—that's us—before they enter a foreign country—that's you—is technically guilty of espionage by implication. I have a copy of the document you signed in London. Are you hearing me better now?"

Gene said nothing. He was out of his depth now. He knew Curtis was right.

"As for Blaha's death, I think the Czech police would be very interested in talking with someone who had been at the scene."

Gene looked up. "Nobody saw me there."

Curtis's gaze was steady. "Are you sure? Do you think it matters? Well?"

Gene stared at the ground. There was no getting out after all. The nightmare was going to continue. Like it or not, he was trapped. His only consolation was that Kate was safe. "Okay," he said quietly. "You made your point."

Curtis relaxed somewhat and lit a cigarette. "That's better. Just so we understand each other. By the way, anything you've been told comes under the classification of national security," Curtis added.

"Yeah, yeah, you don't have to spell it out." He became conscious of the music again filtering out to the garden. The piano had been joined by a saxophone. Somebody was probably digging up a set of drums, but the last thing on his mind was a jam session.

Gene was suddenly struck by the irony of his position. He was in a foreign country, a Communist country, and although the embassy grounds were considered United States soil, he was no safer here than if he'd been in Red Square without a visa. There was no escape. Curtis had thought of everything.

"So what happens now?"

"It's too complicated to explain now and I've been gone too long from the party as it is. All I can tell you is you're going to be working Blaha's granddaughter."

"Lena? Why her, or should I even ask?" But even as he asked he knew the answer.

Curtis shrugged. "Think about it. Blaha must have confided in her, left something with her that could lead us in the right direction. From our point of view it's worth checking out and you're the best choice for that assignment. You've met her already." Curtis paused, looking steadily at Gene. "You're sure Blaha didn't give you anything already?"

"You'd know that wouldn't you?"

"What's that supposed to mean?"

"You or one of your guys didn't search my hotel room?"

"No," Curtis said, looking genuinely puzzled. "Okay, we'll talk about it tomorrow." He was suddenly impatient now, throwing his cigarette on the ground and stamping on it. He started away then turned back. "Hey, I know you'll find it hard to believe, but I am sorry about the story about your sister. We just couldn't—"

"Skip it," Gene said, not even trying to keep the bitterness out of his voice. He wasn't going to let Curtis forget that.

He stood for a few minutes, thinking, wondering how he was going to face Lena now. The sounds of the party filtered down louder now, but that was the last place he wanted to be.

He found another way out of the embassy grounds, a back staircase that led back to the front courtyard and made it possible to leave without going back to the party. Jan Pavel at least would take note of his absence, but he didn't want to answer questions. Another story to come up with, another excuse.

He decided to walk back to the hotel. It was still very warm and muggy and the air was heavy with the threat of rain. He loosened his tie and wandered along, glancing in shop windows, aimlessly strolling in the general direction of Wenceslas Square and the Zlata Husa Hotel.

Having once turned Lena down, he was now going to do what she'd already asked him. Could he convince her he'd simply changed his mind? He would have to. She was the one bright spot in this whole mess he was in, but he didn't want it like this. He sighed. Yes, he could convince her, maybe even help, but what would they find? He wasn't sure he wanted to know.

He passed a narrow alleyway and saw at the other end the bright glow of lights coming from bars and restaurants of Wenceslas Square. He turned into the cobblestone alley. He didn't notice the car until it was nearly on him.

He heard the engine first and turned, facing into the bright glare of the headlights, wondering why cars were allowed on such narrow streets. He moved as close to the side as possible, pressing up against a building to allow it to pass. Instead, it stopped just a few feet past him.

Too late, he realized his mistake. He couldn't go forward. The car was completely blocking his way. He started to back up, but didn't react soon enough. It happened so fast he didn't have time to think.

The rear door of the car flew open and he was yanked inside by powerful arms and thrown to the floor face down. He barely registered three men. A handkerchief was stuffed in his mouth, a heavy shoe pressed on his back. The doors slammed, the car reversed back up the alley. At the corner, it turned and raced up the street he'd been walking on. It had all taken less than a minute.

Gene lay on the floor and felt himself jolted and bounced, panic rushing through him. He concentrated on traffic noise. Eventually it became lighter then faded altogether. Finally, the car began to slow and pulled to a halt after a short stretch of what must have been an unpaved bumpy road. He heard a muffled voice from the front seat, the doors open, then he was dragged out of the car. He stumbled and blinked in the darkness. A hand, smelling of harsh tobacco jerked the handkerchief out of his mouth. He stumbled again, but was held upright by two men.

Looking around, his eyes becoming accustomed to the light, he saw the road had cut through the forest. They were somewhere in the country. How far? Twenty minutes out of Prague? It was hard to tell. Across the road was a small cabin of some kind.

Before he had time to think about it, the two men led him up a path to the cabin. Both were thick set, powerfully built, rough faces. Neither man looked or spoke to him. He glanced back over his shoulder once. The driver had remained in the car. He could see the orange glow of a cigarette.

Inside the cabin, the one room was bare except for a wooden table and chairs. A single bulb on a cord burned brightly. There was a musty smell, like it hadn't been used in a long time. His eyes fastened on a small window opposite the door. It appeared to be a simple pane glass, no more than three feet square. Could he make it? Dive through the window, cut and bleeding and run through the forest? He would have to try.

The two men released him, then he heard a voice behind him. "Sit down, Mr. Williams."

Gene turned around. He hadn't seen this man. He was tall, with a thin angular face and lank hair that hung straight down from the crown of his head. His eyes were a milky blue and he spoke with an accent.

"Who are you?" Gene said. "Why have you brought me here?"

The man spoke quickly to the other men in a language Gene didn't readily recognize. It wasn't Czech. Russian? They pushed Gene down in one of the chairs then backed away. The third man came around and sat down opposite Gene at the table. He took out a package of cigarettes and gold lighter and placed them on the table and studied Gene for a few moments.

"Who I am is of no importance," he said. "If you must have a name, we shall use Ivan. Fitting don't you think? Most Americans persist in the belief that all Russians are named Ivan." He smiled at Gene, pleased with himself, as if he'd just said something very clever. "We are here, in fact, to determine exactly who *you* are, Mr. Williams." He lit a cigarette then pushed the pack and lighter toward Gene. "Please."

Gene hesitated a moment then lit a cigarette of his own.

"It would appear, so I am told, you are a rather talented musician invited to take part in the jazz festival. Is that correct?"

"You know it is, but I don't think you want to discuss music. What is it you think I've done?"

Ivan dragged deeply on his cigarette and blew a cloud of smoke above him. "I didn't say you'd done anything, but you're quite right. Music is not the subject of our discussion, although I have a certain fondness for jazz. You might be interested to know that Premier Kosygin possesses a similar interest. He has quite a collection I'm told. Cool jazz, I believe it's called."

"I'll send him a Gerry Mulligan-Chet Baker album."

Ivan colored slightly, but smiled. "You attempt to provoke me, Mr. Williams. That would be unwise. Be that as it may, you are correct in assuming my interest lies in other matters. The CIA for example. It is in these matters that I intend to discourage you. You have become a nuisance, Mr. Williams, which unfortunately, we cannot allow and so you must be dealt with."

"I don't know what you're talking about," Gene said, knowing Ivan, or whatever his name was, probably knew everything. How? Stall? Bluff? Deny everything?

"Please, don't bore me and insult me with denials, Mr. Williams. Your association with a CIA case officer is—"

"The CIA? For God's sake." He managed a silly grin. "C'mon, Ivan. Do I look like a CIA agent? I'm a musician. You think the CIA trains musicians?"

The Russian's smile was humorless. "If it suited their purposes, yes. But in your case it wasn't necessary. They simply made use of a musician, conveniently traveling to Prague for completely legitimate reasons. You may not be here by choice, but it's been done in the past." He paused, eyes riveted on Gene, searching for a reaction, but Gene knew it was coming and held the man's gaze steadily. Ivan looked away, annoyed.

"Very well," he said. "Do you deny knowing a man named Josef Blaha?"

Gene felt himself relax a little. He could do this. "Of course not. I brought some music with me for the festival. A new arrangement. It had to be copied and Blaha was recommended. Besides, he is a friend of the band leader I'm working for, Jan Pavel."

Gene hoped Ivan would notice he didn't use the past tense in referring to Blaha. If he could convince the Russian he knew nothing about the murder, he might have a chance. It was a crucial point and he'd guessed correctly. The Russian picked it up immediately.

"Is?"

"Sure. I understand they went to school together. Old friends." Gene suddenly realized Pavel had not mentioned Blaha's death since the phone call at the hotel.

The Russian paused again, considering Gene's answer. "A very convincing story. True perhaps, but equally plausible that it could all have been arranged in advance."

Gene caught an almost imperceptible nod from Ivan to the two men behind him. Gene started to turn ,but they already had him. One pinned his arms behind him; the other kneeled in front of Gene and bound his ankles to the legs of the chair. He struggled and kicked, but it was pointless. So much for his chance to run if he'd ever had one. The Russian watched it all calmly, then motioned for Gene's arms to be released.

"I'm afraid you don't take my questions seriously enough, Mr. Williams. Perhaps you'll give the next one more careful consideration."

"Yeah, what's that?" He rubbed his arms and felt the rope biting into his ankles.

"It's a two part question actually," the Russian said. He looked up at the ceiling for a moment as if to consider how to frame the question, like a lecturer posing an inquiry to his class. "Pianists are very careful about their hands, aren't they. On the other hand, an...unfortunate accident would prove equally damaging to a percussionist, I should think, which I wonder, and here is where you can help me, Mr. Williams. Which would be more debilitating? The right or the left hand?" The Russian leaned back in his chair and smiled thinly at Gene.

Instinctively, Gene crossed his arms across his chest and stared back. It wasn't possible. He couldn't do that. God, don't let it be possible.

The Russian's eyes had grown cold and Gene had no doubt he could sit there calmly and watch his two thugs break either or both of his hands with no compunction whatsoever. Gene's heart was racing now. Beads of sweat broke out on his forehead.

"Let me see," the Russian went on. "For a violinist, the left hand would be particularly crucial. But for a drummer, it would perhaps be the right hand, no?" He smiled faintly again.

Gene didn't, couldn't answer. He could only recall a story, widely circulated in Boston about a saxophonist who made a play for a girl at a club he was working. Unknown to him, the girl was the property of a small time Mafia type. He was warned off, but didn't take it seriously.

A week later, he was jumped outside the club where he was on break, having a cigarette. He was robbed and beaten so it looked like a mugging, but the knuckles of both hands had been smashed with a hammer.

The Russian was right, of course. Solos would be out if they broke only his left hand, but the right would be the most damaging. He needed it to lay down the time on the ride cymbal. But then.....no, stop it. His mind was running away. What was he thinking. He could only stare back at the Russian.

"I see I have given you cause for alarm, Mr. Williams." The Russian studied Gene's face now carefully.

Gene felt helpless. "I can't tell you what I don't know," he said.

With slow deliberateness, the Russian lit another cigarette. He held it upright between his thumb and forefinger, letting the smoke curl around his face. "Perhaps you are telling the truth. I had to be sure you understood our concern." He leaned forward. Gene would never forget his face. "Let me give you some advice, Mr. Williams. Stick to music. If you are even considering some ridiculous proposal of the CIA, forget it. The situation in Prague is far beyond your comprehension. If I have that assurance...well, I'm not a cruel man, despite what you might think. I have no wish to antagonize your government."

Gene sat rock still as the Russians words began to penetrate his mind. He felt himself relax slightly. Every muscle in his legs had been tensed against the ropes that bound him to the chair. Had he heard right? Was this a reprieve? It was like somebody holding a gun to your head and squeezing the trigger and hearing merely a click.

He knew they really weren't sure. No one was going to break his hand, not this time anyway. This whole thing had been set up to scare him. Well, the Russian had succeeded. Gene had been scared out of his mind. But what kind of assurances did he want of him? He rubbed his hands together. Whole, unbroken hands. "I don't know what it is you want me to say," he said quietly. "I'm not interested in the CIA or anything they have to say. I told you, I'm just a musician."

How many times had he repeated that statement in the past few days? First to Curtis, then Josef Blaha, Lena, and now to the man who must be Curtis' opposite number. He felt a shudder go through his body. After this, Curtis would be nothing to handle.

"So you say," the Russian said. He placed both hands on the table and rose. "Good. Excellent. I'm delighted we could come to an understanding." He seemed genuinely pleased. "I'm sure I don't have to remind you that we can contact you again if necessary. That conversation, I assure you, won't be nearly as pleasant as this one. I assume you know it would be foolish, futile even, to inform anyone of this meeting." The Russian paused again, looking at Gene. "I have your word then?"

"Sure," Gene said. Did the Russian expect him to say anything else? Goodbye, Curtis, Lena, Jan Pavel. Goodbye, Prague. He was going to make it after all.

"Excellent," the Russian said again. "I suggest we drink a toast to our agreement."

"What?" Gene was instantly on guard again. They couldn't know about that. But watching the smile appear once more on the Russian's face, he knew they did.

One of the men behind Gene produced something from a bag on the floor that couldn't have scared Gene more if it had been a gun or a hammer. He watched hypnotized as the Russian set a bottle and a glass on the table.

"Are you familiar with Slivovitz, Mr. Williams," he asked as he broke the seal on the bottle. "It's an excellent, very potent Czech brandy." He made a show of looking around. "What a pity. Unfortunately, we have only one glass. I hope you don't mind drinking from the bottle." He poured a small amount in the glass and held it up. "Please, join me, Mr. Williams. To our agreement."

Gene hesitated then reached for the bottle. He did know about Slivovitz. He'd been warned by several members of the band, but of course he didn't need anybody to warn him about alcohol. How did they know? He put the bottle to his lips and tilted it slightly, barely letting the clear liquid touch his tongue.

"Oh come now, Mr. Williams," the Russian said when Gene sat the bottle back on the table. "That was hardly a taste at all. Ah, I forgot, your arms are tired. My associates were a bit rough earlier. Perhaps they could help you."

One pinned his arms again, the other grabbed him by the hair and held his head back. He tried to keep his mouth closed, his teeth tightly clenched, but powerful stubby fingers pried his mouth open and poured. A good deal got down his throat, scorching and burning like liquid fire.

He gagged and coughed and gasped for breath, choking on the potent liquor. Some of it ran down his chin onto his suit. They released him for a moment, but the bottle came again and again and again, two, three, four times. He lost count. His eyes watered and he choked again, gagging and sputtering.

"No more," the Russian's voice was distant now, as if Gene were sinking under water. "We've only just begun," Gene heard.

***

There was water running nearby. He could hear it. A faint trickling sound. He tried to open his eyes. They were so heavy, but he could see it now, a tiny stream of water trickling past his eyes.

He tried to raise his head, but felt an immediate stabbing pain behind his eyes. He let his head drop down again and closed his eyes. Yes, that was better. The water was cool, but his head hit something hard, like stone. The water flowed past him. More of his senses revived. His whole body was damp, cold.

He raised his head again then pulled himself up on hands and knees. The water washed over his hands. He tried to focus. The street. He was in the street and the water was flowing in the gutter. His suit was torn and soaked and smelled of Slivovitz so strongly he gagged again. He tried to stand, but only lurched forward, his head in the water again. Lights in front of him, somehow familiar. The hotel? Yes, he was in lying in the rain washed gutter in front of the hotel in Wenceslas Square.

He tried to keep his eyes open and focus. He must get up. Then he saw two blurred figures coming toward him. They were coming again to give him more. "No," but his voice was only a whisper. A muted scream tore from his throat. "No." Then he fell back again.

"Gene, Gene." He could hear the voices calling to him, strong hands lifting him up, but he couldn't stand, kept falling down, then finally he was lifted, an arm over each shoulder. He tried to focus. It looked like....yes, Bartek and another man, Imre, the Gypsy.

They dragged him inside the hotel, through the lobby and into an elevator. The light was so bright, so painful. Talking rapidly in Czech. Why? He didn't understand Czech.

Finally, they got him to his room. Bartek, the tall thin saxophonist, Imre, the burly Gypsy. They stripped off his clothes, put him in bed.

"Slivovitz," one of them said.

"No," Gene moaned.

Then he fell into a chasm of darkness.

NINE

Waking up was agony.

Stabbing pain shot through his head. The room seemingly spun around him if he attempted to stand. He was consumed with a dry parching thirst he quenched greedily from the tap in the bathroom. He vomited repeatedly, violent spasms that racked his body and left him limp and weak until finally he collapsed on the cool bathroom tiles.

He was still on the floor when Bartek and Imre the Gypsy let themselves in with his key. He looked up blankly at Bartek standing in the doorway, having only the vaguest memory of being carried back to his room by the two musicians.

Bartek helped him to his feet and guided him back to the bed. "No problem, Gene," he said. "Imre will fix you."

Gene had no idea what Bartek meant. He was grateful to simply lie down again and cover his eyes with his arm, wondering if he'd ever feel human again.

Imre, like a doctor on a house call, was busy at work on the table beside the bed. He had come armed with a collection of bottles, small tins the size of aspirin boxes and a few selected items from the hotel bar: tomato juice, a bottle of mineral water and a long handled spoon. He measured and poured carefully, frowning in concentration with all the consummate skill of a lab technician conducting a research project. Mixing, stirring everything into a tall glass, he added the final ingredient from a small vial he took from his pocket. Finally, he held the glass up to the light and grunted in satisfaction.

"Gypsy medicine," Bartek explained. He had watched Imre's every move, nodding and smiling. "C'mon, Gene, you must drink."

Gene sat up gingerly. The finished concoction looked as vile as he felt. "You drink," Imre said, hovering over Gene with the tall glass of dark red liquid. "This Gypsy blood," he proclaimed. "Make you strong."

Gene looked at it cautiously, imagining he could actually see it foaming and bubbling in the glass. "I don't want to be strong," Gene said. Whatever was in Imre's mysterious potion, just the sight of it brought on another wave of nausea. He shook his head and waved it away. "No, I can't," he said, sinking back on the pillow. "Go away."

He wanted nothing more than to be left in his misery, to sleep if that was possible. At least then he felt nothing.

"No you must drink," Bartek said sternly. "Gypsy blood always work." He raised Gene to an upright position. As soon as he sat up, the room began to spin wildly, but Bartek held him. Imre approached and gently held the glass to his lips. "You must drink fast," Bartek said. "All of it."

Gene put up a hand to steady the glass and took the first tentative swallow. It had a sweetish, pungent taste he couldn't readily identify, an almost syrupy texture and an odor like burnt rubber. He closed his eyes and swallowed more, finding it immediately cool and soothing to his fiery stomach. He managed half the glass and looked up at Imre smiling down at him. Bartek squinted at the proceedings as if he could trace the route of the drink to Gene's stomach.

"Yah, go, Gene. More." Bartek said, encouraging him.

He drank off the remainder and handed the empty glass to Imre. He lay back on the pillow to await its effect if there was going to be any. He lay still for a few moments then cautiously opened his eyes. It was amazing. The room had already steadied and he felt his body bathed in cool delicious relief.

"Jesus, what is that stuff?" he asked, eyeing Imre who was no longer concerned now as he organized and collected his various bottles and tins, packing them in a small leather pouch.

"Secret," he smiled. "Gypsy secret." He turned to Bartek for confirmation. "Is correct?" *Imre must be learning English*, Gene thought.

Gene opened and closed his eyes rapidly. His head was clearing and the sensation was like a million tiny bubbles exploding in his brain. The effect was instantly pleasing and settling. He sat up and got off the bed carefully, but found he was able to stand unassisted. He took a few cautious steps. The room no longer lurched around him. He smiled at Bartek, who watched approvingly. He sat down again almost literally feeling his brain clear.

"God," he said. "Whatever that stuff is it's incredible. If he bottled and sold it he'd make a fortune. I can't believe it."

Bartek lit a cigarette for both of them. Imre knelt in front of him and pushed up his eyelid, examining and nodding. He said something to Bartek in Czech that made the saxophonist smile.

"What?" Gene said, looking at both of them, grinning now.

"Imre say Gypsy blood also good for when you with woman. He balled up his fist and flexed his arm and they both laughed. Then he turned serious. "So, Gene, what happened? You drink too much Slivovitz, yes?"

Gene averted his eyes. He couldn't tell Bartek what really happened. The less people involved the better, but he owed him some kind of explanation. Brief loss of memory would have to do.

"I don't remember much after leaving the embassy party," he said, improvising. "I just kind of wandered around, ended up in a restaurant and some people invited me to join them and well....we drank. Too much I guess."

Bartek frowned. "You drink Slivovitz with Czech peoples?" It was obvious Bartek didn't entirely believe him. He exchanged glances and translated for Imre. "Slivovitz very bad, very strong." He shook his head, but didn't pursue it further.

"Yes, I know now," Gene said, already trying to piece together what had happened after the session in the cabin with the Russian, but it was all a blank. "How did you find me?"

Bartek shrugged and put out his cigarette. "After embassy party, Imre take me to see his uncle. He have Gypsy band in Prague, all from Budapest. Very good music," Bartek went on stretching out the words. "Make girls cry with cello. We come back to hotel and you are asleep in street. Very bad. Now you need new suit, yes?"

"Was it raining or something? I remember water?"

"Yah, raining very quickly, very hard. How do you call it? Thunder bath?"

"Thunder shower."

"Yes," Bartek said. "Only twenty minutes, but much rain. Is normal in Prague in summer."

Gene dragged deeply on his cigarette, feeling more and more normal himself. So he had been force fed Czech brandy—the whole bottle?—then dumped in the gutter in a drunken stupor. Nice guy, the Russian. But why? To discredit him with the band. Maybe they hoped he'd be found by the desk clerk. Pavel would be alerted and Gene would have to suffer the embarrassment of explaining his condition to everyone. What would Pavel have thought to find his imported guest American drummer drunk and passed out in the gutter? Not a good advertisement for his band.

Whatever the Russian's motives had been, the message was clear: stay away, stay out of it.

"Hey, thanks a lot," Gene said. "I mean it and it won't happen again. I learned my lesson. Does Jan—"

Bartek shook his head. “Pavel know nothing. Only me and Gypsy find you. No problem.”

Gene nodded, wondering what Bartek really thought. Maybe one day he could tell him the truth.

“But why you leave party?” Bartek grinned. “Pretty girls, good beer and, oh, I forget.” He reached in his pocket and gave Gene a small envelope. “Lena Blaha come too. She gave me this for you.”

Gene took the envelope. “Did she say anything?”

Bartek shook his head. “No, she just talk to Jan. You know her grandfather was died?”

“Yes, Jan told me. “

“Mmm, very sad,” Bartek said. “I don’t understand.”

Now, as his mind cleared more and events began to make sense, Gene realized how carefully he would have to balance things. He was still caught up with Curtis and there seemed no way out of that. He had no doubt if pushed, Curtis would indeed set the Czech police on him. But the consequences of defying Curtis were far less worrying than another visit with the Russian.

The panic and fear in his eyes had been real and the Russian must have seen it clearly. He had learned about fear in that cabin and didn’t want to experience it again. Then dumped in the street, drunk and passed out no doubt made the Russian secure in the knowledge that he had done a good enough job on him already. Unless he drew their attention. Next time, there would be no reprieves.

But tomorrow night was the festival. If he could stall Curtis off until then, make it appear he was complying, Curtis would have to agree to let him go after that. He wouldn’t have any legitimate reason for staying in Prague. His perfect cover would be over. It was at least worth a try.

The anger was simmering again, threatening to overcome reason and good sense. He’d been blackmailed, tricked into believing his sister was in danger, forced to become, at least indirectly in Josef Blaha’s murder, and finally humiliated and frightened to death by a Russian KGB agent. All this he could lay at the feet of Alan Curtis and the CIA.

And for what? The remote possibility that a frightened old man, so Curtis said, might have found the answer to the question on the lips of everyone in Prague and the western world.

Was the Soviet Union going to invade Czechoslovakia?

Another more troubling thought occurred and persisted even as he tried to shake it off. Would Josef Blaha have been murdered if he had not been chosen as his contact? Was he in some remote way, responsible for his death? Did Lena think so?

He got up then and went to the door with Bartek. “Gypsy medicine is good, yes?” Bartek said

Gene said, “Where did you learn English again?” He’d noticed so many phrases like ‘no problem’ come up repeatedly.

“From American soldiers,” Bartek said proudly. “They come to my village when I am boy. I help them. One sergeant, he teach me.”

“What happened to him?”

“He go home,” Bartek shrugged. “Then fucking Russians come.” That would make Bartek somewhere in his late thirties although he didn’t look it. “Maybe American soldiers come back if fucking Russians come back again, yeah?”

“I don’t know,” Gene said. “I just don’t know.”

He shut the door and quickly opened Lena’s note.

Gene, I hoped to talk to you tonight. Please call me, Lena.

***

Alan Curtis was already at work when Gene was ushered into his office at the American Embassy. Seated at a broad desk flanked by filing cabinets with combination locks, Curtis was reading from the inevitable file folders. *He looked*, Gene thought, *every inch the title stenciled on his door: Political Attaché.*

“Gene,” Curtis said with a forced smile. “Glad you could drop by.” He motioned Gene to a chair opposite him.

“Thanks,” Gene said, somewhat puzzled by Curtis’ uncharacteristic greeting, especially in light of last night’s talk. The mystery was solved quickly when the CIA man pushed the file across to Gene. A note was clipped to the dark green folder. *This office is not secure*, the note said. *Read the file and we’ll talk about it later.*

Gene nodded his understanding and opened the file. “How about some coffee?” Curtis asked. “You look like you could use some.”

“Sure.”

“Okay, here you go.” Curtis poured coffee from a glass pot on a hot plate in the corner. “Look, I’ve got couple of things to take care of, so if you’ll just excuse me for a few minutes, I’ll be right back.”

“Yeah, no problem,” Gene said. He felt like an actor who hadn’t studied his lines and had wandered into the middle of a play he didn’t know. Exit Curtis. Williams reads from file.

The heading read: Czechoslovakia: Project Analysis. He'd planned to just skim over the printed sheets, but the more he read the more absorbed he became. He saw at once what Curtis had alluded to earlier. It was all there.

A detailed chronicle of Alexander Dubcek's rise to power and the anatomy of a thus far, peaceful attempt to throw off the yoke of Soviet domination in Czechoslovakia. The struggle of a country trying to live its own brand of Communism was reduced to five pages of facts and information. But even as he read, Gene knew there must be more.

In the few days he'd been in Prague, Pavel, Bartek, some of the others had tried to convey their growing excitement over the new found freedoms that he as an American took for granted. The easing of travel restrictions, the abolishment of press censorship. Philip Hastings had mentioned them as well.

The report explained it all in intelligence terms, a dry compendium of information and options that failed to include the pain and joy of change the people of Czechoslovakia were going through. The human element was missing.

Gene found himself moved by the account of Dubcek's emergence as a leader. Here, according to this, was a man really dedicated to his people. It shone through clearly even when couched in the emotionless language of Washington analysts. Here was a man willing to risk the wrath of the Kremlin to achieve his goals.

But reading the conclusion, Gene was more baffled than ever about his own recruitment and importance to Curtis. The Washington prognosis was not encouraging. Soviet intervention probable and imminent employing Warsaw Pact forces currently on standby, followed by dissolution of present administration. Projected date: accurate sources unknown at this time.

What did it all mean? For Dubcek, for Jan Pavel and his musicians? For himself? From deep in his mind Gene conjured up newsreel footage of tanks and soldiers in Hungary. And what about Lena? Her grandfather dead and his death somehow tied to this report. How many would die before and after if it came to pass?

He began to understand what Curtis had meant when he'd said he would see things differently after reading the report. Could he really do anything to help, or should he just play it safe, adopt the all too common slogan of don't get involved? Well, it was too late for that. He was involved.

Curtis came back then, breezing in like an old buddy. "Sorry to keep you waiting. How about letting me show you around the grounds eh?"

Gene stood up. "The grounds, yeah, good idea." Gene took his cue from Curtis, waiting as he put the file back in one of the locked cabinets.

They went outside in the embassy gardens and walked along a gravel path. Curtis was better prepared and donned a pair of aviator sunglasses.

"Is all that security really necessary? I mean this is the U.S. Embassy isn't it?"

Curtis allowed himself a slight smile. "Yes, I'm afraid so. We've found some bugs in the office. We sweep regularly, but you never know." They walked slowly farther down the path. "Well, you've read it. Do you get it now?" Curtis had dropped the friendly tone now.

"No I don't. You've got it all down pat. Why the charade with me?"

"Because," Curtis said, "of that last line. We still don't know when."

"And you think Blaha did?"

"No doubt in my mind, but I think he also found something else, something that prevented him from reporting as usual. What exactly, I'd rather not speculate on now. But it wasn't like him."

"You sound like a press release."

Curtis said, "Yes, I guess I do."

"And that's where I come in?"

"Yes, Blaha was going underground. He'd have spotted a ringer right off. There were other reasons as well. Remember I told you in London about the invasion plans that had been intercepted by West German intelligence? Obviously the invasion didn't come off according to that schedule. We thought maybe they were a plant. The Soviets are good at misinformation, to throw us off the real date or just test our reaction. At any rate, Washington didn't buy it. Plans or not, no action was proposed.

Gene stopped and looked at Curtis. "But why? You mean we, you, just stand by and...let it happen?"

"Any action on our part would mean direct confrontation with Moscow. We want to avoid that at all costs. We might not be as lucky as we were with the Cuban thing in 1962."

"Yeah, I remember," Gene said. They began to walk again, reaching the far end of the gardens. He recalled Kennedy's speech, the world holding its breath. "But if we're not going to do anything, what difference does it make if you know when it's going down?"

"Don't you play poker on those band busses? Sometimes you win a pot with a bluff. The Soviets don't know what we might do. And, there's one other thing, although granted it's remote. There's always the possibility they won't stop with Czechoslovakia. That's what it's all about. Being ready for the worst case scenario."

Gene stopped and sat down on a bench. Curtis joined him. "How did a guy like Dubcek get into office anyway?"

"They weren't paying attention in Moscow. The former President, Novotny, holed up in the castle or took long drives in his limo, put off dealing with things, oblivious to what was happening around him with the liberals. By the time things had started to change, Breshev tried to intercede for him, but by then, the party was split over whether the jobs of head of state and party boss should be held by one person. Dubcek was ambitious and at the next party vote, he was installed. Novotny stayed on as president, but his days were numbered. He was replaced by Ludvik Svoboda. He was a war hero and a Kremlin favorite.

"Dubcek was clear then to start his reform programs. In April, he published a 27,000 word paper outlining unheard of freedoms for Czechs. The people loved it of course and he's always out there among them. You need a ration card for gasoline here and he drives down the neighborhood station and buys his own."

"Are you serious?" Gene asked.

"Yep. Can you picture Johnson doing that?"

Gene shook his head. "Not without a motorcade, Secret Service and all the TV networks."

"Exactly," Curtis said. "He's the epitome of this socialism with a human face thing, returning the power to the people. Moscow was worried, but they figured they had Svoboda in their pocket, sort of their man in Prague to keep Dubcek in tow. There were several summit talks and Kosygin told Dubcek to ease up on the reforms or they'd do something more active. There were more talks, Dubcek and Breshev really got into it, but the other leaders supported him and voted against any support of force. Dubcek walked out of the conference and Moscow promised to let him pursue the reforms. The idea was to give Dubcek enough rope to hang himself."

"So what happened?" Gene asked.

"Just what we're seeing now. This big show of force by the Warsaw Pact Forces. They think now, Dubcek has gone too far."

Gene considered Curtis' words. That an invasion was in the works seemed a given, almost beyond doubt. But there had to be more to it. Curtis' motives for keeping him in the game surely went beyond mere confirmation of something they already expected. Something so valuable or...damaging that Blaha was killed because of it. Once again he had the feeling Curtis was holding back.

"What about your conversation with Blaha," Curtis said. "Can you remember what he said?"

"I've been over it a hundred times. He talked about music and then just told me to meet him. If there was anything else, I missed it," Gene lied, leaving out the copyist's warning *be careful of your own.* What did that mean? There was something there, but he couldn't put his finger on it.

They got up and began walking back toward the building. "What if nothing happens before the festival? I don't have any reason for staying in Prague after that.

Curtis shrugged. "Then you go home and we start all over again. You have my word." Curtis looked directly at him, but his eyes were hidden behind the dark glasses.

They reached the end of the garden and turned back toward the main building. "I'm still not sure what exactly you want me to do," Gene said.

"Just your normal routine. Rehearse, hang out with the band. Spend some time with Lena Blaha, keep your eyes and ears open." Curtis looked away. "For all we know, somebody may contact you. I'm not sure, but we have to keep that option open in case Blaha had a backup plan."

"You really think he confided in his granddaughter?"

"Maybe not directly, but there's something. Blaha knew the score. He would have made some provision if something happened to him."

"What happened to her parents?"

"They were both killed in a car crash," Curtis said. "He never talked about it, but we knew. That's when Lena came to live with him."

"Jesus."

Curtis nodded. "Yeah, and now her grandfather." They walked back without saying anything.

As they neared the main building, Gene glanced up at the American flag fluttering in the morning breeze. "One question. What do you guys do with all this information?"

"Simple. It goes to Washington for analysis. We like to think it helps to make good decisions, but we don't make them. Only that old Texan on the wall in my office does that."

Gene thought of something else then. "I always thought spooks were ghosts."

"They are," Curtis said. "At least they're supposed to be."

***

From an upper floor window, another American watched Alan Curtis and Gene Williams near the exit gate to the street. He saw them shake hands then Williams left. The American picked up the phone and dialed rapidly.

"He's leaving now," he said into the phone. He listened a moment then said, "I don't know. That's up to you. I can't do anymore now." He listened again. "Yes, I know," then he hung up the phone.

He remained for several minutes, pouring himself a large drink from a bottle in his desk and stood gazing out over the embassy gardens, long after Alan Curtis and Gene Williams were gone.

***

On another interoffice extension in another embassy, Colonel Dimitri Polokov took a call relaying information in regard to his memo to the STB. "Well," he barked into the phone. He was irritated, impatient with everyone this morning.

"Nothing, Comrade Colonel. The search revealed nothing. He appears to be nothing, but a musician," the voice on the other end of the line told him.

Polokov paused. Something nagged him like a pesky fly. "You're sure?"

"Yes, Colonel. The search was thorough."

"Very well, but maintain surveillance."

"As you wish, Comrade Colonel."

Polokov hung up the phone. Now there was another decision to make. Where shall I dine tonight?

***

Gene hurried along the tree lined boulevard dotted with bustling shops and restaurants. Distracted by the memory of his conversation with Curtis, the gloomy predictions of the intelligence analysts, the persistent feeling that he was somehow, in some way, responsible for Josef Blaha's death.

Jesus, he was more confused than ever. Adding to what he already knew, the report he'd read left him with a new perspective. Exactly, he conceded, as Curtis had predicted. But there were still a good many blanks to be filled in and he wanted something more, a human contact, someone he could trust, a safe contact. *Now, I'm thinking like Blaha*, he thought. *Philip Hastings could perhaps provide some of the answers.*

The British reporter told him he'd be back from a morning of tracking down sources, so now Gene headed for the Alcron Hotel, anxious to talk with Hastings.

There was no rehearsal until later this afternoon, but the festival was drawing near—less than twenty-four hours away. After that, well, he was gone, his obligation to Curtis fulfilled beyond reason. There was no way Curtis could get out of it then and Gene promised himself to go all the way. But how? Curtis had all the cards.

Yet the jazz festival, his only reason for being in Prague now seemed to have lost its importance when placed alongside the events that had come crashing down on him.

With Kate safe, his purpose for recruitment dead, reason dictated he simply go through the motions for Curtis's benefit for another thirty-six hours. He owed nothing more. If anything, they owed him. Curtis could not be trusted, despite his now good guy attitude. Real or merely a bluff, Gene wasn't going to push it. He could still be implicated in a number of unpleasant things and he knew Curtis would manipulate him in any way necessary.

Interrogation at the hands of the Czech Police was a grim prospect. The publicity alone would bring nothing, but embarrassment to Jan Pavel and the band, and if Curtis decided to abandon him, he would be left out in the cold. But to go beyond these minimal obligations would be drawing the Russian's attention and he didn't want that either.

Yet, the intelligence report had worked some kind of magic on him. He had to admire Dubcek and his reforms. Gene realized he was the complacent American who took for granted freedoms and privileges the Czech people had been denied for years. Weren't they worth some effort? If he could do anything, however minor, shouldn't he?

Turning onto Stephanska Street, he was bewildered at this turn of his mind. What was he thinking? *Man, you're a drummer and that's it.* He'd never been aware politically, never a joiner, an activist, and yet here smack in the middle of a Communist country under siege, which, if the experts could be believed, was on the brink of destruction, something had awakened in him. Issues he'd never confronted, but now he felt obligated to pursue.

He remembered a punishment, once meted out by his father as a small boy. Dragged kicking and screaming, he'd been confined to his room. But once settled in and resigned to it, he found himself almost enjoying it, and on top of that, being disappointed when the sentence was shortened and he was released early.

The feeling now was almost the same, and he conceded, equally foolish thinking he was responsible for Blaha's death. It was absurd to think otherwise. Blaha knew the score, Curtis had said. The old man played a dangerous game and lost. That was the rational, logical explanation. But nagging him, spurring him on was the lingering possibility that Josef Blaha had been killed because he, Gene Williams, had come to Prague, been Blaha's contact. The doubts remained, the web of ambiguity more tangled. He had to know.

But how? As he had repeatedly told himself and everyone concerned, he was just a musician. He had laughed when Curtis had first approached him. He was not a trained agent and really knew so little he didn't know how little he knew. But, maybe this was his one advantage. A stranger to the intelligence community and a naive one at that. An amateur, an unknown commodity floundering in a pool of professionals he both feared and mistrusted. His only ally, if he had one at all, was Lena Blaha. She had to search for answers of her own and was caught in the same web.

Maybe he could bounce all this off Philip Hastings. A sane voice was called for, but he quickly discovered it wasn't going to be Hastings.

"He checked out," the desk clerk told him.

"Checked out?" Gene couldn't hide his disappointment or surprise.

"Yes, I'm sorry," the clerk said. He checked his watch. "About one hour ago."

Gene started to turn away when the clerk called him back, looking at him as if trying to remember a description. "You are Gene Williams?"

"Yes, why?"

The clerk smiled and produced an envelope. "Good. Mr. Hastings said you might be calling. He left this for you."

"Thanks," Gene said taking the envelope. He walked slowly away from the desk, weighing the envelope in his hand. He sat down in one of the lobby's overstuffed chairs and lit a cigarette. The envelope was sealed, hotel stationery and had his name scribbled on the front. There were two typed pages inside. The first was a short personal note.

Dear Gene,

Sorry to cancel our lunch with no notice, but after reading the enclosed, I'm sure you'll understand. It's a draft, but by the time you *read this, it will be a lead story I intend to file within the next day or two. After what I saw this morning, I'm sorry to say I must revise my skepticism about military intervention. The source I mentioned last night not only confirmed the rumors, but also managed to get me a look at a Soviet encampment just over the border. I called my paper and I've been dispatched to Bratislava for a closer look. Regrettably, this means I'll miss the jazz festival—if there is one.*

Gene stopped and looked around the lobby, feeling suddenly exposed. He put out his cigarette and continued reading.

I don't want to alarm you, but I urge the utmost caution if you remain in Prague. I strongly advise you to leave immediately or at least directly after the festival. Friend Dubcek is in serious trouble and barring a miracle, Prague will be no place to be in the coming days. If you cannot get out, seek haven at your embassy. If you make it to London, please don't hesitate to call.

Best regards, Philip.

Gene leaned back in the chair and closed his eyes for a moment. Get out? Seek haven in your embassy? Jesus what the fuck had he gotten himself into. As he read the second page, there was no doubt Hastings knew what he was into or what he was about.

ASSAULT FORCES READY FOR ACTION

Like a giant dog held in check by its master, an amassing army of Warsaw Pact Forces waits in readiness at key points on the borders of Czechoslovakia. Two Hundred Thousand soldiers waiting for orders that will release them on an unsuspecting victim.

The Russians come from Tashkent or Odessa, the far reaching outposts of the mother country. Tall blonds, swarthy Mongolians, or sometimes unmistakably, Armenians. A fully integrated army of farm boys and city cousins suddenly finding themselves thrown together on the front line of an as yet unsought battle. The enemy, an unknown adversary.

The number plates on the tanks and lorries reflect the East German origins of nearly half the forces. But wherever they come from, they share a common bond—boredom. All of them simply want to go home.

The infantrymen carry AK47 assault rifles; the NCOs, revolvers in wooden holsters; the officers, automatic pistols. The tank crews, clad in black leather jackets and padded helmets man the T34 and mammoth T54 tanks equipped with infra-red searchlights. The large cylinders are not, as many think, fuel tanks, but heavy rolls of wire matting to free the mud mired vehicles.

For most of them, the day begins at five o'clock with reveille. The officers sleep in tents or crude temporary huts; the troops make their beds on the ground, on waterproof capes. The meals are also simple and boring. Breakfast is porridge and coffee. Lunch, a greasy pea soup with lard floating on top. Dinner is soup again and bread, one loaf divided among four men and carefully weighed on Russian scales.

Cigarettes are rationed at ten a day. There are no packages from home, no PX and many of the troops have not seen their families for nearly four years, although their service was completed in East Germany. They have been on standby since January.

The long days are passed mending socks, washing clothes, or cleaning weapons. A routine broken only by the occasional game of football or the inevitable singing and dancing that is Russia. For the most part, they seem to stand around, striking poses of ultimate boredom, perhaps thinking of faraway families while waiting for strike orders or the more appealing option of just going home. Most feel word will come soon, but rumors filter through the camp in a multitude of contradictions. Hopes are raised then quickly dashed by counter orders as the endless waiting continues.

And what of their ostensible target? Czechoslovakia and a people who....

Hastings had stopped there, but Gene could finish the sentence himself. A people who only want what has been denied them for so long. Freedom briefly enjoyed and soon to be ended.

Gene could appreciate Curtis' frustration. Jan Pavel should be told, but how? Would anybody believe him? And how would he explain having such information?

He looked around unable to reconcile the quiet scene in the hotel lobby with the picture Philip Hastings had drawn of soldiers waiting to sweep down on the city. Did Alexander Dubcek really know, or was he simply over confident, thinking it all a bluff, designed to force him to alter his program of reforms and liberalization?

One person he knew had to see this. He got up and went to a phone in the lobby and called her. "Lena? It's Gene."

"Yes," she said, her voice quiet.

"I need to see you as soon as possible."

She hesitated only a moment. "I'm at my grandfather's flat. Come here."

"Okay, about thirty minutes."

"I'll be waiting."

Gene hung up, suddenly realizing she hadn't asked him if he needed directions. Well, it didn't matter now, but first it was time to see if he had company.

He walked back to Wenceslas Square, stopping occasionally to glance in shop windows, study reflections, but he couldn't be sure. *Remember, you're an amateur*, he thought. *Let's see.*

He continued on till he came upon a large department store. He found the men's wear section and casually inspected some items while studying the layout of the store. Either they were very good or he was alone. He couldn't decide which, but there was one way to find out for sure.

He joined the small group that had gathered in front of the elevator waiting to be taken to the upper floors. He hung back, waited until the last moment, then crowded aboard. He drew an angry look from the operator and irritable mutterings from some other passengers, but he ignored them all and remained in the front of the car.

On the second floor, he rushed out toward the doors to the stairs he'd spotted earlier. Employees only he guessed, glancing at the lettering on the door. He raced down the stairs to the landing between floors and ducked under the stairwell to wait.

Seconds later, he heard a door slam shut from below, the sound of footsteps pounding up the stairs. He pressed further against the wall and caught a brief glimpse of a man sprinting two steps at a time, then the sound of a door swinging open above.

Gene ran back down the stairs, jerked open the ground floor door and found himself in the middle of the toy department. He pushed through the crowd to the street exit and found a taxi at the curb.

"Kotlarska Street," he yelled at the driver. As the taxi pulled away, he looked back through the rear window. Unless there was a second man, he was clear.

Hey, this was kind of fun.

TEN

"He got away," Arnett said, dropping into a chair opposite Alan Curtis. He helped himself to a cigarette from the pack on the desk.

"He got away? What do you mean he got away?" Curtis had been sitting back in his chair, coat off, tie loosened, his feet on the desk when Arnett came in. He sat up now and scowled at Arnett, who concentrated on the ash of his cigarette and shrugged.

"We picked him up and tagged him to the Alcron Hotel. When he left, I stuck around to see if I could find out what he was up to there. Then he slipped my man at the Maj Department Store."

"He slipped your man. This guy who is just a musician slipped your man. How did he manage that?"

"Hey, how the hell do I know? He just did. Maybe he's seen some spy movies." Arnett continued to avoid Curtis' glare.

Curtis leaned on the desk toward Arnett. "Now listen to me and get this straight. Don't underestimate Williams. We've got him in a corner now and he knows it. Remember, we're not dealing with one of our own. Williams is going to be unpredictable." Curtis sat back then. "Jesus, no telling what he might do. He has no idea what he's into."

"Okay, okay," Arnett said. "I'll get back out there myself."

Curtis got quiet. He'd spent most of the morning on accumulated paper work—cables, memos—distracted, but methodically working through a stack of documents. Eventually, he'd pushed them aside. He wished he could do that permanently, but he was Political Attaché and cover job or not, it was work that had to be done.

He'd begged off lunch with Warner Roberts, puzzled by the man's new found interest, when another telex came in from Washington with Top Secret stamps all over it. The President, it seemed, was becoming increasingly annoyed at the lack of solid information from Prague Station. An updated analysis had been forwarded for confirmation, but Curtis had only looked at it wearily, knowing he could add little to it. And now this. His one puny lead out of contact, at least temporarily.

Williams was going to be harder to control now and not so easily intimidated with the threat to his sister blown. Curtis could only hope the implied threat of exposure to the Czech Police would keep the young musician in line. But, he reminded himself, Williams was a jazz musician. Everything about him was improvised. He had kept his word to Mead and left Williams as much in the dark as possible. If he really knew what was going on, he'd had left the country already and blown off the festival. Well, he'd do that anyway if nothing turned up in the next twenty-four hours.

Curtis looked again at Arnett. "What was he doing at the Alcron anyway?"

"According to the desk clerk, Williams was supposed to meet a British newspaper reporter named..." Arnett dug in his pocket for a piece paper, "Philip Hastings. Hastings had already checked out by the time Williams got there."

"Oh yeah," Curtis said. "I think I met him last night at the reception. He's here covering the jazz festival. Probably doing an interview with Williams."

Arnett nodded. "Yeah, I don't think there's any other connection. He left a note for Williams is all."

"Probably not," Curtis said, but thought he would like to have seen that note. His mind wandered back to the morning cable. The twice daily briefings by the Kremlin watchers were apparently boring the hell out of President Johnson. Curtis could imagine the big Texan bellowing at his aides and dodging the press.

The analysts had been wrong before. All of Western Europe worked on the premise that any major move by the Soviets would be tipped off at least two weeks in advance. If an invasion date was scheduled, it was the best kept secret in the history of intelligence. And now, with his best source dead, his only hope a fucking musician. *Christ, I'm starting to sound like Arnett. No training, no experience, just happened to be in the right place at the right time. A total amateur. One very unpredictable pissed off amateur.*

"How are you going to pick up Williams?" Curtis asked.

"We've got the girl staked out. She's still at Blaha's and I can pick up Williams at the Lucerna. There's another rehearsal later this afternoon."

Curtis thought for a moment. "Okay, but if anything breaks, I want to know."

After Arnett left, Curtis could only think that something had to break soon. Dubcek couldn't keep up this tightrope act much longer. Moscow might just be ready to sever the cord Dubcek was suspended on.

***

Gene got out of the taxi on Kotlarska Street, but had the driver stop a block away from Josef Blaha's apartment. He scanned the street, walked past the building a couple of times. If there was anybody watching the place, he couldn't pick them out. But so what? Seeing Lena was exactly what Curtis wanted him to do.

He walked up to the entrance. It looked so different in daylight. He remembered the other night when he'd discovered Blaha's body and didn't look forward to seeing the inside of that place again, but Lena was here.

He bounded up the stairs and knocked lightly. Lena opened the door almost immediately, as if she'd been watching the street, waiting for him.

"Sorry I'm late," he said, breathing slightly harder than usual.

"Problem?" Her greeting smile quickly dissolved.

"Yeah, I was being followed." He walked in and she quickly shut the door behind him. "I'm not sure if it's Curtis or not, but I think I managed to lose them."

She followed him into the living room and they settled on the couch. He couldn't help glancing down the hall to Blaha's work room, but the door was shut.

"But if it wasn't Curtis' people, who else...unless."

"Listen to me, Lena. Yesterday you asked for my help and I turned you down. I had my reasons, but since then, a lot of things have happened. I'm still in a bind with Curtis, at least until after the festival. I'm supposed to just carry on as normal." He tried to look at her directly. "Curtis thinks your grandfather confided in you."

She nodded and got up and walked over to the window. "And you're here to get the information out of me and then you'll leave. Is that it?"

"No, that's not it." He got up and went to her at the window, turning her around to face him. "I met Curtis this morning. He showed me some things I need to tell you about, but I didn't tell him what you told me the other day, that you already knew about your grandfather's work. I want you to believe me."

She looked in his eyes and then pressed against him as his arms came around her. "I don't know what to believe anymore," she said.

He held her close, aware of her body against his. "I have my own reasons for staying in. I can't explain it, but I want to know about your grandfather too. I have to know if I was somehow responsible in some way, if I did something wrong, put him in danger and—"

She pulled back and looked at him. “No,” she said. “You must not think that.” Her eyes teared briefly. “No one was responsible, Gene, least of all you. My grandfather knew what he was doing.”

Gene sighed. “I hope that’s true. Have you made any...arrangements yet? Can I help?”

“No,” Lena said. “It’s been taken care of. The funeral will be in Plzen. That’s where he was from. I can’t go now, but I will in a couple of days. There is other family there.”

He pulled her close again and she didn’t resist. Then he kissed her, lightly at first, then deeply and she melted against him, her arms around his neck. When they broke, they looked at each other, both breathing hard. He realized in the face of her grandfather’s death, she was affirming life. She too, seemed to realize they had stepped across some indiscernible boundary and neither of them knew what was on the other side.

He held her again. “I’m here, I’m in Lena.

***

The afternoon rehearsal had again been satisfactory, nothing more. The music was under control now and the band was edgy for a live performance, like a football team ready for the big game. Gene’s own playing had been adequate, but uninspired. As he suspected, most of the band had put it down to his drinking bout. Bartek had gotten the word around no doubt.

They knew. He could see it in their eyes and it was impossible to ignore the look of concern in Jan Pavel’s expression. How would he take the news that an invasion of his country was quite possibly just around the corner? But how could Gene tell him, even hint at it? No, not yet. There had to be more.

Before he’d left Lena, he had told her everything. He had watched the shock and concern spread over her face as he related the incident with the Russian and his thugs at the cabin, the search of his room, the meeting with Curtis and the additional threats.

KGB, Lena had pronounced calmly when he’d described the forced drinking party and the Russian. The story had frightened her, but somehow in the telling of it, his own fear had diffused, become a distant thing, as if it had happened to someone else.

Now, stepping out of a taxi, Lena waiting on the corner for him, he knew why he was there. She had a string bag of groceries in her hand.

He watched the taxi pull away and went over to her. Instinctively, he scanned the street and saw a familiar figure.

"You go on," he said to Lena. "I'll be there in a minute."

"What's the matter?" She was suddenly alarmed.

"It's nothing. Just something I have to do. Go on."

He waited till she was on the way, watched her look back once over her shoulder then enter her building. There was no traffic on the street, but some young boys were kicking a soccer ball around on the sidewalk. Their shouts echoed off the walls as he started across the street. The man started away, then stopped, staring at him curiously as he approached.

Gene stopped in front of Karel Arnett. "I don't know what your name is, but if you've got some coins, you can step in that booth there and call Alan Curtis. Tell him I'll be here for the night. Okay?" Gene spun around, crossed back across the street before Karel Arnett could answer or even react.

Unpredictable? Hell, the sonofabitch is crazy!

***

On the border near Poland, three thousand Soviet troops and tanks carrying armored vehicles were less than twenty-five miles from the railroad center of Zilina, one of the seven key entry points to Prague. To the south, a huge Soviet convoy waited just inside Hungary. Air bases in Poland and nearby Baltic states were jammed with Soviet planes, while the tactical Air Army was mustered in East Germany.

The decision to strike still remained locked in the minds of a handful of Kremlin leaders in Moscow, but just two hours earlier, an order had filtered down from Command Headquarters that confirmed the rumors sweeping through the camps. The soldiers greeted the news with almost cheerful relief. At last, they had something definite to combat their boredom. The time for war games was apparently at an end, they concluded, as they listened to field commanders read out the brief directive.

All units were to switch to live ammunition.

***

While Lena cooked dinner, Gene took a shower and changed into the clothes he had picked up and brought in a small bag from the hotel. He'd also brought his practice pad and sticks. He sat now, idly taping out rhythms, playing exercises, rolls, watching Lena move about the kitchen, engrossed in her tasks, looking up at him occasionally, smiling. His hands moved instinctively on the pad, sometime slowly, sometimes a blur as he remembered the afternoon. They had made love almost desperately, clinging to one another, each for their own reasons. Lena, he knew to forget her grandfather's death. He to hold onto something real in all this. Afterwards, they had lain quietly, comfortable together already, both wondering where things were going next.

"It won't be long now," she said, coming over to sit with him. She sipped from a glass of wine and watched his hands. She touched his forearm lightly, felt the muscles flex as he played faster then stopped. "Are you hungry?"

He set the sticks down and moved the pad. He leaned closer to her. "For you, yes, but I guess I can manage some food too. Are you a good cook?"

She laughed and kissed him quickly, teasingly. "You're about to find out." She got up and went back to the kitchen and set the table. "Come on, drummer boy."

They made small talk over dinner, avoiding the subject on both their minds, but over coffee and a cigarette, he wanted to talk. She listened without interrupting as he gathered his thoughts and formed the words to express his frustration, his sense of responsibility he didn't know he had.

"It still bothers me, Lena. Your grandfather's death. If I—"

She cut him off. "That has nothing to do with it, Gene. You must believe that. You could do nothing to control what is happening here, what happened to my grandfather. No one could. Not my grandfather, not Curtis, not anyone. Everything was already in motion, long before you arrived in Prague. It is our destiny and only a question of time now."

"It can't really be that bad can it?"

"Forgive me, Gene, but you Americans are so naive. Your country has never been invaded, taken over. Perhaps that is why you think the way you do. The Soviets must control us as they do others—Hungary, Bulgaria, Romania, Yugoslavia. If not by force, then by coercion of the leaders."

She is right, he thought. *What do I know about politics, Communist politics?* When Hungary happened, he was a senior in high school, drinking his first beer, trying to make the football team and score with his first girl. Hungary could have been on Mars as far as he was concerned. "Maybe as you say I'm naive about things here, but what about that report. It makes sense, doesn't it?" He had shown her Philip Hastings story and told her about the briefing paper he'd read in Curtis' office.

"Those are only words. " She flung her hands in the air. They don't show the suffering the people of Czechoslovakia have endured, nor do they convey the feeling of freedom we've experienced these last few months. How can I make you understand? You've always been free."

He looked in her eyes and felt a response he couldn't fathom. A feeling from somewhere inside him had been awakened. A feeling that transcended his own precarious position and only deepened his involvement. He couldn't be sure if Lena was the instrument of this awakening, but he knew she was a large part of it. "Tell me, Lena. I want to know."

She told him as only one who has lived through it, grown up in it, been told by relatives, seen with her own eyes. Lena told it as a Czech.

"My grandfather told me so much. Before Dubcek, before Novotny, there was Gottwald promising the gains of socialism, but delivering nothing. He was a harsh ruler. Everything was nationalized, taken away from the people in the name of Communism. Farms, homes, jobs, all were given to the state to be doled out like candy to a child. When Novotny took over, it was no different."

He listened to her getting more and more agitated, struck by how different what he was hearing was from the intelligence briefs he'd read. She was wound up now, desperately wanting him to understand.

"It was the artists, Gene. People like you. Why do you think jazz is so popular here and in other countries in Eastern Europe? It is free music from a free country. Willis Conover and his late night Voice of America broadcasts made him a god here. It was the artists who began to change things. They demanded freedom of expression, freedom to write about what they knew to be true and Alexander Dubcek gave it to them. His following quickly developed and, at last, Novotny was gone." She stopped, stared into space, as if remembering something she didn't want to remember.

"But now? What?"

She looked at him again. "For the last eight months, Czechoslovakia has been an exciting place. You must have felt it, even in these few days with the band. There was hope, Gene. Prague was once considered the Paris of Central Europe. Did you know that?"

He remembered something Bartek had said. *Soon our newspapers will be like yours, he'd said. Dubcek has said it will be so.* "Yes I've seen it, Lena," and he had.

"Dubcek has been brave, but he will be broken and we'll return to the old ways, maybe even worse. We cannot fight the Russians." She looked away for a moment then back, managing an embarrassed smile. "I sound like a politician don't I, on a..."

"Soapbox?"

"Yes. I never quite understood that phrase."

"Listen to me, Lena. Maybe there is something, something that can make it possible for Dubcek to continue and maybe your grandfather knew what it was. We have to find out what it was that was so valuable."

She studied him now cautiously. "You're scaring me now, Gene. You don't know what you're up against, what you're saying."

"No, Lena, listen to me. What if the information your grandfather had could change things? We have to find out what it was. You have to tell me everything you know. How he worked? What he did? Anything you can remember."

She pulled back and studied his face, recognized the expression. She'd seen it before, the same intensity, the same determination.

It was the same face she'd seen on her grandfather.

***

"Tell me exactly what your grandfather did." They were sitting up in bed after making love again. It was still warm and there was a slight drizzle outside. Unfortunately, it had not deterred their surveillance. Gene had checked several times and found Arnett taking shelter in the phone booth.

"He didn't want me to know at first, but when he realized there was no hiding it from me, well, it was nothing very glamorous," she said, pronouncing the word carefully. "Just pickups and deliveries. That was how he described it." She grew pensive, her eyes taking on a faraway look as Gene continued to press her.

He reasoned that the only way was by backtracking; learning everything Lena knew if he was to find some clue, some sign that might point them in the right direction. He'd gone over it in his mind a hundred times. There was no way Blaha had given him anything other than the music and he'd checked and rechecked that several times, but there was nothing.

"How did he make these, these pickups and deliveries? Like the one you described in the park?"

Lena seemed uncomfortable with his probing; as if his questions would reveal something about herself she didn't want to give up. Not yet. But with her grandfather gone, there was no one else in her life now. She had to trust.

"My grandfather was what is called a cutout. He would pick up and deliver packages, envelopes, paper—he never knew exactly what—to various hiding places called drops. He would go to a drop, pick up a package, deliver it to another drop to be picked up by someone else and finally, I suppose, it would find its way to Curtis. That's how it works. No one is ever really connected to anyone else, and sometimes he didn't know the package's final destination."

"You mean he never actually saw anyone when he made these deliveries?" He found himself fascinated by the mechanics of the operations.

"Sometimes, like the one in the park I described to you. Sometimes it was what is called a brush drop."

"Brush drop?"

"If the information needed to be passed quickly, a brush drop was used, but they are more dangerous because you must come into personal contact with someone. It's usually at some crowded public place. You bump into the contact, wearing or carrying something to identify him, and in the confusion, the exchange is made."

Gene smiled. "Yeah, just like in the movies. What about the other drops? Where are they?"

Lena shrugged. "They can be anywhere. Under a pew in a church, a seat in a cinema or once..." She paused and started to giggle.

"What's funny?"

"Nothing. I'm sorry, only my grandfather told me once he'd picked up an envelope from behind a mirror in the men's room at the Intercontinental Hotel."

"That's kind of dangerous isn't it?"

"Not really. The package only stays in place for a few minutes, so it's quite safe and the locations change all the time."

Gene lit a cigarette and tried to digest what Lena was telling him. This was a whole new language. He tried to sort it out. It was just like in the movies. But whatever Blaha had hidden, if he'd hidden anything at all, would have to be a secure place, something more long term than a hotel men's room, one that no one knew about. "Any other kind of place?" Nothing Lena had described so far fit the bill.

"For what? What are you saying?"

He took her by the shoulders. "Look, Lena. Whatever it was your grandfather wanted me to have must have been damn important to insist the contact be someone like me. If it was that vital, wouldn't he have written it down, left it somewhere for safe keeping. Somewhere maybe you'd remember so if—"

"The picnic." Lena was suddenly excited now.

"Picnic?"

"Yes. I thought it strange at the time, but now it makes sense. One afternoon, he insisted we go on a picnic. It wasn't far really, just outside Prague. I remember now there was a small inn nearby. We spent the afternoon walking around in the woods. He loved to walk, but I don't think we were ever separated."

Gene got to his feet, excited now. "Think, Lena. That's got to be it. He must have left something there, maybe even that day. The inn, the woods, somewhere. It's worth a try."

She looked up at him for a moment then nestled under his arm, her head on his chest, her breasts pressed against him. "All right," she said. "I'll show you the place in the morning." She slid her hand down his chest slowly, lower and lower until he felt his hardness in her hand. "I think the Gypsy is right," she said. He'd told her about Imre's magic potion.

He felt her stroke him, then her mouth was on him, her tongue, until he moaned then she raised up and straddled him, guiding him into her warm wetness. She leaned forward, her hands on his shoulders as he took her nipples in his mouth. She pushed down on him, moving faster and faster till he exploded inside her, her moans muffled in his neck. "Gene, Gene," she said.

He awoke first, blinking at the gray light streaking in the window. A light rain peppered the glass as Lena began to stir. He kissed her and got up and went to the window. "This rain is a break. It'll give us some cover, but we'll have to split up to get rid of my friend over there." He could still see Arnett, half hidden behind the phone booth, the glow of his cigarette burning.

"Can't we just forget it? I'm afraid of what we might find." She stood in the middle of the room hugging her arms to her chest.

"No, we can't just forget it." He playfully smacked her butt. "Come on. You're going to show me that picnic spot. Whatever we find could clear me with Curtis and tell you why your grandfather died. You want that don't you?" She didn't answer. "Trust me, okay."

***

Across the street, Arnett huddled in the phone booth, his raincoat pulled up around his neck. He was sweating as he fumbled for a coin and dialed the embassy number. Curtis answered on the second ring.

"The girl just came out," he said. His eyes were still on the store. "Probably went to get drummer boy some cigarettes."

"You sure it was her?" Curtis said.

"Oh yeah, I'm sure. She had on a raincoat and a hat pulled over her face, but it was her all right." Arnett was annoyed at Curtis' tone. Williams hadn't come out so what was he worried about.

"How long ago did she go in the store?"

Arnett glanced at his watch quickly. "About fifteen minutes or so. Why?"

Curtis said, "Arnett, listen to me. Is there a back door to that shop?"

Arnett's face contorted in rage. "A back...shit!" He dropped the phone and sprinted across the street to the shop.

***

From the foyer of the apartment building, Gene watched Arnett burst out of the phone booth and race across the street, waiting until he was inside the shop. The rear entrance opened onto an alley way, Lena had told him and, by now, she was already on a tram.

Gene came out of the building and slipped off in the opposite direction. At the corner, he flagged down a taxi and just caught a glimpse of Arnett emerging from the shop and slamming his hat on the ground as the taxi pulled away.

Gene let out a deep breath, leaned back against the seat and thought about how complicated his life had become.

***

"Goddammit, what do you mean they got away?" Curtis was on his feet, shouting and furious at Arnett. "You're supposed to be trained in surveillance."

Arnett had come back to the embassy with the bad news and sat now, head bowed crumpling his hat in his hand. "How did I know he was going to pull that? He's supposed to be a musician isn't he?" He knew his excuse was feeble and waited for the rest of it. Somehow he would make Williams pay.

"So you've been telling me," Curtis said, calmer now, leaning on the desk over Arnett. "Fuck," he said, turning away and lighting a cigarette. He couldn't blame Arnett entirely. He was usually reliable. His nondescript looks, fluency in Czech made him a valuable asset. He'd just underestimated Williams. *We all did*, Curtis thought.

He turned around to face Arnett again. "Look, the man is not stupid. He's cornered and that's my fault, but he's just spent time with the girl, who, do I need to remind you, is Blaha's granddaughter. She knows all about slipping a tail. She learned from an expert."

Curtis began pacing around the office, trying to calm down, wondering what was so important to Williams and the girl that they dodged Arnett. He sat down and briefly glanced at Johnson's portrait glaring at him. The eyes looked almost accusing.

"Williams is a fast learner and probably trying to figure out things for himself, which is exactly what we wanted. But it doesn't do us any good if we don't know where he is or what he's doing. God help us all if he decides to pull off something on his own."

Arnett nodded, sitting up again now. "So what do we do then?"

"What you do is get a team together and cover every place they might show up. The hotel, Lucerna and find out when the band is rehearsing again. Williams has to show up there eventually."

"Right. Where do you want me to go?"

Curtis sighed. "I'm tempted to tell you. All right, you cover the Lucerna. Let me know when Williams gets there and no slip ups this time." *Christ, it would be easier if Williams was working for us. I bet he could tail Arnett anywhere.*

***

"Are you sure this is the place?" Gene looked around, taking in the wooded area. There was a small stream nearby, trickling through the clearing, swollen now by the morning rain. The old inn, a decayed building was all but gone. The jagged pieces of the two remaining walls stood opposite the stream, a relic from another time. A trail, overgrown with high grass, led into the woods. The rain had stopped now, but the ground was damp and muddied their shoes. Strands of wet grass glistening with moisture clung to his trousers.

They had arrived separately. Gene by taxi to a landmark Lena had told him to watch for, then he had walked the last mile or so. His earlier elation had dimmed. There didn't seem to be any place to hide something here. He was grasping at straws and he knew it.

"I'm sure this is it," Lena said. We ate our lunch over there by that building." She stood watching him pace around, huddled in her raincoat, chilled despite the mild temperature.

Gene nodded and went to inspect what was left of the inn. Rotting wood and plaster but no openings or crevices, no hiding places. "What did you do after lunch? Try to remember. It's important." He continued to walk around the building.

Lena shrugged and looked around. "We sat here and talked for a while, then went for a walk in the woods. He was very quiet that day. He talked about my mother a little, but seemed preoccupied, his mind somewhere else entirely."

Gene looked around the clearing once again. "Okay, if you can remember where you walked, let's retrace your steps." He took her by the arm and led her toward the overgrown trail.

"I'll try, but I wasn't paying attention really. I didn't know I'd have to find it again."

"Your grandfather did."

They started up the path. He was convinced it was here. All they had to do was find it.

The morning rain added to the beauty of the area and left the fresh smell of wet grass. In minutes, the trail led them deep into the woods and they soon arrived at another clearing, marred only by a large tree stump.

"There," Lena suddenly said. "We stopped there. He wanted to rest. He sat down on that stump."

"And what did you do?"

"I stood here for a minute, then walked over to where those flowers are." She pointed to some wildflowers about fifty yards away."

"How long were you there?" He was insistent now, like an interrogator.

"I don't know. Five minutes, no more. I told him I wanted to pick some flowers and he said take my time.

Rest or hide something. "Could you see him the whole time?"

"Yes, I guess so. I suppose my back was turned part of the time." She paused now, remembering. "I thought it was strange though. When I came back, he was still sitting on the stump. 'This is how I want you to remember me, Lena. An old man resting in the woods.' He was smoking his pipe. He looked so peaceful. I wish I'd had my camera then. Oh, Gene." She turned away, blinking back tears.

"Okay, go over there and do just what you did that day." Gene sat down on the stump facing the direction Lena was walking. He put his hands behind him, running them over the surface of the tree. The bark was rough, peeling in places, wet from the rain. He got up and examined the back side more closely.

The dirt was packed solidly around the stump. Blaha wouldn't have had time to dig without Lena seeing him. He noticed now some of the bark was loose, but still attached to the stump. One piece could be pulled back, leaving a shallow opening between the bark and the stump. And there, wrapped in cellophane was a single folded sheet of paper. Lena's name was written on the outside.

Gently, he pulled it loose from the stump. The cellophane was stuck to the paper in places from the moisture and flakes of decaying bark. He peeled back the wrapping and called to Lena. "Over here."

She had been watching and ran back quickly. "What is it? Did you find something?"

He stood up and wordlessly handed her the paper, noting her expression as she recognized her grandfather's writing. Gene moved away reluctantly, torn between wanting to know its contents and not intruding on her private moment. He watched her as she began to read. Her face remained expressionless, then a short intake of breath. She glanced up at him, meeting his eyes. "I think this is what you were looking for."

Now, they would know what had killed Josef Blaha.

ELEVEN

Gene stood motionless in the clearing, gazing into the woods, allowing Lena a moment to translate the letter. The sun had burst through the clouds with splinters of light, but the smell of rain hung heavily in the air.

He stole a glance at Lena seated on the tree stump, head bent, coat collar up around her neck. God, she was beautiful. He felt like an intruder, an unwilling witness to some private ritual he had no right to be a part of. Yet, he was as much if not more concerned with the letter than Lena. He paced around the clearing, smoking nervously, trying to contain his impatience.

The legacy of Josef Blaha. Had he died for it or because of it? Gene's thoughts, focused now on his own survival and escape, told him it didn't matter. The secret, whatever it was, would be his deliverance. From Curtis, the CIA, the lies and deceptions, the bizarre nightmare of the past few days that he knew would haunt him forever.

It would all be so easy now. Wrap it up neatly and turn it all over to Curtis. Let him deliver it to his analysts and Gene could go back to being what he was—a musician.

He stamped out his cigarette in the wet ground and turned again toward Lena. It was important to her too. There was something in her eyes. Sadness, but something more. Fear? She looked up at him, caught his eyes on her, letting the letter go limp in her hand, then held it up to him. He took it from her and examined it. Probably done with a music pen, noting the bold script, the heavy black strokes. When had Blaha written it? Late at night in his office? In a park somewhere in Prague?

Gene handed it back to Lena. "What does it say, Lena? I have to know."

She hesitated. Her eyes were still moist, her face a mix of sadness and resignation. She made one futile attempt to dissuade him. "It's too late, Gene. Let it go."

"Let it go?" He kneeled in front of her and gripped her arms. "Your grandfather died because of this, Lena. He wanted someone to know...to do something. This will finish it. This is all Curtis wants." His eyes searched hers for confirmation. "It is something important, isn't it?"

"No, it's...yes, but it won't finish anything." Her voice trembled slightly as she took the letter and began to read.

"Dearest Lena," she began. "You know the work I've been doing is for a good cause. I've hated it, but I hate even more what is being done, what will be done to all of us. Perhaps, in some small way I've helped. Recently, I've discovered something that frightens even me, something too dangerous to keep to myself any longer. It is now impossible for me to continue.

"Dubcek has been betrayed. The meetings with the Russians in Cierna and Bratislava mean nothing. There will be an invasion and Dubcek must be warned about Indra. He is a traitor and behind it all."

She paused and looked up at Gene. He was nodding, the trace of a smile forming. He felt a surge of elation and relief rush through his body. He didn't know what it meant or who Indra was, but he knew this was it. This was what Curtis was so desperate to have. "Go on," he urged. "What else?"

She looked again at the letter and continued. "I have asked for a safe contact to pass on this information because of something else I've discovered. I am sure now one of the Americans is also a traitor and..."

She continued to read, but Gene was hardly listening now. Only vaguely conscious of her voice trailing off, he turned back toward the woods as if he'd been pushed.

One of the Americans is also a traitor.

It was some kind of cruel joke. There was to be no deliverance, no release, no return to sanity. It was like running in a maze. The deeper you got in, the fewer ways there were to get out. And now, as surely as a locked door, the way out was blocked. Escape snatched from his grasp with five words from the past.

Be careful of your own.

"Jesus." He kicked at the ground. Who? How many Americans were attached to the embassy? He knew only Curtis and Warner Roberts. The memory of Roberts at the embassy reception was still vivid. The drunken leer, the fat cigar. The idea of Roberts as a spy was ludicrous. Who then? Someone unknown to Curtis?

Fuck. No wonder Blaha wanted a safe contact. How long had he known? The questions raced through his mind. Slowly, inescapably, he came back to the one question that had to be answered.

Curtis. What if it was Curtis?

The slick recruitment in London, the made up story about Kate, the continued threats to keep him in line. Suppose Curtis was playing both ends and using him as bait to find out if Blaha knew.

One of the Americans is also a traitor.

"Who's Indra," he snapped, turning once again to Lena. She was still far away, her thoughts on another time, another place.

"Alois Indra, a cabinet minister. Very close to Dubcek." Her voice seemed cold, distant.

"And he's selling out Dubcek to the Russians?"

She got up and went to him. "There's nothing you can do, Gene. Stay out of it. Let Curtis deal with it."

"Didn't you hear what you read? It could be Curtis he's talking about."

"You don't know that," she said. "You're only guessing. You can't be sure. It could be anyone."

"Yeah, but what if it is Curtis. He knows everything about me, including the fact that I have a violent reaction to alcohol. That Russian the other night knew it too when he crammed a bottle of Slivovitz down my throat. How did he know? I can't take that chance."

His mind spun out the possibilities. Even if he was wrong, even if Curtis was not the one, handing over this information didn't guarantee a thing. At the very least, he'd be held until Washington decided what to do with him. And who would they believe? A veteran CIA case officer or a jazz musician? He laughed out loud. What would he get? A handshake, a pat on the back. Thanks for all your help. Sure. He would be kept for safekeeping while the information was confirmed, whatever suited their purposes for the moment.

If it was Curtis, well, there was only one answer to that one. There was no way to get out on his own, much less with Lena. Where would he go? Once he surrendered the information he would have no leverage with Curtis.

Until they knew exactly what he'd found, they would have to keep him...alive. It was down to that. He had refused to admit, even to himself the reality of his position. But Josef Blaha's lifeless body was no illusion. There was no escaping it. He'd been set up from the beginning.

He had only one choice.

Gradually now, things came into focus, the one corridor in the labyrinth became clear. One way out of the maze. He knelt beside Lena again. "I know this is going to sound crazy and maybe it is, but I don't see any other way." He took a deep breath. "I've got to see Dubcek, warn him about this, go public, make a scene that will get everybody's attention."

Lena's eyes grew wide. "Dubcek? Do you know what you're saying? You can't be serious. How? He won't believe you even if you could get to him. My God, Gene, please, you're acting crazy."

"Maybe. I haven't worked it all out yet, but I will." He paused and looked away for a moment. "Look, I didn't ask for this. I came to Prague to play at the jazz festival because that's what I do. Now you, Jan, the musicians, everyone in Czechoslovakia is in for some really hard times if there's an invasion. I can't just sit on this and I can't turn it over to Curtis if he's the one your grandfather is talking about."

He was tired of being manipulated, being used, lied to and now he realized he had to do something about it. Unless he could eliminate Curtis as a suspect, he was on his own. Well, he'd been there before.

Lena shook her head and looked away. Gene glanced at his watch. "C'mon," he said. "I've got a rehearsal. I want you to think of everything you can about Alexander Dubcek."

***

Arnett had been waiting for over an hour. He'd watch the saxophones rehearse a difficult part—well, he guessed that's why they played the same passage over and over—while the rest of the band looked on in boredom, talked quietly and continually glanced at the vacant set of drums like a crew without a navigator.

Where the fuck is he? Arnett thought. Then just as suddenly, there was Williams, walking in and things heated up. Pages of music were turned, valves oiled, mouthpieces adjusted, cigarettes ground out. Now, they could all begin.

Arnett felt relief. He was still burned at the thought of how the young musician had humiliated him again. Curtis was right. The prick was getting good. The girl wasn't with him, but Arnett didn't care. His mind was only on Williams. Once the rehearsal was well underway, he went to the pay phone in the lobby.

"Okay, he's here. I don't know about the girl."

"I do," Curtis said. "One of the team called in. She's back at the apartment." Curtis sounded a lot calmer than the last time they'd spoken.

"What now?'

"You stay put. Don't let him out of your sight. If he goes for a leak, you go with him. It doesn't matter now. He's made you. I'm coming over with Roberts. He wants to talk with Pavel so I'll tag along."

"Okay, I'll be here." Arnett couldn't see the stage from where he was, but he could hear the drums.

"You better be and so had Williams or I'll have your ass this time."

Arnett hung up the phone. "Yeah, yeah." He walked back into the hall. "Prick." He took a seat in the back rows. "You too, Williams." He hoped he didn't have to wait long. Christ, how he hated jazz.

***

On stage, Gene stared at the music, trying to recall what his part was at letter C. They'd gone over this before, but his mind was suddenly blank, the concentration gone, diverted to Lena, Curtis, the glassy stare of her grandfather and the letter, always the letter.

The music spread open before him seemed meaningless. He realized suddenly there might not even be a jazz festival. If Blaha's letter was accurate, there might not be a country. He'd thought about destroying it at first, but then, if he did manage to somehow get to Dubcek, talk to him, the letter was his only proof.

He had to go directly to Dubcek somehow, with Lena to corroborate her grandfather's allegations. But until then—he had it now. Letter C. Improvised solo.

He needed some insurance in case—in case what? He was never seen or heard from him again? Dubcek could have him arrested. The CIA could hold him. He could have an "unfortunate" accident. He needed something to keep Curtis backed off at least temporarily. If he failed, it all went wrong, someone would know and hopefully investigate.

He looked up from the music, out over the immense hall. Was Curtis or the man from the phone booth out there somewhere now, watching him, wondering what he'd found? Curtis could bust in on the rehearsal and take him away and nobody could do anything about it.

"Gene, you are ready please?" Jan Pavel's voice jarred him away, sent him back to the music. He glanced at the rest of the band, conscious of their puzzled stares, saw the disappointment in Jan's eyes. Since that first day, his playing had been mediocre at best. He had nearly missed one rehearsal, been late for another, but Jan had been reluctant to probe, allowing him to work out whatever was bothering him on his own. He owed these guys, he owed Jan.

"Yeah, sorry, Jan." Gene grinned at Bartek seated next to him, hugging his baritone saxophone. "Thinking about a girl I just met." He held his hands cupped in front of his chest.

Bartek laughed and punched him on the shoulder. He translated for the other musicians and even Pavel was laughing as they began to play. It was false, a spur of the moment gesture, but it worked. The tension was broken.

Gene willed himself to throw aside everything but the music. The festival was important to Jan, to the band. There would be extensive press coverage and good reviews would mean tours in the west. Western currency that unlocked the doors to the special Tuzex shops he'd been told about, where imported goods could be purchased. The band needed a strong showing and Pavel was counting on him to be the catalyst. This was his thing. This he could do.

"Prague Dance" was a jazz waltz arrangement. *Concentrate, concentrate*, he told himself. With a slashing of cymbals he threw himself into the music in a frenzy of motion, driving, pushing, kicking the band toward the coda.

"Fuck yes," Bartek said and grinned. The rest of the band nodded. This was how it was supposed to be. Pavel broke into a grin as the music began to gel and reach that elusive quality that nobody has ever been able to rotate. Swing! Thirteen musicians playing as one.

They roared through three more charts before Pavel called a break. Beer bottles popped open, cigarettes were lit and a relaxed feeling filled the air. Gene looked at Jan Pavel and got a wink and approving nod. There was no doubt about the band's excellence, with or without Gene, but he was providing the spark.

He stood up, stretched his arms overhead and caught sight of Curtis and Warner Roberts approaching the stage. They had obviously been listening. Roberts waved to him and motioned him down. He jumped off the stage, wiping his face with a towel. The heat in the hall was oppressive and the rain had increased the humidity.

"Williams, how you doin' boy? The band sounds great," Roberts' voice boomed and echoed in the empty hall. Some of the stage hands turned to stare in their direction.

The ever present cigar and the strong scent of expensive cologne loomed around Roberts like a cloud as he hurried over to shake hands with Gene and pound him on the back. Gene was again struck by the image of a campaigning politician. "You're doin' it, boy!"

"Yeah, it's starting to come together." Gene's eyes flicked to Curtis, hanging back, glaring at him over Roberts' shoulder.

"You remember Alan Curtis? I think you two met at our little embassy shindig the other night."

"Sure I remember," Gene said, going through the motions, shaking hands. Curtis' grip was vise-like and his eyes bored into Williams.

Roberts seemed momentarily puzzled by the unspoken exchange. Gene looked more closely at Roberts, taking in the puffy eyes, the flushed face, the too hearty voice. Roberts was a drunk, he realized.

"Well," Roberts said, breaking the silence. "I've got a couple of things to go over with Pavel about the festival and I can see you two have some business so I'll see you in a few minutes. Okay, Alan?"

Curtis nodded sullenly as Roberts went off. He motioned Gene to walk toward the rear of the hall. Once out of earshot, he turned on Gene. "That was real cute this morning. I told you I wanted you in close contact, not ditching my man," Curtis said. "He's for your own protection, I might add. It seems the KGB is interested in your activities."

Gene tensed. "I'm getting tired of being followed, but if your man is so good, how come it was so easy to lose him?" He glanced back toward the stage. He could see Roberts talking to Jan Pavel, waving his cigar, gesturing around the hall. There would be nearly three thousand people here tomorrow night, Gene had been told.

Curtis ignored the remark. "Look, Williams, we're not playing games here. This isn't some training exercise. Now where the hell were you all morning? We know you were with the girl. If you found something I want—"

"Her name is Lena," Gene said. "What if I did find something? Am I supposed to trust you?" They were playing games, a kind of psychological chess. Only Curtis knew all the moves.

Curtis arched his eyebrows. "What's that supposed to mean? Are you saying—"

"I'm not saying anything. Using me was your idea, not mine. Don't forget that. I haven't decided what to do yet. If, and when I do, I'll let you know."

Curtis sighed and shook his head and looked off into space for a moment. "I'm not getting through to you am I. You are not by any stretch of the imagination remotely qualified to make that decision or any decision." He faced Gene and pointed his finger. "I'm warning you. Don't try any grandstand plays on your own. You're out of your league, Williams, way out of your league."

Gene held his gaze. "Maybe, but what guarantee do I have if I cooperate with you?" He'd already said too much. He could sense Curtis felt he was on to something.

Curtis took off his glasses and rubbed his eyes. He put them back on and looked again at Gene, his voice less edgy now. "Look, I made a mistake pulling you in the way I did. But we're talking about information that could be vital to this country, our country. So think about what you're doing, okay? That's all I ask."

Gene felt his fists clench at his sides. "You can save the patriotic speech. I've heard it all before, in London. Remember? We both know where you're coming from. You blew it with Blaha and now you want to save your ass and the CIA embarrassment. I'm betting you have to answer to somebody in Washington." He wheeled away and walked off back toward the stage before Curtis could say another word.

"Not very cooperative is he," Arnett said, coming up alongside Curtis.

Curtis was still staring after Williams. "Deliver me from amateurs," he said.

"You think he found something?"

"I know it, but he's scared. He thinks we tossed his hotel room. That's all I need, a scared amateur."

"KGB?"

"Probably. C'mon, I have to call Langley. They can decide what to do about Williams."

Within the hour, Curtis was back in his office, coding a flash message and waiting for a reply.

```
REDSKIN OUT OF BOUNDS. ADVISE.
```

It took only a few minutes for a reply. Curtis could imagine Walter Mead in a quick conference with the director.

It was out of his hands now. He cleared his desk and winked at President Johnson on the way out.

***

Alexander "Sacha" Dubcek was the youngest party leader in the Communist world. But the strain, the tension of continuing the reform programs he had implemented over the past few months, and the equally tiring task of keeping Moscow at bay, had taken their toll on the forty-six year old leader.

His already slim frame was twenty pounds lighter than it had been in January when he had taken office as Chief of the Czechoslovak Communist Party, and now, as he sat in his office at the Central

Committee building, he felt only exhaustion and weariness. His milky blue eyes reflected the eighteen hour days necessary to stay one step ahead of the Kremlin.

He swiveled in his chair to look out over the Square, taking in the shoppers, students, the workers—his people. *Yes*, he thought, *there had been change.* The people were euphoric over the new freedoms and there was hope in the air for even more.

Great strides toward his goal of "socialism with a human face" had been made. No one could deny them. "The people want a change," he told friends when he took office. "And since you can't change the people, the leader must be changed."

Had he moved too quickly, changed too much? Some of his colleagues said so. "Don't push Moscow," they said. "Slow down, Sacha. You want too much too soon." He brushed their reservations aside. How could he slow down? The people deserved change and he was determined to give it to them.

He had gone to the meetings in Cierna tired and battered. Concessions were made, but he had not been intimidated. He had shown them his resolve even when the talks had started badly. Breshnev had attacked his new policies for almost four hours. He had countered with assurances that he was in accord with the Soviet position, but he was not going to be bullied. This was their country.

Breshnev had retired then, saying he was ill, leaving Shelest, the Ukrainian hard liner to take over. It had gotten ugly then as Shelest had attacked Dubcek's friend and advisor Kreigel. "You just agree," snapped the Ukrainian. "We don't have to explain why."

For Dubcek that had been too much. He broke then, banging his fist on the table. "You're not going to treat us as underlings," he shouted and stalked out of the conference.

It was later that Svoboda told him, "You'll get used to it, Alexander. They do it to me too." Then, just as suddenly the atmosphere changed. Breshnev returned, miraculously recovered, and Dubcek had been overjoyed as the terms were hammered out. Concessions were made on both sides. He knew it had all been a test. He had called their bluff and he had survived.

But now, as he gazed at the photo of his wife Anna and their three sons, he realized the real fact to emerge was the Bratislava meeting earlier this month was no different and some of his cabinet sensed trouble.

"Careful, Sacha. Remember Hungary," they said. But he could not, would not believe Moscow would do the same with Czechoslovakia.

After all, hadn't he himself lived in Russia for many years? Didn't he speak Russian and hadn't he always supported the Soviet line? His optimism would not allow him to even consider such an act as his supporters feared might be a real possibility. Moscow would keep their word, and he had President Svoboda, a favorite of the Kremlin and a military hero as his staunch ally.

He turned back to his desk and sighed wearily, feeling the exhaustion wash over him. He wanted to go home for a while and why not? Maybe even time for a nap before the evening meeting of the Central Committee. Perhaps at the weekend, he would take Anna and the boys to the country. He slapped his palms flat on the desk. "Yes," he said aloud. But first he would stop for some petrol, chat with the people. It always made him feel better and how long had it been since his last walkabout? Two weeks? Then a quiet dinner with Anna.

Suddenly energized now, he pressed the button on the intercom and informed his secretary he would be leaving shortly. He got up and glanced once again over the square, feeling as always the responsibility of office and to the people. *We will win*, he thought. *We must.* And tonight, when they discussed the coming Party Congress, he would also assure the Presidium that he could handle the Soviets. He grabbed some papers and stuffed them in a satchel and walked out to where his car was parked.

Gahdos was waiting for him. "Can I drive you?" he asked.

Dubcek smiled at his long trusted friend and bodyguard. "No thank you, I'm only going home for a while before the session tonight. I think I will drive myself."

Gahdos frowned. "I wish you wouldn't. I don't like it."

Dubcek laughed at his friend's apprehension. He got in his car and started the engine. "I am a popular leader, am I not? What could happen to me in Prague?"

He waved and drove off before Gahdos could think of anything further to say.

TWELVE

The airport shuttle left from the Intercontinental Hotel. Gene crowded aboard the coach with the other travelers leaving Prague, wishing he could join them. He took a seat in the rear and looked around, trying to guess the nationality of the travelers. He thought he recognized snatches of French, German, but no Czech. What he wanted was an American or Englishman. Maybe at the airport. He had to find someone traveling to London for what he had in mind.

After the rehearsal, he'd written a short note to his sister Kate, briefly outlining what had happened. Nothing too detailed, just enough to put his family in the picture with instructions to go to the authorities if they hadn't heard from him by the time they got the letter. He hoped they wouldn't have to open it.

Meager that it was, this was his insurance. It wasn't much, but it would have to do for now. Curtis was sure to be keeping an even closer eye on him now after the scene at the Lucerna. He had no doubts about where he stood with the CIA man. He would just have to keep him guessing a while longer.

His idea was simple and also he realized, maybe naive. Slip the letter in someone's luggage, let them wonder how it got there, but mail it anyway since it was sealed and stamped already. There was no other way to get anything out of Czechoslovakia now. For all he knew, anything going out of the country could be intercepted, confiscated, or end up in Curtis' hands. The telephone was out as overseas calls had to be booked in advance and could easily be monitored. He'd already checked on that.

He turned and looked back out the rear window of the coach. If anyone was tailing him—and he was sure somebody was—they would be in a taxi or car. *They probably think I'm making a run for it*, he thought. Bailing out, forgetting the festival, just taking off. Well, he was going to make it easy. This was one time he wanted to be seen.

At Ruzyne, the coach deposited the passengers and Gene joined the throng of foreign tourists and business types. There were some Czechs as well, enjoying some of their new found freedom. Was it only a few days ago he'd arrived here, meeting Philip Hastings, demonstrating his practice pad to the customs officer? It all seemed like a dream now.

He stood for a minute watching people mill around, gathering up bags for departure and reviewed it again, just as he'd practiced it with Lena. What had she called it, a brush drop?

He checked the departures board and found two flights scheduled for London. One on British Airways; one on the Czech Airline. BEA would be the best bet. There must be some British tourists in Prague.

He glanced around trying to spot Arnett. He was there somewhere, he was sure. Gene walked to the gift shop to browse over cheap trinkets, souvenirs of Prague, newspapers from around Eastern Europe. Nothing that made sense for him to buy except...he suddenly remembered the English language paper. What was it? *The Morning Star.* He fumbled in his pocket for coins and shoved them at a bewildered cashier. Carrying the folded paper, he roamed the terminal again, looking, listening. Then he saw them.

Two men and a woman, obviously traveling together. The woman had a small flight bag with the BEA logo emblazoned on its side. They were talking loudly, almost arguing but good naturedly in German. Gene moved closer. They had boarding passes in their hands, LON in large letters.

He circled to the other side, keeping them in view and making himself as visible as possible, still trying to spot his tail. He had to be seen. There might not be another chance. It would have to be now. Their plane would be called soon.

He took out the letter and slipped it into the folded newspaper in his hand.

The three Germans were still talking and occasionally glancing toward the boarding gate. As Gene came near, he noted the position of the woman's flight bag. Another larger bag next to one of the men would do for his faked clumsiness. He walked toward them quickly.

Suddenly, he was nearly in the arms of the woman as he tripped over the other larger bag. She cried out, startled. Some people nearby turned to look. He got to his feet quickly, careful to pick up the woman's flight bag that she'd dropped in the scuffle and mumbled apologies. With all the confusion, it was easy to slip the letter in the side pocket of her bag.

Gene walked away quickly. With any luck, it would be in Kate's hands in a few days.

***

At the Embassy, Alan Curtis was still at his desk. No reason for him to stay around, but he couldn't pull himself away. The ashtray was overflowing with butts even as he lit another and blew smoke rings at the ceiling. The telex hummed in the corner and was flanked by a coffee pot on a long table, littered with sugar packets and stirring sticks. Curtis got up and rummaged through the debris, finally rescuing his mug and filled it with the hot black liquid and thought once more about Gene Williams.

How could it have gone so wrong? When he'd pitched the idea to Walter Mead in London, he was confident they could pull it off with no hitches. Now, it had deteriorated, fallen apart at the seams into a mess maybe nobody could clean up. Josef Blaha was dead and now a hostile, unpredictable, scared amateur was on the loose in Prague. "Keep him in the dark," Walter Mead had said. "I don't want some Goddamn musician running around Prague thinking he's James Bond." He sighed. That's exactly what he had now. It was no way for a case officer to run an agent.

He'd handled Gene Williams wrong from the outset. He knew that now. He'd made Gene an adversary, not an asset and he had only himself to blame. Brash, impulsive, naive, Christ, Williams might do anything now and Curtis couldn't afford that any more than the Company could.

If Williams were picked up by the Czech Police or somehow stumbled into one of the KGB networks, he'd be too big an embarrassment. They'd be screaming U.S. intervention all the way to Washington. So what had he done? Covered himself, taken the easy way and asked Langley to bail him out even when he knew what the answer would be.

The order had been clear: REMOVE REDSKIN FROM GAME.

He was amused by the football jargon that had crept into the agency directives, but they were right, of course. Cut their losses before it was too late. Still, some gut instinct told him that pulling Williams now would be a mistake. He was close, so close. If only he could have let Williams in on the whole story from the beginning. It was too late for that now.

It was risky, giving Williams his head, but he'd allow it a while longer and justify it to Langley later, keeping Arnett on him, if he could manage it. Williams had learned fast. It was worth a chance. Maybe he could get lucky.

Somebody had said it many times before. You go to all kinds of trouble to obtain vital intelligence and then the real battle begins: trying to get the powers that be to act. There wasn't enough yet, but maybe Williams would turn out to be like the beggar in Cairo, who for days tried to tell embassy officials the Deputy Ambassador was marked for assassination. No one had listened and the ambassador's wife became a widow.

The phone startled him as it rang. It was Arnett reporting in.

"He just left the airport."

"The airport? What's he doing there?"

"Beats me. He took the shuttle bus, wandered around awhile then left. He's back at the girl's place now." Arnett sounded bored with the whole thing.

Curtis considered for a moment. Why would Williams go to the airport? Storage locker? Meet someone? Maybe he got cold feet and decided to bolt then changed his mind again. "Anything out of the ordinary happen? He talk to anyone?"

"No, nobody. Oh, just some German woman. I had him in sight the whole time. He tripped over her bag."

"Goddamn, Arnett. What German woman?" Curtis shouted into the phone. Someday he would kill Arnett.

"Hey, it was nothing. He bumped into some people. Fell over the woman's suitcase."

Curtis let out a long sigh. "All right, all right. Get back over to the apartment and stay with them. Call in anything new."

He decided to give Williams another twenty-four hours. The second call came fifteen minutes later.

"Curtis? Your man checked in yet?"

"Williams? What are you—"

"Save it, Curtis. How did he like my clumsy act with the Germans. That's what it was, an act."

Curtis gripped the phone tighter. "What are you talking about?"

"Those people were going to London. They're carrying a letter to my sister. You remember my sister, the one who was arrested on drug charges in Spain. I told her what's going down here and who to contact if she doesn't hear from me real soon."

"You're bluffing Williams."

"Am I? You'll have to call it then." Williams hung up.

Curtis slammed down the phone.

Now it was a challenge.

***

Arnett sat hunched down in the Fiat across from the cafe, his cap over his eyes, a cigarette jutting from his mouth. Williams and the girl were still there. He could see them through the glass. They'd tried to slip him again, but not this time. He wondered why they'd ever made the effort. It looked like they were just having dinner. How sweet? A romantic dinner in Prague. Why this particular cafe? There was nothing much here. Couple of shops, the gas station across the street.

But after the airport, Arnett was suspicious of anything Williams did now.

He watched the line of cars slowly edging toward the pumps, the drivers with ration coupons in their hands. The early evening traffic was heavy and the sidewalks were crowded. Arnett looked at his watch and contented himself with watching the parade of young Czech women homeward bound in miniskirts. His eyes followed one tall blonde flashing thigh as she ran for a bus.

He looked to his right and noticed a sudden flurry of activity at the gas station. Several people were hovering around one car. The driver was obscured from his view for a moment, but then finally, some of the people moved aside and he could see what all the fuss was about. He sat up straighter and stared. He'd never seen it himself, but he'd heard all the stories, read the articles. It had been well publicized and now, fuck, it was true. Alexander Dubcek, head of the country driving in and buying his own gas.

He watched the scene unfold as Dubcek got out of his car and began talking, shaking hands, smiling at everyone. Arnett glanced back at the cafe. Williams and the girl were on their feet now, Williams paying the check. He continued to look from the scene at the gas station to the cafe. The attendants were busying themselves with Dubcek's car, filling the tank, cleaning the windshield, checking the tires, under the hood. The crowd kept a respectful distance, but were obviously enjoying the close contact with their leader.

He looked back at the cafe, then gripped the wheel. Williams and the girl were coming across the street—straight for Dubcek's car. Arnett watched frozen, trying to decide whether to jump out of the car or stay where he was. What the hell is this crazy bastard up to now?

He watched mesmerized as Williams and the girl approached the curious onlookers and melted in with the crowd. The impulse to move was too great. He swung around in the seat, frantically looking for a phone booth, spotted one and got out of the car, walking quickly. Jesus, he hoped Curtis was near a phone.

"He what?" Curtis was yelling crazily.

"It's the craziest thing I ever saw. Williams and the girl walked right up to Dubcek's car and got in."

"You're positive it's Dubcek?" Arnett was breathing hard and Curtis could hear the panic in his voice.

"C'mon man, it was Dubcek all right. Jesus..."

"You better tell me you can see them right now."

"Oh yeah, I can see them." Arnett wiped sweat off his forehead. The phone box was like a sauna.

"You stay with him like your life depended on it because it does. Wherever they go, you stay with them and..." And what? He didn't want to spook Williams. "Just stay with them. If Williams looks like...never mind. I've got to call Washington. That's the ball game."

***

"The Director will see you now, Sir." Walter Mead followed the secretary into the expansive office at CIA Headquarters in Langley. The Director was seated behind a massive desk. He looked up at Mead only briefly.

"This had better be as important as it sounded, Walter. I've got a briefing with the President in—" he looked at his watch"—twenty minutes."

Mead cleared his throat and stood in front of the Director's desk. "It is. Just came in on the wire from Prague. Our Redskin is with Dubcek."

The Director looked up at Mead. "What do you mean he's with Dubcek?"

"Surveillance says he walked right up to his car at a gas station and got in, both he and the girl."

The Director got to his feet. "Jesus H. Christ. What the fuck do I tell the President? We've got a musician going for a drive with the head of Czechoslovakia? He doesn't even know about this project. What happened to the removal order." The Director was pacing now, chewing on the end of his glasses. He spun around and pointed at Mead, his glasses in his hand.

"Okay. Have Prague maintain the surveillance, as many people as it takes, but don't get close enough to spook him. What's this guy's name?"

"Gene Williams."

The Director nodded. "We don't know if he's got a gun or what the fuck he's doing. The second he's clear, get him. Jesus, can you imagine Johnson driving down to the local Shell station and buying gas?"

Mead didn't know whether to answer or not, but he couldn't imagine anything of the kind. "Sir, what if...what if something happens to Dubcek?" Mead said.

"I don't even want to think about that."

***

"All right, Mr. Dubcek," Gene said nervously, "drive very carefully, just the way you always do." His eyes scanned the crowd of puzzled people staring at them as they pulled out of the gas station onto the main road. Gene sat in front with Dubcek; Lena huddled in the back.

It was getting dark now and a light rain was starting to fall, at least partially obscuring the interior of the car. Gene had been expecting the car to be swarming with police at any moment, but there was no one.

"My son, what about my son? Who are you? What do you want?" Dubcek's eyes flicked from Gene to the road to the rearview mirror and Lena. "She said my son was in danger and you were responsible. Do you know who I am?"

Gene was relieved Dubcek's English was good, just as Lena had said it was. Over dinner she'd filled him in on the Czech leader's personal and professional life from what she knew personally and from the dozens of articles recounting his rise to power. His unheard of eccentricities amazed Gene, such as driving himself much of the time, stopping for his visits with the people, buying his own gas. Gene could hardly believe it, but this was Prague, not Dallas.

"I'm sorry about that. Your son is in no danger. I made her say that. It was the only way I could get to talk to you alone," Gene said.

Dubcek glanced in the mirror again and spoke rapidly to Lena in Czech. She was visibly shaken and avoided his eyes in the mirror. "This is an outrage," Dubcek said, turning his attention once again to Gene. "My security people are not far behind. You will be arrested and—"

"With all due respect, sir, you are traveling alone as you often do in your own car." Dubcek's anger was undiminished, but Gene could see his shoulders relax slightly, his grip on the wheel loosen. "Take the next turn and go up the Lenin Highway." He turned around to look through the rear window, but he could only see the lights of cars in the drizzle.

Dubcek, still unsure, complied. Only the set of his eyes betrayed his anger. "Who are you?" he demanded.

"Who I am is of no importance. I have something very urgent to tell you, about your government. Please, just listen for a few minutes."

"Very well," Dubcek said. "It seems I have no choice. I will listen, but then you will be arrested."

Gene had no doubt about Dubcek's determination or his intentions, but he had come this far. There was no turning back now and maybe Dubcek would listen. "This girl's grandfather worked for American intelligence. He came into some information vital to the safety of your country. Information so vital he was killed for it."

Dubcek glanced sharply at Gene and again at Lena in the mirror, but said nothing as Gene continued. "It's not important how, but we've discovered what that information is." He paused, shifting in the seat and took a deep breath. Everything hinged on Dubcek believing him.

"The Soviet Union is preparing to invade Czechoslovakia, maybe in the next day or so, I don't know exactly when." He paused and took a deep breath. "One of your Cabinet Ministers, Alois Indra, is betraying you, giving the Russians advance information." There, it was out. Even as he said them, the words seemed implausible.

Dubcek began with Lena, again speaking rapidly Czech. She leaned forward, obviously pleading with him to believe that what Gene said was true, but he could see the leader wasn't buying it. Well, why should he? A maniac jumps in his car, says his son is in danger and then babbles about invasions and traitors.

"This is absurd," Dubcek said, as if echoing Gene's thoughts. "Indra is a trusted member of the Presidium. He opposes me on some issues, but he is not a traitor. As for an invasion, it is out of the question. If you are with American intelligence, as I assume you must be, you know about the talks in Cierna and Bratislava. I have assurances from Moscow. No, you are mistaken." His voice was firm and Gene knew there was nothing more he could say.

"I don't know about any talks, but I don't think a man who was about to die would leave such information. There must be some way you could verify it. Confront Indra. I'm only trying to warn you in time."

Dubcek was incredulous. "Confront Indra? On the word of a...a kidnapper! How do I know this isn't some plot to weaken my government?"

"Sir, how do you know it is? Why would I go to the trouble and risk of seeing you like this if I didn't believe it myself? Her grandfather was a loyal Czech."

"Loyal Czechs do not spy for American intelligence," Dubcek snapped. Gene looked back at Lena. His words stung her like a slap in the face and deflated Gene's hopes in the same breath.

He slumped against the seat. It was no good. Dubcek wasn't going to buy it and why should he? "Turn here," he said. They were in a residential section now, blocks of flats bordered by a small park. The rain continued in a monotonous drizzle.

"Stop here by the park," Gene said. He waited until the car halted then handed Dubcek Josef Blaha's letter. "At least read this, Sir."

Dubcek took the letter and read it quickly and tossed it back to Gene. "Anybody could have written this," he said. "It proves nothing."

"Suppose I could show you proof," Gene said, trying one last ditch effort as he remembered the invasion plans Curtis talked about. He shot a warning glance back at Lena. Dubcek's face remained impassive, but Gene knew he'd struck a nerve. He could feel it. He doesn't want to believe me even if it is true. And he knew why. Alexander Dubcek had worked too hard and too long to see it all go down the drain.

"What proof? You have such proof?" A slight faltering, a tiny speck of doubt had crept in his voice.

"I can get it." Gene heard a sharp intake of breath from Lena in the back.

Dubcek gripped the wheel tighter. There was no sound for several moments other than the hypnotic whir of the windshield wipers.

Then like a man who has just been told he has cancer, Dubcek said, "I'm not saying I believe you. Not for a moment, but..." He turned off the engine and faced Gene. "I must see this proof. You must bring it to me. Then I will consider things."

"Fine," Gene said. "You just tell me where and when." They were still alive, but he had no idea how to get those papers from Curtis. He watched Dubcek stare out the window, deep in thought. Gene twisted in his seat. The longer they spent in a parked car, the more chance they had of being spotted.

At last Dubcek broke the silence. "At Party Headquarters." He turned to Lena again, speaking to her in Czech. She nodded. Then again to Gene he said, "She knows where it is. My car will be outside. My driver will be waiting at midnight." He nodded toward Lena again. "She will bring it and give it to him. If it is as you say, then we will talk further."

Gene nodded his understanding, not trusting his voice to betray the relief he felt. He started to open the door, but Dubcek put a hand on his arm.

"If she does not appear, I will personally have you both found and arrested and charged with espionage. Is that clear?" Dubcek's eyes had turned a steely blue and bored into Gene with intensity.

As they got out of the car, Dubcek leaned over and said something to Lena in a quieter, softer voice. Then he started the car and drove away. Gene watched as the taillights disappeared.

"What did he say to you?"

"He said he was sorry about my grandfather and..."

The car rushed toward them, tires screeching, engine whining and bright flashes from a window. Shots, chipping at the wooden bench near them.

Gene threw Lena to the ground and more shots were fired as the car roared by, the bullets chewing up grass only inches from their faces. Then just as suddenly, it was gone.

Gene gathered up Lena and they ran blindly behind a block of flats, down an alleyway and finally to a street that ran parallel to the Lenin Highway. They stopped out of breath and leaned against a wall.

Dubcek was going to have him arrested and now somebody was shooting at him. Curtis? KGB? Take your pick. Lena was trembling as he held her. He felt the panic in his gut again. What had Curtis said?

"You're out of your league."

***

"I don't know who it was." Arnett was breathing hard from running. "I was right behind them all the way when they got out of the car. Then this other car, behind me I guess pulled around and passed me. It was too dark to get a look, going too fast."

"Well, that ties it," Curtis said. "At least nothing happened to Dubcek. Let's hope he doesn't make an official complaint to the Ambassador. Pavel's band is on tonight. We'll pick Williams up there and get him out immediately. They're having heart attacks in Washington."

Curtis hung up, relieved, but there were sure to be repercussions and he could only imagine where his next assignment would be, if there was one at all. What the hell did Williams think he was doing? He was baffled by the shooting. He hadn't ordered it so that left only the KGB. Someone was on to Williams, but how could they know unless he was...Maybe this was some outside action. Whatever the case, Williams was in a heap of trouble. What could he have gone to Dubcek for? It was time to reel him in, way past time. Right after the concert. Williams wasn't going to miss that and to do it before would mean too much explaining unless he wanted to bring Jan Pavel and Warner

Roberts into it. No, that would just be more complications. Williams had to go and as quickly as possible.

Before somebody kills him.

THIRTEEN

The Lucerna Hall was filled to capacity.

An enormous banner was strung from the ceiling that proclaimed: JAZZ PRAHA—1968. On stage, a quartet from Bulgaria, the opening group, huddled together at center stage in tuxedos and did an impressive imitation of the Modern Jazz Quartet.

In an enclosure directly in front of the stage, scores of photographers and reporters, cameras whirring, pens scribbling on pads, clustered together to record the night's events for newspapers and music magazines around Europe.

As Gene and Lena arrived and pushed through the crowd, the charged atmosphere churned up memories of a rainy night at Carnegie Hall, years past, when Gene had witnessed his first major jazz concert. He'd tried to imagine then what it must be like for the musicians. Now, seeing his name again on one of the many posters, he realized he was going to find out.

There was no way for Alexander Dubcek to connect him with the jazz festival and after the shooting incident, a concert hall crammed with three thousand noisy jazz fans seemed the safest place in Prague for both he and Lena. Jostled by late comers still finding their seats, Gene and Lena kept pushing toward the stage area. He spotted Alan Curtis and Warner Roberts seated with the other embassy staff in a special reserved section a few rows from the stage. Roberts was chomping on his inevitable cigar, listening intently to a woman next to him. Curtis' attention was riveted on the Bulgarian quartet. Then he looked up, caught sight of Gene and their eyes locked briefly. Curtis gave a brief nod and turned back to the stage. Gene would be allowed to play.

At the passage way leading to the back stage area, a festival official stopped them, then just as quickly ushered them inside as he recognized Gene. They ran up the steps and Gene's first sight of Jan Pavel was of the leader pacing, looking at his watch and smoking nervously. It was close. They were on in thirty minutes.

Pavel's face flooded with relief as he saw Gene and ran over. "Hurry please, Gene," he said rushing toward them. "I checked your room at the hotel. No one had seen you, but they gave me this." He reached for a plastic bag with Gene's suit. He'd left it for a quick cleaning after his night in the gutter. Jan looked at Lena for a moment, then embraced her, said something in Czech, about her grandfather Gene supposed.

Gene read the disappointment and concern in Pavel's face. *He thinks I don't care. They all do*, he realized, looking past Jan at the other musicians gathered together, instruments in hand, ready to play. Most of them nodded in desultory greetings. Only Bartek came forward and put his hand on Gene's shoulder.

"You are okay, Gene?" The saxophonist studied him for a moment.

"I'm sorry," Gene said. "I'm okay. Let's play some music, man."

Bartek broke into a grin and turned to the band, speaking rapidly to everyone, pumping his fist in the air.

Lena stayed with Jan while Gene was herded off to the makeshift dressing room by the band boy Milan. Gene thanked him and shut the door behind him.

A single light bulb hung from the ceiling. The room was littered with clothes, instrument cases, empty beer bottles and smelled of sweat and stale tobacco smoke. *Band rooms are the same the world over*, Gene thought, as he doused his face with cold water and examined himself in the cracked mirror over the stained sink. His face was drawn, pale, his eyes like marble. The sleepless nights and strain of the past few days had taken their toll.

He shuddered now, remembering the speeding car, the grass flicking up in their faces as he and Lena lay sprawled on the ground in the rain. The image of Josef Blaha's face still haunted him and brought a fresh wave of revulsion and fear. He leaned on the sink and thought how easy it was to die.

He began to change into the dark suit, still seeing Dubcek's piercing blue eyes. Proof, he had promised. From where? The plans he had tempted the Czech leader with were safely locked in those innocuous file cabinets in Alan Curtis' office at the embassy. Who was he kidding? He had nothing to show Dubcek. It had been an idle desperate gesture, an impulse. Playing for time and how much was there now?

And who had shot at them? Curtis' interests could only be served by keeping him alive and in the picture. But suppose Curtis had been overruled? He was sure his latest escapade was already in the books in Washington. Kidnapping Dubcek—there was no other description for it—was only further proof of his liability to the CIA. What had Curtis said at the embassy reception about Blaha's death? "We cut our losses and go on. That's how the game is played." Maybe it was already too late to go to Curtis even if he could. If there was just some way to eliminate Curtis as a suspect.

The alternative was just as chilling. From what Lena had told him, what he'd seen done to her grandfather, what he'd experienced himself at the hands of the Russian in that cabin, he needed no convincing to believe the KGB would do anything if he got in their way. If the attack tonight was simply another warning, it was not meant to be ignored.

He finished dressing and looked in the mirror again. Suppose though, he could link Indra with the American informant, whoever that might be. If Indra was collaborating with Moscow, he must also be connected with the American mentioned in Blaha's letter. If he could make that connection, expose them both—but how would he get to Indra? It wouldn't be like with Dubcek. There would be security, a wall he'd never get past.

Lena knew a girl who actually worked in Indra's office, but that had been a dead end. She was off somewhere in the country and not expected back for several days. They might not have several hours and Dubcek's words still echoed in his mind. "If she does not appear, I will have you both arrested and charged with spying."

He looked up as he heard muffled applause fill the hall and then there was a knock on the door. Gene opened it and found Milan, the band boy. "Gene," he said. "Now."

Gene nodded. It was almost time. He couldn't remember when he felt less like playing. Then the door was kicked open. Gene spun around half expecting to see Curtis, but instead it was Bartek, a mug of beer in either hand.

"Hey, Gene, we drink one toast yeah?" He handed one of the beers to Gene who smiled. Jan was not only worried, he'd sent Bartek to check on him.

Bartek watched him closely as they stood facing each other and clinked the glasses together. Gene closed his eyes and took a deep gulp of the cold beer.

"Gene, you okay? You have some troubles yes. You tell Bartek. I fix it." His expression was so open, so vulnerable Gene had to look away.

"No, I'm fine," he said nodding, wishing it were that easy. He put a hand on Bartek's shoulder, moved by the saxophonist's touching attempt to help. It reminded him once again of his obligation to Jan, to the band. At least this was something he had control of, something he could salvage.

"We're going out there and play the best fucking jazz they've ever heard in Prague." He spoke quietly in mock seriousness.

Bartek was quiet for a moment, looking in his eyes then he slapped his leg and his body shook with laughter. "Okay! We drink one more toast." He looked at Gene carefully to see if he'd remembered. They'd taught it to him early, an old joke to signify everything was okay. Bartek told him it had started when the Czechoslovak hockey team had defeated the Soviets four zero. Gene hoped the toast was prophetic, as they raised their glasses high.

"Fuck Russia!" they shouted.

They went back out to join the other musicians to pass the final few minutes. The Bulgarians had left the stage and a crew was setting up music stands for the band while the festival director made some announcements to the crowd.

Bartek grabbed his baritone sax and blew phrases against the wall. Imre, the Gypsy, stood in a corner staring at his bass as if it were a stranger, idly plucking at the strings. The brass players silently blew into the horns, clearing the spit valves, loosening their lips, checking mouth pieces. Like runners waiting for the starter's gun before a race, the butterflies are always there until the first note is played.

Gene found Lena at an improvised bar, talking with Jan, smiling nervously at him, sipping a glass of wine. Jan turned toward him, his eyes searching Gene's face. He seemed satisfied with what he saw now.

"So, Gene, you are ready now, yes?" Jan was as keyed up as any of them although they'd all played this festival many times before. "It will be good, yes?"

For an instant, Gene considered telling Jan everything. But there was too much explaining to do and not enough time. After the concert perhaps. He owed Jan that much, but now said only, "Yes, Jan. It's going to be very good."

Suddenly, an image flashed through his mind of Soviet soldiers storming Prague, rushing into the Lucerna Hall. Here, backstage before a performance of a jazz festival, the idea seemed sheer fantasy. But Josef Blaha's letter was real. He had held it in his hands.

Another wave of applause swept over the hall as the quartet took their bows in the isolated glare of the spotlight and quickly went off past a maze of cables, curtain lines and stage lights. To the left, Gene could see the drums and piano flanked by neatly arranged music stands.

Dr. Jaromeir Melenik appeared at Jan's side. He carried a clipboard with the festival schedule. Melenik was the festival director and coordinated all the logistics involved in hosting an international jazz festival.

"So Jan, we go, yes?" he said in English for Gene's benefit. He winked and gave the thumbs up sign, then walked back on stage to introduce the Prague Jazz Ensemble.

"Panove, ye dem. Let's go, gentlemen." Jan clapped his hands for the band to assemble. Gene smiled at Lena, gave her a quick kiss as they lined up to file onstage.

It was time.

***

It was time in Moscow as well.

The last of the Zil limousines sped through Borvitsky Gate and into the Kremlin for an emergency meeting of the Soviet Politburo. It was just after ten o'clock.

Party Chief Lenoid Breshnev joined Premier Alexi Kosygin, President Nicolai Padgorny and the other members of the politburo in a large conference room adjacent to Lenin's former office. Also in attendance were Pyotr Shelest, the Ukrainian Party Chief and a junta of military generals and marshals who had recalled the Soviet leaders from their holiday on the Black Sea.

As they took their seats around the massive green felt-covered table, the portraits of Lenin and Marx looked on like silent observers. It was immediately evident an impasse had been reached on Czechoslovakia.

Shelest, one of the most militant, wasted no time in stating his case for decisive action. "Comrades, it is clear that despite the meetings in Cierna and Bratislava, Dubcek is not containing the reforms as he promised. The situation is deteriorating daily. We must act now," he roared and pounded his fist on the table.

Breshnev flicked a glance around the table. He took in the impassively cool Kosygin, chain smoking as always, and the sharp frowns of the military strategists. There would be a vote and soon.

Mikail Suslov rose. "Comrades," he began. "We must keep in mind that the World Communist Party Conference is near at hand. Intervention at this time could pose serious problems with other world members," he said in opposition to Shelest's hard line tactics. He paused, looking around the table, but was greeted only with silence. "There is also the Western press reaction to such an act as Comrade Shelest so passionately argues for. It could damage our position worldwide." He looked around again, but there was only an embarrassed silence and eyes avoiding his own.

"Nonsense," Breshnev snapped. "The West will do nothing. A formal protest will be issued. Nothing more. Johnson is too busy with Vietnam." The others nodded their silent agreement.

"Comrade Breshnev is correct," said one of the most militant generals. "It is Dubcek and his policies that pose a threat to us all. The very workings of the Communist Party are at stake. Dubcek cannot be allowed to continue. Besides, this is an internal problem. It is not the business of the West."

The argument raged on for nearly an hour, but the end result was never really in question. Finally, Breshnev threw up his hands. "Enough, Comrades. It is time for a vote."

The ballot was quickly tabulated and Breshnev read the results. "Very well, Comrades. We are in agreement."

There was a murmur of approval around the table. Orders were issued to General Pavlovsky, the Commander of Soviet Forces on alert in Czechoslovakia. A statement was hastily drafted to be relayed to the Soviet Ambassador in Washington D.C. and to be personally delivered to President Johnson.

Finally, Breshnev stood and addressed the meeting solemnly. "Czechoslovakia will be an example to our other little brothers. The unity of the Communist Party must not be jeopardized."

Mikhail Suslov sighed wearily and leaned toward his seat mate, his voice barely audible over the din of approval for Breshnev's announcement.

"He seems to have completely forgotten about Hungary."

***

The audience jamming the Lucerna Hall in Prague had given Jan Pavel's jazz ensemble a tremendous reception. The applause and cheers swept through the great hall in waves and now the band was at the end of their performance. Pavel was a favorite and had been for years, but when he introduced Gene as "our distinguished American guest," the crowd was completely won over. Jan walked over to Gene and embraced him as the crowd yelled for more.

The press enclosure, crammed with photographers exploded with a blinding barrage of flash between each number, hoping to record a uniquely candid moment during the band's performance. The soloists came in for even more close range attacks when they ventured to the microphone at center stage.

Now, with one number to go, Jan flashed a grin at Gene. He had saved the best for last, the arrangement Gene had brought from New York. Pavel surprised them all when he dedicated "Message To A Friend" to the memory of Josef Blaha. Pavel turned toward Gene and smiled almost sadly. *Maybe I won't have to tell Jan anything*, Gene thought.

Gene made a slight adjustment to his cymbals and glanced toward the wings. Lena stood watching, her hand over her mouth. He waved and she smiled back. He looked toward the rows closest to the stage and could just make out Warner Roberts, leaning forward intently, Curtis still there staring impassively, but now they didn't matter. He shut them all out of his mind, blocking everything, but the music, the pageantry of the festival. The band was never more sharp, honed to a fine edge by the days of rehearsals and spurred on by the enthusiastic crowd and inspired by Gene's playing.

The audience hushed as Jan counted them in. Imre's bass boomed in Gene's ear as they roared through the intro like a runaway freight train. The tempo was up, a shade faster than they'd rehearsed, but it felt perfect. Gene's hand flashed on the cymbal as the brass screamed their entrance at letter A and was punctuated by his short, sharp accents on the snare. Gene felt it, knew he was in the zone.

The saxophones waited patiently, then five sets of fingers flew over the keys of the horns in a flurry, driven on by the relentless cymbal beat, then reined in like a team of horses. Then, a sharp break, tension suspended for four agonizing measures of silence, then a crash and wave of sound as Bartek stood and made his way to the microphone for his solo and brought the house down with four scorching choruses.

The applause and shouts still lingered as he returned to his seat. He shouted something to Gene, but it was lost in the crowd and whirring cameras. Now, it was his turn.

He began with a hypnotic patter between the tom-toms. The cylinders of wood and metal, stretched taut with skin, took on a life of their own, as he stirred the drums, his hands blurring, pushing up toward the crest, then teasingly dropping back to a whisper soft roll on the snare drum that said, not yet.

The audience, silenced now strained to hear as he climbed yet another summit, another crescendo, slashing at the cymbals, his hands like the wings of a hummingbird. Somewhere in the distance he heard the band calling his name. Then mercifully, with a final crash of cymbals, the band joined him for the final chord. Jan, his hands overhead, held them on the chord, then dropped his hands toward the floor to end it all.

Gene slumped back, his jacket soaked through with sweat. Jan pointed to Gene as the ovation rose and intensified and three thousand voices washed over him. The band stood, horns aside, clapping to add their approval. Gene stood and bowed and grinned at the band, then Jan took him to center stage for a final bow before they filed off, the crowd still applauding.

Backstage, he gratefully took a cigarette from someone and slumped in a chair. The band filed by, shouting, clapping him on the back. A hand appeared from somewhere with a beer. He drank thirstily, savoring the moment, knowing he would be able to recall every detail of this night forever. The crowd backstage had swollen with friends and family as they pushed their way in to congratulate the band. He saw Lena embrace Jan, blinking back tears, then she found her way to him and clasped him to her.

But it was all over too quickly. Over her shoulder, he caught a glimpse of Warner Roberts and Alan Curtis, trying to fight their way through. "Meet me outside," he whispered to Lena. "I'm going to change."

On the way to the band room, he grabbed Bartek and quickly explained what he wanted. The saxophonist was puzzled, but readily agreed and left Gene to round up the band.

Minutes later when he left the dressing room, he could see the entire band crowded around Curtis and Roberts. He would have at least a few minutes jump on them. No one noticed as he slipped out the side door.

Lena was waiting for him, talking with another girl. Gene barely glanced at her. "Let's go," he said to Lena. "We've got to get out of here."

"Gene, wait. This is my friend Eva."

Gene stared blankly for a moment then suddenly realized this was Eva who had been in the country. Eva who worked in Indra's office. Maybe there was a chance.

"C'mon," he said, pushing both girls ahead of him. "I want to talk to her."

FOURTEEN

The Soviet Army was on the move. Near Bratislava, Colonel Alexis Savin's tank battalion was already underway, rumbling toward the Slovak capital. Engines whining, the T-54 tanks roaring through villages at nearly thirty miles per hour, waking residents and triggering a flurry of telephone calls to Prague two hundred miles away. The smoking treads of the tanks churned up asphalt and knocked down anything in their path—lamp posts, street signs, even some automobiles.

For Savin, it was like another journey twelve years earlier on the road to Budapest. Tonight, he rode in the lead car as commander, surprised at how swiftly the order to strike had come down the chain of command. By morning, they would be in position and the citizens of Czechoslovakia would awaken to find their country occupied with thousands of Soviet and Warsaw Pact forces.

Yes, Savin thought, *it was just like Hungary all over again. Even the results would be the same.* Savin was sure of that.

* * *

"Ask her if there is any way she can get into Indra's office," Gene said, impatiently pacing around, looking at his watch. Midnight was fast approaching and Dubcek was waiting.

He watched Eva's face turn white as Lena translated Gene's request. She looked at Gene wide eyed and backed away as if she'd been slapped. Lena tried to calm her down, but she continued to stare at Gene with frightened eyes. She kept repeating the same phrase over and over.

"What's she saying?" Gene asked.

"Who is he, who is he?" Lena said. Eva had already confirmed to Lena that while working one Saturday, she'd forgotten something, went back to the office and discovered Indra receiving coded telex messages from Moscow, the Soviet Ambassador. Indra had been furious that she'd seen the message and she had been too afraid to tell anyone.

Gene paced again, glancing up now and then to make sure no one was around. They were in a small park just off Wenceslas Square. Eva's news was all Gene needed to confirm Blaha's allegations as being correct. Indra was probably in daily contact with Moscow, detailing Dubcek's every move, every idea. Indra, Gene guessed, would also want to keep Moscow appraised of U.S. intentions. What better way than to have an informant in the American Embassy? But who?

If he could connect Indra with the American informant, he could blow the whole thing open. At the very least, delay the invasion plans. Once the informant was exposed—assuming it wasn't Curtis—then he could go to someone for help and turn it all over to...He was so close. He could feel it.

He turned back to Eva and Lena, both talking rapidly. "So what does she say?" he asked impatiently.

Lena took Eva by the shoulders and shook her, telling her to be quiet and calm down. "She says the Central Committee is meeting tonight. They'll be there late, but Indra won't be in his office." She looked at Gene. They both knew about that meeting already. She looked back at Eva. "She's afraid, Gene. She wants to go."

"Okay, I can see that." The midnight meeting with Dubcek was sneaking up on them and Curtis no doubt had everybody out looking for him. The band couldn't have held them up that long. But he had nothing to show Dubcek. There was however, one thing that might get Indra back to his office. He sighed. It was another long shot and just as crazy as kidnapping Dubcek, but he'd have to try.

"You'll have to do some convincing, but this is exactly what I want Eva to do. I need a pen and some paper." He watched Eva's face fall as Lena translated his instructions. She shook her head, refusing at first. Lena grabbed her and shook her and snapped at her harshly until she reluctantly agreed.

"I need the key to Indra's office," Gene said, holding out his hand. Eva handed it over then turned and ran off down the street.

Gene closed his hand over the key. "What did you say to her?"

"I told her if she didn't do what I said, I'd make sure Indra knew she'd been talking to an American spy."

***

At the Bryanston Court Hotel in London, Peter and Marie Hoffer were about to join Peter's brother Hans for a drink at the bar. Peter waited in silent irritation, while Marie searched her flight bag for the mate to the pearl earring she held in her hand.

"Peter, what's this?" She held up a blue airmail envelope.

"It looks like a letter," Peter said dryly.

Marie sighed. "I know it's a letter, but how did it get into my bag." She looked at the address. "I don't know anybody in California named Kate Williams. I don't know anyone in California."

"Darling, how does anything get into your bag? Maybe somebody left it here by mistake, maybe the maid thought it was yours and put it in your bag." He took the letter from her. "It has stamps. You probably picked it up somewhere. I don't know. Now come on. Hans is waiting."

"Well, should we mail it?" Marie asked, still not convinced.

"Yes, we'll mail it. First thing in the morning. Leave it here on the table by the door." He set the letter down and took Marie by the elbow and guided her out the door and slammed it behind him.

The force of air from the closing door picked up the flimsy letter perched on the edge of the table. It hung suspended for a second, then took a downward course to the floor and sailed under the bed.

When the Hoffers checked out five days later, they had completely forgotten about Gene Williams' letter to his sister Kate.

***

In the yellow stucco building of the Communist Party Central Committee, the Presidium of Alexander Dubcek was two hours into its regular Tuesday night session. The agenda included, among other things, plans for the party congress due to be held in September. But there was other pressing business as well that had, thus far, taken up most of the time, causing Alexander Dubcek to look more closely at his colleagues and especially fellow member Alois Indra.

Indra's insistence that a new memorandum he had brought to the meeting must be acknowledged had dominated the proceedings. The party was losing control, Indra argued. A quick vote was taken, but Dubcek's majority overruled this proposal and reaffirmed the earlier position of continued liberalization programs.

Still, Dubcek thought, there was the letter he'd received from Breshnev three days earlier, accusing him of not living up to the Cierna agreements. He hadn't told anybody about the letter. An idle threat, he'd decided. One of many and typical of Breshnev's bullying. The Kremlin leader always had to talk tough. But they had gone too far to be stopped by threats and so far, the rest of the committee was with him. There were only three holdouts: two who feared the Soviets. The third was Alois Indra.

It was not fear that drove Indra, Dubcek was sure of that. He eyed his minister closely, thinking back to his earlier encounter with the Czech girl and the young American. He had told no one about that either, not even his wife Anna. She had been puzzled by his insistence on knowing the boy's whereabouts when he'd arrived home.

He wondered how the other members of the Presidium would take the news that he had been abducted, told of an impending invasion and that comrade Indra was a traitor. No, that information was better kept to himself. There was enough apprehension as it was. He had no doubt that he would never see either the girl or the American again. Yet, what motive could he...Dubcek looked up, the knock on the door interrupted his thoughts and the session. A messenger came in, handed Indra a folded slip of paper. While the other members around the table stood and stretched, grateful for the break, Dubcek watched Indra read from the paper. He saw nothing in his face to betray anything significant.

Indra rose. "Please excuse me, Comrades. It seems there is a small matter I must attend to immediately. I shall return shortly." He nodded at Dubcek and left the room.

Everyone was tired and welcomed the break. Coffee was served, cigarettes were lit. "Comrade Indra seems rather busy this evening," remarked Dr. Sik, one of Dubcek's chief supporters.

The others nodded and laughed nervously. Indeed Indra had left the meeting several times already for phone calls and messages. Brief absences that caused the other members to speculate on his activities.

"Maybe he's got a mistress," one of them quipped. Others got up to stretch and walk around, talk in small groups. Several lifted their eyes to the ceiling as the sound of aircraft over head filled the room.

"Sounds busy at Ruzyne tonight," Cernik said. He was trying to remember if he'd heard planes earlier. He was sure he had. Dubcek was about to answer when the messenger came in again, this time summoning him to his office adjacent to the conference room. Something about a telegram from the ambassador in Budapest.

What's this now, he thought, ripping open the envelope.

REPORTER AT PRESS AGENCY HERE RECEIVED ANONYMOUS

CALL THAT INVASION BY SOVIET FORCES TO BEGIN TODAY. NO

CONFIRMATION. THOUGHT I SHOULD ADVISE.

REGARDS, STEPHAN.

Dubcek angrily crumpled the telegram in his fist and flung it into the wastebasket near his desk. Is there no end? First I'm kidnapped by a deranged foreigner and now this stupid telegram. He got up and walked back into the meeting. Indra had not yet returned, but they would have to start without him. There was still so much work to do.

* * *

In the darkened office, Gene and Lena waited for Alois Indra.

It had taken all of Lena's persuasive powers, but Eva had finally agreed to help them. All Gene wanted was for her to leave a note with the Duty Officer at the Central Committee building. He would never remember her.

Eva had also confirmed that many of the Presidium members were routinely called out during sessions for messages or phone calls, so such a request would arouse no suspicion. If Indra was as busy as Gene suspected, his message would be nothing out of the ordinary. He could only guess at Indra's reaction to the note.

"Call me immediately from your office. Urgent," he'd written. He hadn't signed it, but written in English, Indra would know it was from one person only.

But now huddled in the darkened office, jammed in their hiding place behind some filing cabinets, he was having second thoughts. They'd made a hurried search of the office, but Gene didn't know what he was looking for and Lena said of what she'd seen, there was nothing unusual. Of course, Indra wouldn't leave anything incriminating and if they were discovered here, well, he didn't want to think about that.

They both tensed at the sound of hurried footsteps coming near the office. A key hastily inserted in the lock, the door thrown open, the light snapped on, flooding the room with a fluorescent glare. Indra slammed the door behind him and strode to the telephone.

Gene could just make out the angry set of Indra's face as he dialed, hear the nervous fingers drumming on the desk while he waited for an answer. Finally, the words spilled out in a torrent. Gene knew only a few words of Czech, but he didn't need Lena to translate Indra's anger and the first word told the whole story.

The name. Now he knew the informant's name.

It remained only to unravel the last bits, put all the pieces of the puzzle in their proper place. But someone else could do that. He was finished. He had all he needed. He felt the same elation as when Lena had first read her grandfather's letter, only this time it was different. The way out of the maze was suddenly clear.

He watched Indra slam down the phone and sit for a moment, puzzled, unsure. He got up and walked around the office, staring blankly. He stood in the center of the room for a minute then wheeled away, flicked out the light and left, locking the door behind him.

Gene and Lena let out a collective sigh of relief, but stayed in position in the cramped space a few minutes longer until they were sure Indra was gone and not coming back. They stood up and Gene went to the phone. He had a call of his own to make.

He dialed then waited an agonizingly long time as it rang and rang. "C'mon, c'mon," he said out loud. Finally, someone answered. He left a curt message without even waiting for a response and hung up the phone. There was no time to argue or explain.

"You go back to the apartment and wait for me," he said to Lena as they ran down the stairs to the street. He waved down a taxi and pushed her inside.

"But, Gene—"

He cut her off. "Don't worry, I'll be okay. Everything is going to be fine."

He watched the taxi pull away and set off across the Vltava River Bridge. He hardly noticed a formation of Russian MIGS overhead, streaking over the spires of Prague.

***

The night duty officer on the embassy switchboard didn't know what to make of the call. The party had hung up so quickly he wasn't even sure he had the message right as he'd hastily scribbled down the name on a pad.

The board was already swamped with incoming calls from all over Czechoslovakia. The winking lights flashed at him accusingly, demanding his attention. He ripped the message from the pad and handed it to the first embassy officer he saw passing by the switchboard. There was so much confusion with everybody suddenly arriving. He didn't have time to worry about it now.

***

It was seven-fifteen in the evening in Washington, DC and Walt Rostow was still in his office. As President Lyndon Johnson's special assistant for national security, it was not unusual for him to be working late. With Vietnam escalating daily, the recent assassination of Robert Kennedy and the growing student unrest over the war, Rostow was used to sixteen hour days.

But tonight, he was caught up. He remained in his office for one reason only: a telephone call that would confirm what he already knew. The information from the twice daily intelligence briefings was not surprising. It only remained to receive official word through the proper channels. The call would change nothing, but it was required.

It came moments later from Mr. Dobryin, the Soviet Ambassador. "Good evening, Mr. Rostow. Working late as usual?"

"Yes, aren't' we all, Mr. Dobryin? What can I do for you?" Rostow asked, although he knew exactly what Dobryin wanted, he had to go through the formalities.

"I would like to speak to the President as soon as possible. It's very urgent."

"I'm sure it is," Rostow said. He'd already alerted Johnson and he too was waiting for a call. "I'll call the President. Can we expect you within the hour?"

"Yes, excellent," Dobryin said.

Rostow hung up the phone and once again went over in his mind the information the CIA report had earlier revealed, and more importantly, the report's implications.

There had been photographs of large-scale refueling of Soviet military aircraft in the Ukraine and NATO Headquarters in Brussels had confirmed previous reports the Warsaw Pact maneuvers were only a front for a possible invasion of Czechoslovakia. In addition, the West German electronic surveillance devices along the Czechoslovak border had been humming with unusual activity.

Wearily, Rostow locked his desk, alerted the President of the Soviet Ambassador's imminent arrival and headed for the cabinet room. At eight o'clock precisely, Dobryin was ushered into the anteroom and seated opposite Rostow and President Lyndon Johnson.

The Ambassador accepted a drink, small talk was exchanged between the three men and then, the usual courtesies aside, Dobryin produced a prepared statement from a black attaché case and began to read.

"Troops of the Soviet Union and four of the Warsaw Pact allies have entered Czechoslovakia in fraternal response to an appeal by the Czechoslovak Communist Party and other government leaders. They have done so," he continued in a monotone voice, "to defend the country from counter revolutionary forces hostile to socialism."

Rostow and Johnson exchanged glances, but their expressions registered no response.

Dobryin concluded the statement, emphasizing the final words. "This action was, and is, an internal affair and concerns only the Soviet Union." He stood, thanked both men for their time and the three shook hands.

Minutes after Dobryin's departure, the President called a special meeting of the National Security Council for ten o'clock. He also sent an urgent message to Secretary of State Dean Rusk, who was at the time preparing to speak on Vietnam at the Statler Hilton. Rusk canceled his appearance and rushed back to the White House.

The final call of the evening was made to the U.S. Embassy in Prague. Alan Curtis took the call and relayed the message to the Ambassador. As discussed in an earlier dispatch, all embassy staff were put on alert and standing by to evacuate any U.S. citizens in the area.

Classified material was to be readied for possible destruction in the event of an attack on embassy premises.

***

The Lucerna Hall was strangely quiet as Gene Williams slipped in through a side door. On the dimly lit stage, two phantom-like figures swept and stacked chairs and music stands until only the drums and piano were left. The hall was deserted, lit only in shadows that plunged into almost total darkness in the rear.

He shut the door behind him and leaned against the wall. Why the Lucerna? The choice had been an unconscious one. Or had it? It had simply flashed in his mind when he'd called the embassy. A return to the scene of his only triumph in Prague? The symbol of his official legitimate reason for being here? Familiar ground? He couldn't explain it, but returning to the place where only hours before he'd been cheered and applauded for one moment of greatness seemed somehow appropriate.

He looked around the great hall, now in silence. The music still echoed in his mind as he took in the empty seats, the lingering smell of smoke and beer, the residue of debris left by three thousand jazz fans.

Accustomed now to the light, he glanced at his watch and began to walk up the aisle. Come on, where are you? He was impatient to be done with this last bit of business. He climbed up on stage and walked over to the drums. He picked up one of the sticks and struck the cymbal, listening to it echo about the empty hall. He sat down and began to play, moving around the drum set, remembering the night's music.

"Getting in some extra practice?" The voice came out of the darkness. At the embassy reception, here in this hall two days earlier and again now, it was the same. He couldn't see the smoke, but the orange glow was visible, the aroma of cologne and the whiskey unmistakable.

"How you doin', boy?" Warner Roberts said.

FIFTEEN

"Lucky for me you called," Roberts said. "I guess that was you got Indra to telephone me, eh? You're a smart boy, Williams. Pretty smart." Roberts' laugh was grim, without humor.

As Roberts came closer, Gene saw him also looking back over the empty hall. He was obviously drunk, his clothes disheveled, his voice slurred and even now, he took a long pull on the bottle of whiskey he held in one hand. In his other hand was a gun he carelessly waved in the air.

"Goddammit, Williams, why couldn't you stick to playing your drums?" He stopped and turned toward Gene, gazing at him. "God, you were good tonight. Do you know how good you were? " He turned back toward the seating area of the hall. "All those people cheering and applauding for you. What does it feel like to do something really well?" Roberts sighed and shook his head.

Gene looked around. The cleaners were gone. There was nobody but he and Roberts. "Where's—"

"Curtis?" Roberts smiled and sat down on the piano bench. "He's pretty busy right now. All hell is breaking loose. We were all called back. Lucky for me you phoned. The duty operator gave me the message, just like I expected." He looked at Gene. "You're too late, boy, not that you could have done anything anyway."

Gene sat at the drums, the sticks still in his hands as he watched Roberts, looking for an opening, gauging the man's reflexes. "What do you mean, too late?"

Roberts looked over at him with heavy lidded eyes. "I mean it's already started. Embassy's on full alert. Nobody's gonna care what you have to say now. Czechs will be running for cover."

Gene let out a sigh. It had all been for nothing. He felt himself slump down, leaning one hand on the snare drum. Then he looked up at Roberts again. "Why? Why did you help them?"

"This is why," Roberts said, holding up the bottle. "I can't handle it." He sighed and shook his head. "It's such an old story and I'm not the first. I got drunk one night at a party at the Soviet Embassy. Nothing unusual in that, but this was a beauty. Ended up with a young girl, set up really, only I didn't know it at the time. I hardly remember it at all." He stood up and walked around the stage, looking out over the hall again. "At first, I thought I was going to be okay. Didn't hear anything for a while. That was the hell, the waiting."

Gene's eyes never left the gun in Robert's hand. It was now pointing toward the floor.

"I was almost relieved when they came," Roberts continued. "I guess I always knew they would. They had everything. Photos, tapes and either I would cooperate or they would see the Ambassador and my wife got copies. The KGB loves blackmail."

"But why didn't you go to the Ambassador yourself? Tell them you'd been set up, drugged, whatever. You could have explained. "

Roberts shook his head. "Yeah, I could have explained it and they would have accepted my explanation right along with my resignation. Early retirement without the pension, the privileges...the honor." Roberts shook his head and stared at the floor.

"Honor? How can you talk about honor? You killed Josef Blaha."

Roberts wheeled around. "Not me, no sir. I didn't kill anybody. I'm not like you, Williams. I don't have any talent. I've been hanging on by my fingernails for years. This would have finished me. Twenty-seven years down the drain. I've got a daughter in college. I could never face her again."

"You think you can now?"

Roberts finally steadied the gun. "She isn't going to find out. Nobody is. That's why I have no choice with you." He started to walk closer, the gun wavering in his hand.

Gene threw the drumstick. It caught Roberts high in the cheek. He lunged toward Gene. Dodging to the side, Gene pushed one of the cymbals toward Roberts. It crashed to the floor, echoing throughout the empty hall. Roberts, trying to scramble to his feet, dropped the gun. Gene leaped off the stage and vaulted over the first two rows of seats.

Roberts got to his feet, staggered and fell into the drums, blood dripping down his face. He crawled toward the gun, got it and stood up, walking to center stage. "You won't make it out of here, Williams. You'll just be another casualty of the invasion. They're coming, Williams, they're coming." He fired twice, blindly into the seats.

Gene kept low, moving behind the row of seats toward the aisle, watching Roberts nearer the edge of the stage. Suddenly, the spotlights flashed on, piercing the darkness. Roberts wheeled around, putting his hand up to his eyes in the blinding glare.

"Drop the gun, Warner." Curtis' voice came from the left side of the stage.

Panicked, Roberts fired blindly again, the shots ringing out through the hall. Gene caught sight of Arnett, on the stage, coming toward Roberts from behind, grabbing his arm, twisting it behind his back, the gun dropping to the floor. Roberts twisted and kicked and struggled in Arnett's arms, pushing back, his foot on the edge of the stage. Then he was falling back into the press enclosure ten feet below, hitting the floor with a sickening thud.

Gene ran up as Arnett jumped off the stage and joined Curtis.

Roberts was still conscious, but his arm and leg were twisted under him. His eyes were wide with fear. "I had no choice. What else could I do?" His eyes searched out Gene and Curtis. "You can see that, can't you?"

"Hang on, Warner, we'll get you to the hospital," Curtis said. He turned to Arnett. "You have to make a couple of calls." Arnett nodded and took off.

Curtis looked at Gene. "Now you know everything."

* * *

Later, Gene sat with Curtis in the front row of seats as Roberts was taken away. "What happens to him now?" Curtis ignored the question.

"You hit him with a drumstick?"

Gene shrugged. "That's all I had."

Curtis looked around the hall. "You know your girlfriend has more sense than you. She called again to make sure I actually got your message." He paused, gazed at Gene. "Why here?"

"I don't know," Gene said. "I guess I'm getting used to secret meetings. Hey, Roberts said—"

Curtis nodded. "It's on. Johnson's already had official word in Washington. We'll be evacuating people tomorrow, you included. The Czechs are not going to stand for this and it's not our fight." He stood up. "C'mon, I'll have somebody take you to the apartment. Lena's waiting for you. And one more thing." Curtis looked hard at Gene. "Stay off the streets until you hear from me, understand?"

"Sure," Gene said. There was nothing left for him to do anyway.

* * *

The citizens of Czechoslovakia slept unsuspectingly, the majority of them unaware of the Soviet onslaught that was already in motion.

Sweeping through key points around the country, Soviet and Warsaw Pact forces broke into Czechoslovakia like burglars in the night.

While some two hundred fifty tanks raced across the border from Hungary to the Slovak capital of Bratislava, the industrial city of Ostrava was seized quickly by Polish and Soviet troops. The East German units smashed to the south.

Bratislava was taken only an hour or so after the invasion order was issued. The hospital was secured immediately, mute testimony that resistance was taken for granted. Casualties were expected.

A hostile crowd gathered in the main streets, some even sat down in an attempt to form a human barricade against the tanks. They quickly dispersed, however, when it was apparent that a few crushed bodies were not going to stop the tanks. Similar scenes were repeated all over the country.

At Ruzyne airport in Prague, seven miles from the capital, the control tower was quiet. The last flight, an Illusion from Polish Airlines, had disappeared into the night sky. The controllers relaxed, drank coffee and smoked, waiting for the next scheduled flight that was not due in for nearly three hours. There was a Russian Antonon civil aircraft expected earlier, but that posed no problem for the airport staff as the same plane had landed in Prague the previous day on a similar arrangement with Aeroflot.

At approximately ten thirty, the AN24 touched down and rolled to a stop near the terminal building. The passengers, some in Soviet uniforms, climbed down and strode to the waiting cars and drove off.

Inside the lounge, a group of men in holiday dress, ostensibly waiting for the Ankara flight, stood in unison. On a prearranged signal, they drew guns and took control of the lounge. A second group broke into the control tower and the surprised controllers found themselves at gun point.

“No talking,” the Soviet officer said. “Shut down the equipment.” He pointed to the radar scopes and talk down facilities.

While the frightened controllers looked on, a constant stream of aircraft descended over the skies of Prague. They were directed by controls on the AN24 that had landed earlier. The Russian MIGS streaked overhead and were followed by heavy transport planes emptying men and equipment—tanks, armored cars and various other heavy vehicles.

In twelve minutes, Prague airport was under complete control of Soviet forces.

General Pavlovsky set up command headquarters while the infantry, armed with machine guns and flashlights, assembled for the march into Prague. A battalion of marine paratroopers dropped into the suburb of Sporilov along a new section of the motor way.

Columns of tanks rumbled down the four lane Lenin Highway and joined the rest of the forces, then split into three groups on the outskirts of Prague in Deyvice. One group turned south toward Hradcany Castle. The largest force was directed to Wenceslas Square, ignoring the construction site of a pedestrian subway, and crashed through the wooden barriers. The infantry took up key positions at main roads, bridges and the central train station.

Prague was occupied.

* * *

At Central Committee Headquarters, the Presidium session was interrupted by a phone call informing Alexander Dubcek of the invasion. "This is not possible," cried Cernik, who took the call. But a second call minutes later confirmed the worst.

Ashen faced, Dubcek threw up his hands. "How could they do this? I have served the cause of the Soviet Union all my life."

The other cabinet members rushed to the windows to view the spectacle of tanks and soldiers surrounding the building. They watched in horror as one man, shouting insults at the soldiers, was quickly cut down by a burst of gunfire.

Cernik turned from the window to his friend Dubcek, who sat slumped in his chair. "Sascha, it's over," he said.

Moments later, soldiers broke into the conference room to announce that the entire Presidium was under arrest. Several began to protest. "What is the meaning of this?" they demanded.

"Quiet, all of you. No talking," the officer shouted. "Stand up against the wall." They were all searched at gun point then told to sit down again at the conference table. Only Dubcek was missing.

After the first call, he had slipped out of the room to call the Soviet Ambassador. He never completed the call. Four soldiers crashed through his office door and ripped the phone out of the wall.

A startled Gahdos, Dubcek's driver and bodyguard, rushed the soldiers and threw himself at the officer in charge. The officer pushed him aside, calmly drew his pistol and shot him. He then turned to Dubcek, held by two of his men and put away his gun.

"Inside with the others," he snapped to Dubcek. The Czech leader was shoved into the conference room and held under guard with the others, all awaiting their fate at the hands of their Soviet captors.

Stunned, having just seen his friend Gahdos shot in front of his eyes, Dubcek nodded his head slowly, remembering now Alois Indra had been curiously missing when the soldiers arrived.

While news of the invasion poured into the world's capitals, early risers in Prague found instead of their morning coffee, convoys of tanks and their city occupied. Telephone calls from friends and relatives in other parts of the country had brought everybody to the streets to see for themselves. They watched in disbelief and searched for reasons as they watched the clock being turned back once again.

At Prague radio, broadcasts continued warning the people while staff members barricaded themselves inside the station. Three city bus drivers placed their vehicles in the street to block the Russian tanks. A large crowd gathered as snipers fired at the radio station building. Their efforts were hampered by groups of youths, incensed at the Soviet presence, who threw hastily prepared Molotov cocktails at the tanks stalled on the street. Finally, the tanks broke through, soldiers rushed the building and the radio station was taken over by the Soviets.

By mid-morning, Prague was a battlefield. As the tanks moved about Wenceslas Square, groups of students chanted, "Long live Dubcek!" They surged around the tanks, taunting drivers and crews with fist shaking insults and several students climbed atop the statue of St. Wenceslas and defiantly waved the Czechoslovak flag.

Under questioning by more passive onlookers, the tank crews told the people of Prague they were there to protect them from the counter revolution, but some of them, as young as the students protesting against them, had little understanding of their mission. They were clearly confused and bewildered by the hostile reaction of the Czech citizenry.

"We're only following orders," they said.

The people of Czechoslovakia had heard it all before.

***

The white-haired president of Czechoslovakia, Ludvik Svoboda, seventy-two years old and Hero of the Soviet Union, also saw and heard the tanks and soldiers. He was awakened in his bedroom by an aide at Hradcany Castle as telephone calls and radio reports about the invasion poured in.

In his pajamas, Svoboda rushed to the window to see below Russian soldiers disarming the palace guards. A ring of armored vehicles had been set up around the castle. Svoboda swore as there was a knock at his door.

"Yes, what is it?" he said, his anger growing by the minute.

"Comrades Lenart and Indra are here, Sir," the aide said.

"Are they indeed. Show them to my office," Svoboda said, reaching for his robe. He sat on the bed for a few moments longer, listening to the radio reports. Lenart and Indra could bloody well wait.

Ten minutes later, still in pajamas and robe, Svoboda went to his office to find the two men impatiently waiting by his desk. He did not offer either a seat.

Indra, a satisfied smile on his face, stood next to Lenart, who had been Prime Minister during the Novotny regime. He placed a sheaf of papers on Svoboda's desk. Svoboda sat down and did nothing to hide his contempt for the two men as he eyed the documents.

"As you see, Mr. President," Indra began, "that is a list of members for the provisional government of workers and peasants."

His rage building, Svoboda scanned the list. Indra was to be Prime Minister, Lenart his assistant. The others were leftovers from the Novotny era and all opponents of Dubcek's reform programs.

Svoboda scowled at both men. "And which are you, Comrade Indra? Worker or peasant?" He rose from his chair and threw the papers in Indra's face. "Get out, both of you!"

"You are making a mistake," countered Indra. "The change is inevitable." His words reflected the promises he had already secured from the Soviets.

"No, Comrade," Svoboda shouted. "It is you who have made the mistake. Now get out!"

Indra shrugged and exchanged glances with Lenart. The two men left without another word.

Svoboda slumped back in his chair and covered his face with his hands.

"Sascha, my friend. What have they done to you?" he said aloud.

SIXTEEN

Gene heard them first. Engines. Straining, whining, steel treads crunching on asphalt. Voices shouting orders. Boots trampling the cobblestones. The sounds were getting louder now. How far away? One, two streets over. It didn't matter. It was all a reminder of his feeling of failure, his blind stupidity in thinking he, one person, could have done anything to stop one country invading another.

He lay on the bed, blinking at the morning light filtering in through the flimsy curtains, not moving until the most recent convoy had passed. Lena, still asleep next to him, curled on her side, one arm flung out, draping over his body.

After Arnett had taken him back, he had wearily climbed the stairs, not knowing what to say to Lena. But in the end, he didn't need to say anything and he didn't try. She knew. She had simply fallen into his arms. They'd tried to forget everything, find comfort in each other, this unlikely couple. An American jazz musician from New York, the granddaughter of a Czech spy for U.S. intelligence. But nothing else mattered. They were at last free of the bonds that had bound them, constricted their feelings, numbed all thoughts of the future while they had lived in the moment of the past few days. Then they had collapsed together, exhausted and drained.

Now, with morning, the future they couldn't think about was upon them, rolling by outside their window. Not bright, not hopeful, but depressingly dark and violent. Gene had decided whatever happened, whatever argument was offered, he would take Lena with him if she'd have him.

Gently, he eased his body from under her arm and slipped out of bed. He went to the window and looked out, staring fixedly at the tail end of the departing convoy. Lena was right. Nothing in his experience could have prepared him for this, the sight of soldiers and tanks and heavy armored vehicles rolling through the streets of Prague.

He tried to imagine a similar scene in Los Angeles or New York. To Americans, invasion was an abstract word, undefined, locked away in history books or flickering on television screens in warm, safe American living rooms. But there, with his own eyes, he could see the grim reality that to the people of Czechoslovakia was nothing more than a rerun, a bad episode repeated once again.

He stood for several minutes peering through the glass, long after the last columns had passed. There were plumes of smoke in the sky in the direction of what he guessed was Wenceslas Square and his hotel. As he finally turned away from the window, he saw Lena watching him, sitting up in bed, her arms clasped around her legs. He didn't know how long she'd been like that.

"I'm glad my grandfather is dead," she said. Silent tears streamed down her face. "I'm glad he doesn't have to see this again. It's not a pretty sight, is it?"

He went to her, held her, tried to console her, feeling helpless as he did so, but not fully understanding. He was a mere observer. His role had been a minor one, a walk-on part and not even done very well. Lena, her grandfather, all the people of Czechoslovakia were the real players and now they were all victims.

"Lena, what can I do?"

"You're already doing it," she said. "Just stay with me." He felt her heart beating against him, the rise and fall of her breathing.

"What will happen now?" She hardly stirred in his arms.

"Now? Every good thing that has been accomplished will be wiped out. Our time is over, Gene. There will be no more conferences, no concessions, but the result will be the same." She lay back down and stared at the ceiling.

Gene got up, dressed and went to the kitchen to make coffee. He turned on the radio. There was a crackling of static, then an announcer's voice, hurried, agitated, as if he expected to be cut off at any minute. Gene stood motionless, listening then turned to Lena.

"What's he saying?"

She turned her head. "What we already know. News of the invasion. Prague is occupied. Remain calm." She laughed. "Listen to him. Does he sound calm?" She laughed again. The sound was hollow, chilling. "What else could we do?"

Gene nodded. There was nothing for him to say.

***

Two hours later, they had still heard nothing from Alan Curtis or anyone at the embassy. He paced back and forth like a prisoner in a cell, waiting for release, stopping every few minutes to make Lena translate the radio reports, but it was always the same. Scattered bits of news with the same reminders over and over: Remain calm. Do not resist.

He went to the window and looked out. The streets were strangely quiet, but they could hear sporadic gunfire in the distance and over the city center, billowing clouds of black smoke.

"I don't understand it," he said. "We should have heard something by now."

"Maybe there's trouble at the embassy," Lena said. "The phone lines could be out of order."

"I've got to find out what's happening. I want to get us out of here, Lena."

"Where, Gene? Where am I to go?" She was numbed by the invasion he realized. Her strength had faded with the sure knowledge that he could go, she could not. "This is not your problem, Gene, not your life."

He sat down facing her. "Look, Lena. I want you to go with me. A lot of people will be leaving now. Everything is in confusion. There are probably hundreds, maybe thousands who have left already."

"I don't know. I have to think," she said. "I've never lived anywhere else. I don't know if I could."

"Even if you got to your relatives in Plzen, it won't be living. A lot of Czechs will go now if they can. There will be a lot of sympathy in the west for what's happening here."

"Yes, sympathy," she said coldly. "But nothing more."

He nodded, knowing she was probably right. "Look, I can't help that. That's the way it is, but I can help you if you want, if you trust me."

She looked in his eyes in a way he knew she wanted to. "Look, pack some things and I'll be back as soon as I can. I want to see what's happening at the embassy. Curtis said they would be getting people out of here today." He looked at her. She was drained of all hope. In the course of a few days she'd lost her grandfather and her country was now occupied. Too numbed to resist, she listened, but he didn't know if he was getting through to her.

"Lena, I know it's happened so fast, but you know how I feel about you, how much I want you with me. It can be arranged, I'm sure. Curtis owes me. He owes us both. He can get us out of here then you can decide what's best, what you want to do. Just trust me, okay?"

She stared back at him blankly, wanting to believe. Her voice was almost a whisper. "All right, but be careful. They don't care who they shoot."

"Hey," he said, pulling on his shirt and shoes. "I'm not about to argue with a tank, and anyway with all the confusion out there, nobody will take notice of me."

He leaned over her for a moment, holding her face in his hands. When he kissed her, her lips were cold. She smiled faintly at him, touched his face and then he left her.

She stood at the window for several minutes, watching him walk up the street. He turned once and waved, then he was gone. She turned back into the room, struck suddenly with a sense of forbidding, a premonition that she would never see him again.

***

It took Gene nearly forty minutes to make his way to Wenceslas Square. The August sun beat down on him with intensity, as if to make up for the previous days of humid drizzle. He walked along, alert, listening, looking for signs of what he'd been hearing, mopping his brow with his shirt sleeve.

Stay off the streets, Curtis had said. But they seemed deserted. All the shops were closed. No trams or buses were running, although he'd seen several abandoned where they stood, like relics from another era. The occasional taxis he saw sped by as if they were on some emergency mission. There was little other traffic and seemingly, no people. The once bustling streets of Prague were like a ghost town.

He could feel the eyes though, from behind half drawn curtains and cracked doorways, eyes that flicked over empty streets, searching, questioning, making him feel exposed, vulnerable in the glaring sunlight. But he was alone, accompanied by only his own shadow and an increasing sense of urgency.

He'd heard no other gunfire since the earlier sporadic bursts, but as he drew near the square, he could see smoke again and people now, crowding in doorways and alleyways that spilled off the square. The sound increased, as if he were approaching a football stadium. Now he could hear shouting. Then someone near him yelled, "Dubcek!"

He turned to look and saw a motorcade—three cars led by a policeman on a motorcycle. He shielded his eyes and there, in the back seat of the second car was Alexander Dubcek. Gene stepped back on the curb as the cars passed. Dubcek was staring blankly out the window, but as the car passed, there was a spark of recognition. For a moment the fallen leader's eyes locked with Gene, then just as swiftly turned away.

I tried, Gene mouthed silently. *I tried.*

When the motorcade disappeared, he continued on into the square itself. Huge tanks with open hatches ringed the square. He caught sight of some of the crews, warily peeking out, or sitting on top of the tanks, nervously eyeing the increasing crowd of angry Czechs, looking as surprised by their presence as they were.

Several burned out vehicles, some still smoldering, lay over turned in the street. The once beautiful National Museum was riddled with the evidence of the earlier battles. Its facade was chipped and many windows were broken and shattered.

Further up the incline, a group of teenage boys had mounted the statue of St. Wenceslas. They waved a Czech flag and chanted, "Dubcek! Dubcek!" Their cry rang out over the square. More people joined and marched behind a tank as it rumbled around the square.

Gene could only watch, transfixed, feeling as if he'd stumbled onto a movie set, his mind unable to comprehend the scene of destruction. He was about to move on when shots rang out from above. A tank crewman clutched his chest and rolled off the tank he'd been riding on. The crowd scattered in a hail of shouting and screaming, scrambling for cover. Gene was shoved backward and nearly trampled by the panicked crowd. He kept his balance and dived behind a parked car and rolled under it.

More shots. Another crewman fell from a tank. The other crews dived for safety inside their tanks. Hatches slammed shut and from under the car, Gene watched one of the soldiers look wildly about the square then point to a window across the street. A sniper was picking off the surprised Russians from the third floor of an office building. The lone gunman continued firing. Bullets pinged off the tanks even after crewmen were safely inside.

The tank guns began to swing in a wide arc, sweeping the area with random fire. Two women carrying straw baskets and an old man went down in a hail of bullets. Fragments of glass rained down on the square as more windows were shattered.

From behind the cars and tanks, the Soviet paratroopers tried to pinpoint the sniper's position, blindly firing a barrage at the office windows. As one soldier took more careful aim, a middle-aged couple charged him from behind, carrying a bloodstained Czech flag tied to a broomstick.

The startled trooper warded off the man, then butted the woman in the face with his rifle. She staggered back and fell near the car Gene was under. The trooper then turned on the woman's enraged husband and shot him down before returning his attention to the sniper.

Gene crawled from beneath the car to reach the unconscious woman. She lay bleeding a few feet away. He managed to drag her limp body back behind the car where several other people began to attend to her wounds.

The tanks now turned their attention to the chanting youths atop the statue, chasing them into alleyways off the square with a volley of gunfire. The sniper's shots halted momentarily. Seizing the opportunity, several troopers stormed the office building, but returned minutes later empty handed.

Still another tank was attacked by a different group of young men. Flying bricks ricocheted off the tank while they jumped on. They crawled under the gun turrets, smashed bottles of gasoline on the hatch covers and lit soaking rags. In seconds, the tank was a blazing inferno.

The hatch cover flew open and the crew scrambled out, coughing, choking on the black smoke. Completely out of control and still running, the tank crashed into a parked car, shattered the car's gas tank and exploded into flames. Black smoke and flames shot into the air while the youthful fire bombers escaped down an alleyway. Just as suddenly as it had begun, it was over.

An eerie silence descended over the square, broken only by the sobs and moans of the still conscious wounded. The troopers regrouped and pushed the crowd back, vying for control, but they all looked scared, Gene thought.

He stood up shaken and dazed, but unhurt. His eyes burned from the smoke. Several bodies littered the square, perhaps fifteen or twenty. He couldn't tell for sure. Fear, anger, nausea and bitterness welled up inside him and fought for dominance as he surveyed the carnage of the brief battle, sure to be repeated over and over as the day wore on. He stared, senses dulled as angry orders were barked, bodies dragged away and weeping women huddled over victims, saying, "Why? Why?" over and over.

He turned away from the square toward the Zlata Husa Hotel. He must find Jan, but turning the corner he almost collided with the band leader. "Jan," he said taking Pavel's arm. His face was creased in a grim frown that told Gene he too had witnessed the brief battle.

"Gene," Pavel said, relief spreading over his face. "We were worried. We looked in your room when we heard the news." He spoke softly, his voice dull with resignation.

"What about the band? Is everyone okay?"

Pavel nodded. “Yes, most have gone to their families. Some are going to Austria today until...” He merely shrugged and pointed toward the square. The troopers had restored order now and had the crowd under control. “It is terrible, yes?” Pavel shook his head.

They walked the short distance to the hotel together. Gene picked up his passport at the front desk. “You must go to your embassy, Mr. Williams,” the shaken clerk advised.

He stood with Jan in the lobby, now crammed with people and luggage. Everybody was getting out. He could only guess when he’d ever see Pavel again.

They shook hands solemnly, then Pavel pulled him close. “The music, it was good, yes?” Gene looked in his eyes; saw some of the old twinkle still there.

“Yeah, Jan, it was good, very good. I’m...glad to have known you, to have played with your band.” He couldn’t think of anything more to say. “Will you be okay?”

Jan sighed. “Yes, we will make it. Someday, it will all be different. Then, maybe you will come back.” He turned and started for the door. “Ahoy, Gene.”

Gene watched him go, pushing through the crowd. He didn’t doubt for a moment that it would be.

***

The U.S. Embassy was in chaos. The outer courtyard was jammed with people, some tourists, some business types from in and around Prague. Somehow they had managed to find their way to what they hoped was the relative safety of the embassy compound.

They stood in groups, waving passports, demanding assistance from the small contingent of embassy personnel who were doing their best to calm the worried travelers.

“Please, if everyone will just stay calm. There will be buses here soon to take you all to Vienna,” announced one official.

“How are you going to get buses through here with all the goddamn commies shooting up the place?” demanded a red faced man in a plaid jacket.

“Sir, I assure you the buses will be here shortly if you’ll just be patient,” the official countered. The anxiety of the crowd was contagious, rising steadily, but there was little the official could do.

“Patient? We might be attacked any minute,” the man shouted. He turned away in disgust as his wife tried to placate him

"Attacked? Did you hear that?" a stout woman in a print dress said. "The embassy might be attacked."

"Please, please," the aide shouted, glaring at the red faced man. "There is no reason to believe the embassy is going to be attacked. This...this is between the Soviet Union and the Czechs," he said, repeating a directive that had obviously been prepared for this situation.

The rest of the crowd milled about the courtyard, nervous, frightened. Others were clearly excited by the sudden turn of events that had turned a somewhat exotic holiday into a full scale adventure.

"Wait till my sister hears about this," one woman gushed, clutching her handbag to her. She's always bragging about how wonderful and exciting her vacations are. Why I remember..."

Gene watched it all in disgust. They had no idea what was unfolding or what it all meant. You want some excitement lady? Go back out on the square. He wanted to grab them, shake them, tell them people were bleeding, being shot on the streets of Prague. But what was the use? They had no idea what was going on.

He climbed the stairs to the reception area and found it worse inside. A harried young Czech girl, fighting back tears was trying to explain to yet another irate tourist why the excursions he held vouchers for had been canceled.

"Sir, I'm sorry," she said tearfully. "Our country had been invaded."

"I don't care about that. That's your problem," he said. "All I know is I paid for this tour and I better damn well get my money's worth." He pounded on the desk, further frightening the young girl.

Gene and another man reached him at the same instant. They spun the man around and shoved him toward the stairs.

"Hey, take your hands off me," the man said. "Who do you think you are?"

Gene and his newly found ally continued to escort the man farther and sent him tripping down the stairs. Outraged, the man turned to them for a moment, glaring, starting to say something, thought better of it, then finally retreated down the stairs.

Gene and his compatriot looked at each other for a moment and both smiled. They shook hands acknowledging the unspoken thread of understanding that had passed between them. The rest of the group waiting their turn who had witnessed the brief scene were quiet now and listened respectfully to the young Czech embassy employee as she explained what was being done about travel arrangements. Gene caught her eye as he passed. She smiled in gratitude as he went off in search of Alan Curtis.

Inside, telephones were ringing continuously. Typewriters clattered and the embassy staff rushed about in all directions, answering questions, filling requests, reassuring the worried.

Walking toward Curtis' office, Gene glanced in the open door of another office and recognized a famous actor. He did a double take and the actor looked at Gene and smiled and shrugged, realizing Gene had recognized him.

Gene found Curtis in his office. The CIA man had obviously been up most of the night. His shirtsleeves were rolled up, his tie loosened and he needed a shave badly. A cigarette burned in an ashtray as he bent over the telex machine that spewed several yards of yellow paper.

Gene knocked on the open door. Curtis looked up, scowled at first, then nodded Gene to a chair. He turned back to the telex, jabbed at the keys. A bell rang; the machine ceased. Curtis dropped wearily in his chair and poured coffee for both of them.

Gene thumbed toward the office he had just past. "Was that—"

"Yeah it was," Curtis said. "Just what I need. A movie star who wants the first plane out of here."

Gene took a sip of the coffee and made a face. It tasted like it had been made the night before. "That an open line?" he asked Curtis and pointed to the telex. "No more secrets, huh?"

Curtis rubbed his eyes. "Christ, Williams don't start with me this morning. I don't need it." He glanced at the telex. "It's all common knowledge now. That's our embassy in Vienna. I'm a travel agent now, trying to get that mob outside out of here."

"Have you seen what's going on in the square, in the streets?"

Curtis nodded. "I thought I told you to stay off the streets and stay put." He looked away for a moment. "Yeah, not a very nice thing to witness is it?"

"I saw a Russian soldier butt a woman in the face, shoot her husband and—"

"What did you expect? The country's been invaded. There are going to be casualties." He suddenly sounded like he had when he'd talked about Josef Blaha's death.

"How bad is it?'

"Twenty or thirty killed so far that we know about. The reports are spotty. Another three hundred injured, some seriously. You can get hurt trying to stop a tank with bottles and bricks."

Gene nodded and lit a cigarette. "So where does this leave me?"

"I want you, Washington wants you, out of here as soon as possible. I've got a man to drive you across the border to Vienna. There's enough confusion for you to get away before anybody starts putting pieces together."

Gene suddenly realized with the invasion a reality, he was no longer a concern of the CIA. Free at last, free at last. The Soviet forces, the upheaval in the Czechoslovak government had ironically returned him to the status of tourist, visiting artist, to be evacuated like the scores of other foreigners caught up in the country's turmoil.

"You mean Dubcek?" It all seemed so long ago now. The drive with Dubcek, Indra's darkened office, Roberts, the Lucerna. Had he really done all those things?

"No, I'm not worried about Dubcek," Curtis said. "Not now. We know he's under house arrest. By now he's on a plane to Moscow, wondering what's going to happen to him and his country."

"Which is?"

"It's too early to tell," Curtis shrugged. "The Soviets have their own problems now. They have to field the western press, install their new government. I think they miscalculated the Czechs though, and Dubcek. He was too popular to just dump. But if it follows the usual pattern, all the reformers will be eased out, most of the controls restored and like Hungary, it will all be forgotten until next time."

Gene looked at Curtis. "Aren't you even curious to know what I told Dubcek?"

Curtis smiled. "Let me guess. Blaha left a report, a tape, something that incriminated Indra and an American collaborator." He saw Gene's surprised expression. "How am I doing so far? He also left some kind of warning about the invasion."

"But if you knew the—" He leaned forward and stared at Curtis.

Curtis cut him off and continued. "Oh, we knew the invasion was pretty much a sure thing and I suspected someone here in the embassy, but Blaha's request clenched it. He was an old pro. The only reason he would suddenly ask for an outside contact would be to confirm his suspicions that someone here on staff was feeding Indra. You just helped smoke him out."

'And I was the..."

"Confirmation? Right. What we didn't figure on was the KGB taking out Blaha or you running wild on your own. Blaha would have simply passed on the information and I would get it from you. Simple."

"But how was I to know you weren't Indra's insider?"

"You couldn't I guess," Curtis conceded. He seemed stuck for an answer. "I don't know, maybe I would have done the same thing in your shoes. Anyway, consider yourself lucky. The KGB was only trying to scare you off. Washington will be satisfied with your immediate removal from the scene. They're not going to press charges. They don't even want to know you. Keep that in mind if you have any ideas about giving interviews when you get home."

Gene sat back, getting angrier by the minute. Lucky? Washington wasn't going to press charges? After being used and knowingly placed in a dangerous situation. He suddenly remembered the letter he'd written to Kate.

"What about Roberts? What happens to him?"

Curtis's eyes grew cold. "Warner Roberts is a State Department affair. He's under house arrest and when he recovers, he will quietly resign. No trial, no publicity. Indra wanted a hotline to the embassy and Roberts was an easy target."

Gene sighed. It wasn't worth fighting. He just wanted out, but there was one last thing. "Lena is going with me. I want it arranged."

Curtis looked up before answering. "I thought that was coming. Not now though, give it some time." Gene started to protest, but Curtis cut him off. "There will be plenty of offers of asylum in the West. The British have started already. But if she goes now, she may not be able to get back in later."

"Why would she want to?"

"It's her country, Williams, occupied or not. There's a lot of strong feelings you don't understand. There will be a rebuilding process and she may want to be a part of it."

Gene considered. He knew what Curtis said made sense, but how could he be sure she'd be allowed to leave later? How would she take him telling her to wait? She'd think it was just an excuse to get away, leave her. He couldn't just walk away and hope she would follow later. It would have to be her decision, he realized, but he wanted the door open now.

He stood up to leave. "She'll go. You just make sure there's room in that car for two."

Curtis stared at him for a long moment, then looked away, shaking his head. "You've got it bad haven't you? Come to Prague, play the jazz festival, fall in love with the beautiful granddaughter of a spy. Come on, you've only known her a few days."

"The only thing you left out is it was you who introduced me to her. She's going with me."

"Okay, I won't argue with you now. Oh, by the way, there's one more thing. That letter, the one you said you sent your sister."

Gene felt his stomach tighten. "Yeah, what about it?"

Curtis watched him carefully. "Did you really send it?"

Gene smiled. "No, you were right. I was bluffing."

SEVENTEEN

Lena had waited long enough.

From the moment Gene had gone, she'd done nothing, but pace about the tiny apartment, waiting, worrying, her apprehension growing by the minute. She should have heard something by now she reasoned. He'd been gone two hours. She stopped suddenly. Maybe he was being held, kept from contacting her. Maybe the phones weren't working. No, he would come back then. Maybe the embassy had been attacked.

The radio reports streaming in didn't help. It was like an assault, but she couldn't bring herself to turn it off. Shootings, explosions, injuries, deaths, all interspersed with the inevitable instructions: avoid confrontations, remain calm. Occasionally, a report would halt in mid-sentence only to continue again a few minutes later from a new location. Passive resistance. That was all the people of Czechoslovakia could muster.

For the hundredth time, she went to the window and looked out. There was still smoke over Wenceslas Square, but the street below was deserted. She went back and sat on the bed, leaning over, her face in her hands. What had happened? Why hadn't he called or come back? She sat up again, trying to push a more horrible thought aside. What if he simply decided it was all too much? No, she couldn't think that, but she remembered her premonition when he'd left. She must go to him. She knew that now. She couldn't stand another minute in the apartment, thinking, worrying, wondering. She had to know. There was nothing for her here. Her grandfather was gone, the aunt in Plzen she hardly knew. What kind of life would she have now in Prague? What kind of life could anybody have?

Gene was right, she realized. A return to the old ways, the hope gone, Gene gone. She could not survive any of it. She went to the window again and looked out. More smoke hung over the square. What if he'd gone already? She might already be too late. She scooped up the small bag she'd packed earlier, looked around the apartment once more and ran out, down the stairs to the street, not even bothering to turn off the radio.

She must get to the embassy.

***

It was like a magnet. For the second time that morning, Gene found himself in Wenceslas Square. It was not even really a square, but more a long wide boulevard and now, because most of the side streets were blocked off, going through the square was the quickest way back to the apartment and Lena.

The narrow winding alleyways leading into the square were clogged with hundreds of confused angry Czechs and too late, he realized, once in, there was no way out. Shoving and pushing from behind him, the crowd surged toward the square like a herd of cattle to the corral.

He'd left the embassy with one thought. He and Lena were leaving. It was not that he trusted Curtis any more than before, but it was clear the CIA man wanted him away as much as he wanted it for himself. With the invasion a reality, he was of no further use other than to serve as a reminder of a botched plan to use a musician as a spy. That part was at least over and Gene's insistence that Lena be allowed to go with him had been met, if not with enthusiasm, then at least with silent reluctant approval.

As for his actions in Prague, no one would care now. The principals involved were in no position to concern themselves with him, much less know who or where he was. All that remained was to pick up Lena and get back to the safety of the embassy for the drive across the border to Austria. From there, they would go to London, then perhaps the States. Lena had relatives in Chicago. He would take her there. Let her get used to another country among familiar people. Then they would see.

From somewhere inside the square, he could hear the chanting again. "Dubcek! Dubcek!" The leader's name was scrawled on the sides of buildings in chalk or spray paint. Gene felt himself be pushed along until at last they broke free of the bottleneck and emerged into the main part of the square.

Thousands of angry shouting, jeering citizens of Prague had spread out filling the square. It had become the focal point of confrontation with the invading Soviet forces. The dead and wounded had been taken away from the earlier battle, but the soldiers and tanks were very much in evidence still.

The relative calm was deceptive. He could feel the violence and tension bubbling beneath the surface, mounting as the angry crowd continued to question and taunt the soldiers. Their country had been violated, their people wounded or killed and for what? Most of them didn't know and now they demanded answers.

Gene fought and pushed to the edge of the crowd, trying to make his way across the square. A tank loomed directly in front next to an overturned car that was charred and gutted, still smoldering from the earlier collision. Down the incline from the statue of St. Wenceslas, he could see more tanks rumbling toward them. Reinforcements. The anger flashed through the crowd like a brush fire, fueled by the sight of additional armament.

All around the square, slogans and makeshift signs were scrawled on buildings in paint and chalk. Windows were broken, cars were overturned, the street was littered with broken glass. The once impressive square was now in shambles.

As the new convoy of tanks drew closer, the shouting and chanting increased and grew louder. Sensing a new wave of anger, the tank crews already in place, retreated to their vehicles. The armed troopers nervously watched the crowd, guns ready, still wary from the earlier encounter.

But sensing the soldier's apprehension only increased the crowd's boldness and anger. "Dubcek! Dubcek!" they chanted as one. Men, women, old, young, all joined in shaking their fists in the faces of the soldiers.

Gene felt himself being pushed ahead again as someone shoved a leaflet in his hand. Several young boys were passing through the crowd handing them out. Instructions? Underground press? Gene glanced at it, but recognized only Dubcek's name. The radio was still broadcasting. Many people had brought portable radios to the square, passing on news to anyone near them.

Next to Gene, a woman shouted. He turned to look where she was pointing. The chanting stopped suddenly as the crowd hushed. The sound of straining engines echoed through the square. All eyes were riveted on an old man on crutches. He was dressed in a shabby suit. Medals were pinned on the coat, colored ribbons and gold leaves. One pant leg was pinned up. He broke from the ranks of the crowd, hobbling on one leg and the crutches, making a pathetic charge toward the lead tank as it rumbled closer.

The crowd gasped as the old man suddenly stopped, balancing on one leg and a crutch. He held the other crutch aloft, like a saber, high in the air waving it defiantly, challenging the approaching tank, daring it to run him down. *Oh man, get out of there*, Gene thought.

It was only at the last second that someone pulled him to safety. One of his crutches clattered to the ground, crushed by the treads of the tank, reduced to splinters as the tank rolled by, oblivious to everyone.

It was one small incident, one futile gesture that underscored the anger and frustration felt by everyone in Wenceslas Square, but it was the spark the jeering citizens of Prague needed. Gene felt it immediately. The crowd reacted to the old man's blind show of courage and surged forward as one, as if in tribute.

Caught in the wavelike movement of the crowd, Gene was pushed along, pressed up against bodies, the din of chanting in his ears. It took all his strength to untangle himself, fight his way clear to the very edge of the square.

Alarmed, the soldiers cautiously backed up, shouting at the crowd moving toward them. The tanks were fully armed. Then from out of a mass of people, a brick flew through the air and landed at the feet of one of the troopers. Then another and another. The trooper wheeled in the direction of the flying bricks and saw only a young boy scrambling through the crowd handing out more leaflets. The trooper meant to fire into the air, over the boy's head, but in the panic of the moment, his rifle went off a fraction of a second early. The boy dropped to the ground, the leaflets flew in the air and cascaded down over the crowd.

The shot triggered panic among the troopers. More shots were fired in the same direction. The people closest dived for cover or simply dropped to the ground. The rest panicked, ran and shoved and pushed in all directions. Nearly knocked to the ground, Gene stumbled and pushed into a doorway. More gunfire erupted and windows above him shattered, raining glass as the tank guns raked the square.

Another youth charged a tank and rammed a makeshift flagpole, a Czech flag fluttering, down the turret of the tank. He was joined by another cluster of young men who jumped aboard two tanks, emblazoned with swastikas somebody had drawn on them with chalk.

The young men blocked the viewing slits of the tanks with handfuls of flour. The visionless tanks swerved, careened off parked cars and slammed into a building on the other side of the square. As if on signal, it was bombarded with bottles of gasoline. A flaming rag was thrown into the air and in seconds the tank was a sheet of flames.

Close behind, a second tank veered to avoid the burning wreckage, its crew scrambling out of the hatches to safety. It turned sharply. Soldiers clamored on board, bayonets fixed and crouched near the viewing slits, shouting orders to the drivers who remained inside. Other troopers formed a cordon around the remaining tanks.

Gene watched, mesmerized as bricks, bottles, even bags of garbage pelted the tanks, filling the air with a burning stench. The soldiers panicked and fired mindlessly in all directions now. Several people fell, some shot, some trampled and crushed by the marauding mass of people.

Gene looked around in all directions, searching for a way out, then he caught sight of a young woman. She stood motionless at first, then stopped to pick up something in the street. She crawled under the fixed bayonets of the soldiers riding on top of the nearest tank and scrawled a swastika on its side. She then turned defiantly and flung the chalk in the face of one of the soldiers. As she turned toward the soldier, Gene felt his stomach contract, the blood pound in his ears.

It was Lena.

Without thinking, he pushed people aside and ran toward the tank, stumbling over people, pushing, fighting his way clear. As he ran, he could see Lena crawl back under the bayonet, tears streaming down her face, only to run into another soldier who was alarmed by her shouting.

"Lena!" he shouted as he ran. "No!" The words tore from his throat as the soldier fired. Lena doubled over, clutched her side, her eyes staring back at Gene in wonder and pain as the bullets cut her in two. She fell in a heap like a crumpled doll. The tank rolled by, heedlessly, passing within inches of her body.

Gene skidded to a stop, unable to comprehend what he'd just seen. He whirled toward the tank, but before he could take another step, he felt a burning searing pain as he was struck by a bullet, spinning him around backward, slamming his head into the side of a car.

He lay still for a moment, the noise and shouting grew more distant as he sank deeper and deeper, as if he'd fallen into an abyss.

Then there was only silence and darkness.

***

He opened his eyes and blinked several times, his vision blurry. He was immediately aware of a throbbing in his shoulder. Blinking again, he tried to focus on the shadowy figure looming over him.

"Think he's coming around," the voice said from far away, in the corner of the room. He stirred slightly as the room came into sharper focus, zooming in and out from sharp to hazy. The voice now he recognized as Curtis, looking down at him and Arnett, the man from the phone booth. He turned his head to the window. It was dark outside and strangely quiet.

Suddenly, it all flooded back. Wenceslas Square, Lena, the soldier on the tank. He sat up quickly, too quickly and felt the throbbing pain, the room spinning again. He dropped his head back, waiting for the nausea to pass. Lena crumpled on the cobblestone of Wenceslas Square. He knew. There was no need to ask.

Eventually, the dizziness subsided. He was on a couch, somewhere in the Embassy he guessed. The shoulder throbbed more now, searing pain. With his other hand he felt his head, the cloth bandage. He didn't remember anything after being hit.

"Take it easy," Curtis said. "You're full of drugs. You were lucky."

His eyes sought Curtis'. Maybe she was all right. "Lena. I..."

Curtis sat down on the couch and lit a cigarette for him. He put it between his lips, let him take a deep drag then took it away. He stared at the floor. "She didn't make it." He looked back at Gene, his gaze steady. "I'm sorry, I really am." He saw Arnett shift at the window and glance toward him.

"You're sure?" He knew the answer, but couldn't accept it.

Curtis nodded. "Arnett was there, saw the whole thing. I had him tag along, just to make sure you made it okay. Lena came from the opposite direction. She must have been on her way here. The Square was chaos and..." He looked away unable to hold Gene's blank stare. "Like I said, you were lucky. The bullet went right through your shoulder. Tore some muscle, but didn't break a bone. The embassy doc patched you up. You're going to be okay, but we need to get you some proper medical treatment."

"Yeah," Gene said quietly. "I was lucky." His voice was lifeless, flat. He stared at the ceiling. Curtis handed him the cigarette. He dragged on it deeply, forcing the hot smoke deep in his lungs.

Curtis went on. "You won't be playing drums for a while and the doctor says you'll probably be able to predict rain from now on with your shoulder. The bump on your head happened when you hit the car. Slight concussion is all." Curtis looked at him again, met his gaze. "I'm sorry."

Gene closed his eyes again as Curtis took the cigarette from his fingers. It had burned down now. "You'll have to have that looked at as soon as you get back. Arnett will drive you across later tonight, after you've had some more rest. The doctor gave you some sedatives and..."

He was drifting away again now, like he was sinking under water. Curtis' voice faded, became more and more faint. The images blurred. Lena, soldiers, tanks, Dubcek, Jan Pavel. He was on stage, playing, a tank with soldiers on top, the crowd chanting in the background.

Then nothing. More blackness.

EIGHTEEN

He was awake instantly; the room was dark. His watch was gone, but on the desk he could see a clock glowing in the darkness. Just after midnight. He sat up slowly, relieved to find the dizziness all but gone now, replaced by a dull throb in his head. He touched his shoulder. The pain was still there, but not as much.

He found cigarettes and matches on the arm of the couch. He fumbled with one hand clumsily, but managed to strike the match and light the cigarette. The glowing orange ash illuminated the room when he took a drag, outlining the desk, chairs, a coat rack. From somewhere in another room he heard a radio. Voices rising and falling, gradually getting louder. Then Curtis coming into the room, turning on a small desk lamp, carrying a small transistor radio and a mug of coffee.

Curtis handed him coffee and sat down behind the desk. "How are you feeling now?"

"Better. What's that?' The voices on the radio were in English.

"Voice of America broadcast," Curtis said. "It's a debate going on in the United Nations. That's our Ambassador, George Ball."

Gene sipped the coffee and listened as Curtis turned up the radio.

"...and once again, as all too often in history, a small nation, seeking only to live in peace and freedom, has been brutally attacked by a more powerful neighbor. Once again, the victim is that unfortunate country whose name was once the shining example, a symbol of self-determination. Czechoslovakia..."

Gene sat up slightly and listened as Ball continued. His voice was strong, heavy with conviction.

"...the grim parallel between Hungary in 1956 and Prague 1968 is only too apparent. Clearly the allies of the Soviet Union live under a harsh code—conform or perish. This invasion by the Soviet Union is contrary to the United Nations Charter and all international law. It is a gross act of perfidy. It would be universally and rightfully condemned by world opinion no matter where in the world it occurred...."

Later, Ambassador Ball was answered by Jacob Malik, the Soviet representative who denounced what he called Mr. Ball's "torrents of slander and insinuation," and claimed that the "ill smelling wind of the cold war had blown through his statement."

Gene and Curtis listened in silence as the debate raged on. The emergency session had been in progress for hours and would, according to Curtis, probably continue for several days. "Then they'll take a vote to decide whether or not to officially condemn the invasion," Curtis said.

"They have to vote on that?" Gene said. "What does it all mean?"

"Not much really," Curtis said. "Not much at all."

Arnett appeared shortly. It was time to go. Gene felt Arnett regarding him with something like respect and deference. Had he seen him run across the square? He stood up cautiously. The grogginess was gone, but not the memory. Never the memory. Arnett put out a hand to steady him as Curtis rose from behind the desk.

"There's still one thing I don't understand," Gene said. "With all your spies and analysts...why didn't you know this was going to happen and when?" He looked at Curtis intently waiting for an answer.

Curtis shrugged and flicked a look at Arnett. "Washington wants to know the same thing. We knew, but we didn't know they could move that fast. I guess they can keep a secret better than we can. It's something we have to think about."

Gene laughed grimly. "The whole thing won't get more than a few minutes on the six o'clock news will it?"

"Would you give it more if you hadn't been here?"

The two men gazed at each other for a moment, searching for some glint of understanding, but one was a jazz musician, one a CIA officer. Two different worlds, two different views.

Curtis reached behind the desk. "Thought you might want this," he said. It was his cymbal bag. "They're all there," Curtis said. "Arnett went back to the Lucerna for them."

Gene looked at Arnett. "Thanks," he said, taking the bag.

"Here, let me take it."

Curtis opened a drawer in the desk and took out an envelope. He weighed it in his hand for a moment, then held it out to Gene.

"What's this?"

"Your passport, an open ticket from Vienna and five thousand dollars in traveler's checks. No argument, okay." Without another word Curtis walked out of the room.

Arnett looked at Gene and shrugged. "Hey, you earned it." Gene nodded and went to the waiting car.

It was well after midnight when they drove through the streets of Prague. Even this late, the traffic was heavy. Foreigners leaving the country, Czechs headed for relatives and friends out of Prague. As they passed a gas station, Gene could see a line of cars stretching around the corner.

The tanks and armored vehicles were still very much in evidence, deployed around the city. Several hundred according to the laconic Arnett. But it was quiet now as they passed through the suburbs, down the Lenin Highway, into the country side, through village after village on the way to the Austrian frontier.

Gene rode in silence, occasionally nodding off, only dimly aware of the passage of time as he tried to absorb Lena's death. It was too soon, too final. He couldn't deal with it yet.

He felt Arnett watching him, flicking his eyes from the road to Gene and back. Finally, he said, "Hey, I know you don't feel much like talking, but well...shit." His eyes went back to the road. "You know, Williams, I never thought I'd admit this, but you're good. Damn good."

Gene turned to look at Arnett. In the glow of the dashboard light, his features were creased in a frown, as if he was embarrassed by his disclosure.

"Oh, I don't mean just the drums. I never liked jazz, but fuck man, I know a good drum solo when I hear it."

Gene smiled and leaned his head back against the seat. "Thanks. I appreciate it." They saw a road sign then that said WIEN 65.

"No problem," Arnett said, "but I don't mean just the music. You made me look bad a couple of times. I lost you. I underestimated you." He shook his head and laughed. "You ought to think about it. Perfect cover."

Gene continued to stare at the road ahead. A full time spy who played jazz? "Curtis put you up to this."

"No, but I bet he thinks the same thing." Arnett looked at him again. "Hey, I'm sorry about the girl too, Williams. That was a tough one."

Gene nodded again, feeling the pain. "Thanks."

He dozed off, then sometime later felt the car lurch as Arnett braked hard and squinted through the windshield. They were just short of the border checkpoint. "What is it?"

Ahead, outlined in the car's headlights, he could see a convoy of armored cars parked across the road. Several soldiers were clustered around something on the ground. As they drew closer, he could see the beam of a flashlight. The soldiers were studying a map.

"Look at that," Arnett said. "The stupid bastards are lost."

It was one of the Czechs most effective means of resistance, Arnett told him. All over the country, they had removed street signs confusing and frustrating the occupation forces.

Gene's mind was numb. The shoulder still throbbed, but he ignored it, struck by the obscene picture before them: the peaceful countryside of Czechoslovakia marred by presence of Soviet tanks and soldiers. *How long would they stay?* he wondered.

The soldiers looked up as Arnett stopped the car. "Let me do the talking," Arnett said.

Gene watched as the soldiers conferred briefly, then one of them approached the car cautiously, carrying an assault rifle. When Gene saw his face, he looked to Gene to be no more than nineteen or twenty.

The soldier eyed Gene curiously for a moment, then his gaze flicked to the Austrian license plate. Gene rolled down the window.

"Tourist," he said.

The soldier hesitated for a moment, then waved them on. One of the armored vehicles pulled off the road to make room for them to pass. Arnett, looking straight ahead, put the car in gear and pulled away slowly.

Gene leaned back against the seat. What was next? New York? California? Later. He would think about it later.

Arnett shifted his shoulders and smiled. "No sweat now, man. We'll be in Vienna in an hour."

There you go, Gene thought.

CODA

Gene Williams paused on the steps of the American Embassy and took in the expanse of Grosvenor Square. His gaze was drawn to the statue of Franklin Delano Roosevelt and the young blonde girl standing, reading the inscription.

He crossed the street and walked up to her. "He was a great man."

She didn't look up. "Yes, but he didn't help us much at Yalta."

Gene didn't answer. He handed her a sheaf of papers and they sat down on a nearby bench. "Everything is there," he said. "No problems. Takes a couple of weeks for the visa to clear."

He looked up at the eagle hovering over the embassy where it had all started. Even now, he could not believe it had all happened. His shoulder had healed well and it only gave him occasional twinges, perhaps more so because of the rainy London winter. It was five months now and still difficult to believe he was sitting, talking with Lena.

Arnett had arranged a hotel and medical treatment for him through the embassy. He had stayed in Vienna a few days, then returned to London. He hadn't wanted to go home, not then. He'd called Kate. They'd all seen it on television. She'd never received his letter and he wondered what had happened to it.

In London, he'd stayed with Graham, the English pianist. Recovered from the wound, Gene talked little and was grateful to Graham for knowing to leave him alone.

He lost himself with long walks around London. Sometimes, he would take the underground several stops, then walk, working his way back to Picadilly Circus or Trafalgar Square, undeterred by rain and the approaching winter, as he sought to understand what had happened and what he was going to do next. He hadn't played in all that time except for the occasional session on the practice pad.

Then, out of nowhere, a brief note from Alan Curtis via the embassy. Lena was alive.

Taken for dead with the other casualties from the battle of Wenceslas Square, someone realized she was still breathing and rushed her to the hospital for surgery. She was critical for a while, but miraculously, she'd recovered and got word to Alan Curtis. A week later she joined him in London as part of a Czech émigré contingent, one of many. Thousands of Czechs had fled the country after the invasion. Lena was just another name on a list.

"How long will you be in Chicago?"

"I don't know. There are many Czechs there. They will want to hear about everything. I'll stay with my aunt's relatives and..."

"And then?" She was still beautiful, but she was changed. Gene could see that from their first awkward meeting. She had recovered physically, but the other deeper wounds were still sensitive, not yet healed. Maybe they never would be.

"I don't know, Gene. I just need...time." She took his hand in hers and pressed it to her cheek. "Can you understand that?"

"Sure." He tried to keep the disappointment out of his voice, his face impassive.

She managed a smile. "Promise me one thing," she said.

"Of course."

"You must start playing again; you must get back to your music."

"I know. I just needed time too. I'm going to California for a couple of months. My sister is getting married and I haven't been home."

She nodded and leaned against him, put her head on his shoulder. They sat like that for a long time, neither moving, neither wanting to speak. Finally, they got up and walked to her hotel.

"What time is your plane?"

"At three. I should go I guess," he said, turning toward her. He put his arms around her and kissed her, much as that first time in Prague. He pulled back and looked in her eyes. "Lena, I—"

She smiled and put her finger over his lips. "Not now," she said. "I was wrong about one thing," she said.

"What?"

"That morning in Prague, when you left the apartment. I thought I'd never see you again. Even when I woke up in the hospital."

He nodded and looked away. "Call me when you're ready, Lena."

"I will, Gene. I will."

He watched her walk in the lobby. She turned once and waved and he began looking for a taxi to Heathrow.

***

The departure lounge was crowded for the New York flight. He bought a newspaper and was about to sit down when he noticed a group of people in one corner of the lounge gathered about a portable television tuned to the news.

He walked over to see what was happening. "What's going on?" he asked a couple.

"Something about Czechoslovakia," the woman said.

His eyes went to the screen. "...a grim reminder," the anchor intoned, "of the Soviet invasion five months ago. In Prague's Wenceslas Square, the site of several pitched battles during the occupation, Jan Palach, a Prague University student, set himself afire before horrified onlookers. Sources in Prague say..."

Then there was file footage—Wenceslas Square, tanks, the mob of people, still photos of Dubcek. He didn't need to see more.

"How awful," the woman said, as Gene walked away.

"You have no idea," Gene said. "No idea."

ABOUT THE AUTHOR

Jazz drummer and author Bill Moody has toured and recorded with Maynard Ferguson, Jon Hendricks and Lou Rawls. He lives in northern California where he hosts a weekly jazz radio show and continues to perform around the Bay Area. The author of seven novels featuring jazz pianist-amateur sleuth Evan Horne, Bill has also published a dozen short stories in various collections.

http://www.billmoodyjazz.com/

OTHER TITLES BY BILL MOODY

Evan Horne Series

Solo Hand
Death of a Tenor Man
Sound of the Trumpet
Bird Lives!
Looking for Chet Baker
Shades of Blue
Fade to Blue

OTHER TITLES FROM DOWN AND OUT BOOKS

By J.L. Abramo
Catching Water in a Net
Clutching at Straws
Counting to Infinity
Gravesend (*)

By Trey R. Barker
2,000 Miles to Open Road
Road Gig (*)
Exit Blood (*)

By Richard Barre
The Innocents
Bearing Secrets
Christmas Stories
The Ghosts of Morning
Blackheart Highway (*)
Burning Moon (*)
Echo Bay (*)

By Milton T. Burton
Texas Noir

By Reed Farrel Coleman
The Brooklyn Rules

By Don Herron
Willeford (*)

By Terry Holland
An Ice Cold Paradise
Chicago Shiver
Warm Hands, Cold Heart (*)

By David Housewright & Renée Valois
The Devil and the Diva

By Bill Moody
Czechmate: The Spy Who Played Jazz

By Gary Phillips
The Perpetrators
Scoundrels (*)

By Bob Truluck
Street Level
Saw Red
The Art of Redemption
Flat White (*)

By Lono Waiwaiole
Wiley's Lament
Wiley's Shuffle
Wiley's Refrain
Dark Paradise

(*) - Coming in 2012

Made in the USA
Middletown, DE
04 December 2014